A Sinister Duet: Book 1

Una Dove

Contents

For those of us who do it for spite.
Let's get this party started.

Trigger Warnings.

Please do not skip the trigger warnings. These warnings are important for your mental health as there are graphic scenes of sexual assault.

Sexual Content
<u>Non Consent</u>
Graphic violence
Domestic abuse
Mental and Emotional abuse
Financial Abuse
Psychological manipulation
Dub Con
Mask Play
Spanking
Praise
Breath Play
Degradation
Stalking
Voyeurism
Damsel in Distress
Choking
Murder
Somnophilia

I

Lila

THE OCEAN STRETCHES OUT before me, endless blue meeting the horizon in a view that should take my breath away. Instead, I stare through the sliding glass door with dead eyes, my fingers pressed against the cool surface as if I could push through it and escape. This view, this house... it was supposed to be my dream. Now it's just another pretty lie hiding the ugliness of my life with Eli.

Pressing my forehead against the glass, letting the coolness seep into my skin. The early morning light dances across the water, creating shimmers that once made me gasp with delight. When Eli first brought me here ten years ago, I thought I'd stepped into a fairy tale. The two-story house with its perfect ocean view, the library he promised I could fill with books, the balcony where we'd drink coffee and watch sunrises together.

What a fucking joke.

I pull back, seeing my faint reflection in the glass. Even that's too much. I turn away, unable to look at myself. This ghost of a woman I've become. Twenty-nine years old and I feel ancient, hollowed out from the inside by Eli's constant criticism, his unpredictable rages, the nights I've spent wondering if I'd wake up at all.

My gaze drifts to the security camera in the corner, on the ceiling. One of many he installed 'for our protection.' I know better. They're not to keep others out, they're to keep me in. To monitor my movements when he's away on his 'work trips.' To make sure I'm behaving. To catch me if I try to leave.

I've tried before. After one of his assaults, I packed a bag while I thought he was streaming. I made it to the car before he caught me, dragged me back inside by my hair. The bruises lasted weeks. The fear never left.

"No one else would want you, anyway. You're lucky I keep you around."

His words echo in my head, a constant soundtrack I can't turn off. The worst part is I've started to believe him. Who would want this version of me? This broken shell who flinches at loud noises and has forgotten how to smile without calculating the consequences?

I glance at the clock. 8:05am. I need to get ready for work. I'm not sure how I convinced him to let me get a job. Maybe it was because I threatened to kill myself if I couldn't have time away from the house? He agreed, but he made sure I didn't make enough to live on my own. At least at the print shop, I can breathe for a few hours. Valerie and Mia don't know everything, I've gotten good at hiding the worst of it. But they give me something Eli can't touch. Friendship. Purpose. A reason to keep going.

Moving silently through the house, avoiding the creaky floorboard near the stairs. Eli might be up already, streaming or editing videos, and I don't want to disturb him. The bathroom door closes behind me with a soft click, and I exhale, my shoulders dropping an inch from their perpetual hunch.

The first thing I do is throw a towel over the mirror. I can't bear to see myself anymore. My reflection has become an accusation, a reminder of how far I've fallen. The glimpses I catch are bad enough: the steel-blue eyes that used to spark with life now dull with resignation, the distinctive red hair with blonde streaks on either side that Eli once called "exotic" and now calls "attention-seeking."

Stepping into the shower, letting hot water cascade over me. It's the closest thing to comfort I get most days. As I wash my hair, I can feel its heaviness, the weight of it against my back. I used to love my hair. Now it feels like one more thing Eli uses to control me when he thinks I'm out of line, or won't give him what he wants. He won't let me cut it, says it's the only attractive thing about me anymore, but then complained about the cost of my hair care.

The soap runs down my body, over curves that Eli has deemed "disgusting." I've gained weight since we married, not much, but enough for him to notice, to comment, to use as ammunition. My hourglass figure, the one that once drew appreciative glances, is now something I try to hide under loose-fitting clothes.

I step out of the shower and dry off quickly, keeping my eyes averted from the mirror even through the towel. Dressing in the dark blue jeans and a black babydoll shirt I laid out last night, nothing that would draw attention, nothing that would show my figure too clearly but nice enough for work. Applying minimal makeup in the small compact mirror I keep in my drawer, concealer and mascara. Just enough to hide the perpetual tiredness around my eyes.

My hands shake slightly as I finish getting ready. I need to check if Eli wants anything before I leave. The thought makes my stomach clench, but it's easier to ask now than face his anger later for not asking at all.

I pad down the hallway to his office door. The sign he hung there reads "GENIUS AT WORK" in bold red letters. I've fantasized about replacing it with "ASSHOLE AT PLAY" but never worked up the courage.

My knuckles hover over the wood. I should knock. I know I should knock. The last time I didn't, he screamed at me for an hour about respect and privacy. But part of me, the small rebellious part that hasn't completely died, wants to catch him off guard. Wants to see what he's really doing in there when he claims to be "working."

I push the door open without knocking.

The room is dim, lit only by the glow of multiple monitors along the back wall. The air is thick and stale, smelling of sweat and something else I don't want to name. Eli's hunched over in his expensive gaming chair, headset around his neck. The moment the door opens, his hands fly across the keyboard, closing windows.

I wonder what was on there he didn't want me to see. He normally leaves the windows open and insults me for not being as good as the women on screen. Except they look like they're in pain. I'm not supposed to care about it, so I choose not to mention it. Mentioning it could also start something I don't want to finish.

"Fucking knock!" His voice is a whip crack in the quiet room. He spins his chair to face me, face flushed with anger.

"Sorry," I say automatically, the word worn smooth from overuse. "I just wanted to check if you need anything before I leave for work."

His eyes narrow, assessing me like I'm some kind of defective product. "Where are you going after?"

I hesitate. I had planned to stop at the bookstore. A new romance book releases today, but telling Eli feels like handing him a knife.

"The bookstore," I admit, hating how it sounds like a confession.

He snorts, turning back to his screens. "Another trashy book? Don't you have enough of that garbage?"

I bite my tongue. My books are my only joy, the only escape I have. In their pages, women like me find love, adventure, sometimes even revenge. They're not garbage—they're survival.

"I won't be long," I say instead of what I'm thinking. "What do you want for dinner tonight?"

"Pizza," he says without looking at me. "Order from that place on Fourth, not the shitty one you got last time."

I nod, though he can't see me. "Do you need anything else? Coffee? Breakfast?"

Now he turns, a smirk playing on his lips. It's the expression he gets when he's about to say something he knows will hurt. "You know what I need? A wife who isn't a lazy, unorganized slob."

The words hit their mark, but I've built calluses over my heart. Still, I flinch slightly.

"What's with that stupid book scanner thing you bought anyway?" he continues, warming to his topic. "More junk cluttering up the house. As if your 'system' of book piles everywhere isn't bad enough."

My book scanner. The one purchase I made for my-self last month, ordered in secret and paid for with money I'd been squirreling away from my paycheck. It helps me catalog my collection, keep track of what I've read, what I want to read next. It's mine. Just mine.

"It helps me organize," I say, my voice small.

"Organization would mean getting rid of half that shit." He waves dismissively. "You don't need more books. You need to read the ones you have or sell them. They're taking over the house."

My books are all confined to the library, the one room he rarely enters because there's nothing in there for him. No games, no computer, no TV. Just books and a comfortable chair and a throw blanket where I sleep most nights to avoid our bed. He just wants something to complain or fight about.

"I need to go or I'll be late," I say, retreating toward the door.

I close his office door harder than necessary, not quite a slam but close. The sound echoes through the hallway.

"Don't slam my fucking door!" he shouts through the wall.

I keep walking, grabbing my purse and keys from the hook by the garage door. My hands are shaking, but not from fear this time. From anger. From the indignity of being treated like a child, like a servant, like less than human by my husband. So much for the promise to 'honor and cherish.'

Outside, the morning air hits my face as the garage door opens, fresh and clean compared to the oppressive atmosphere inside. I slide into my car, a practical, boring

SUV that Eli approved because it "doesn't draw attention," and grip the steering wheel.

"Fuck him," I whisper to myself, the words a tiny rebellion in the quiet car. "He can't tell me how to spend my own money."

I start the engine and back out of the driveway, feeling the familiar weight lift slightly from my shoulders as I put distance between myself and the house. Work awaits. Valerie and Mia will be at the shop. For a few precious hours, I can pretend I'm someone else. Someone who deserves kindness, someone who might one day be brave enough to leave for good.

As I drive away, I glance in my rearview mirror at the house growing smaller behind me. From the outside, it looks like a dream home. No one would guess the nightmares that live inside. By the time I get to the print shop, I'll have plastered a fake smile across my face, the same one I always use for work. The one my best friends can see right through.

But as I drive toward my few hours of freedom, I can't help but wonder: is this all there is? Will I spend the rest of my life hiding bruises and flinching at sudden movements and sleeping in my library to avoid Eli?

2

Lila

T HE STEREO SCREAMS AT full volume, bass thumping through the speakers of my hatchback as I press the gas pedal harder. Arankai's "Heavenly Bodies" drowns out my thoughts, drowns out Eli's voice that always seems to linger in my head. This is my ritual. The moment I'm far enough from the house, I crank the music to levels that would have earned me a lecture about "destroying the speakers" if he were here. But he's not here. For the next eight hours, I'm free. Not completely free, but free enough to breathe without calculating each inhale.

I sing along, voice cracking occasionally. My singing voice is terrible, another thing Eli never fails to remind me about. But in this car, on this stretch of road with the windows rolled up tight, I can be as terrible as I want. I can take up space. I can exist without apologies.

The road curves ahead, and I ease off the gas, checking my watch. I'm early today, despite the confrontation with Eli. Being early is another ritual. I'd rather be at the print

shop alone for twenty minutes than spend an extra second in that house.

I make a sharp U-turn onto the side street leading to
the back of a small strip mall. *By the Bay Print and Mail*
is through an alley. It's a little bit of a walk, but parking
back here means more room for customers in the front.
To most people, it probably looks unremarkable. To me,
it's a lifeline.

The back lot is empty except for a delivery truck
pulling away. I slide into my usual spot nearest to the
alleyway entrance, killing the engine and letting the
sudden silence wash over me. For a moment, I just sit
there, hands still gripping the steering wheel, savoring
the transition from one world to another.

My phone buzzes in my pocket. My heart jumps. Is it
Eli checking up on me already? But it's just a notification from the bank. I exhale slowly, hating how my body
reacts to every small sound, how deeply the fear runs.

I grab my purse and climb out of the car, fishing the
shop keys from the side pocket. The morning air is cool
against my skin, carrying the salt tang from the nearby
bay. Another deep breath. Then I unlock the back door
and step inside.

Fluorescent lights flicker on automatically, buzzing
softly overhead. The familiar smell greets me—paper,
ink, the faint chemical scent of toner. I drop my purse
behind the counter and hit the main light switch. The
shop comes to life, shadows retreating to corners as
light floods the space.

"Good morning," I say to the empty room, a habit I've
developed on the days I open alone. Sometimes I think it

helps set the tone for the day. Speaking my voice into the silence, claiming the space before anyone else arrives.

First things first. I move to the corner where the steel deposit box sits bolted to the floor. Customers can drop off packages after hours through a secure slot, and it's my job to process them first thing. I twist the key in the lock and pull out a handful of padded envelopes and small boxes. Someone's left a note attached to one: "Please rush, my grandmother's birthday!" and I smile, setting that one aside for priority processing.

Next, I boot up the two desktop computers that run our operation. One for customer service, one for processing online orders. They're old and temperamental, but Valerie hasn't had the budget to replace them since buying the business. We've been doing so well though. I bet she could in no time.

While the computers start up, I sort through yesterday's mail, separating bills from advertisements from the occasional personal letter addressed to Valerie. The mindless task soothes me, ordering the chaos into neat, labeled piles. Then I fill and start the coffeepot for myself. Since I hadn't been able to at home.

I log into the business end of our website on the first computer, navigating to our order system. Three new orders came in overnight. A rush print job for wedding programs, a set of business cards for a local real estate agent, and fifty copies of a community theater playbill. I print the invoices and clip them to their respective folders.

The coffee machine beeps, and I pour myself a small cup, savoring the bitter warmth. Eli always complains about my coffee. Too strong, too weak, too hot, too cold. Just another excuse to act the way he does. Usually, Valerie shows up with fancy coffee in the mornings, but since I was here first and needed some, I decided to go ahead and make some.

I line up sheets of "Do Not Bend" stickers on the counter, placing them next to stacks of mailing labels I'd printed yesterday for the local cafés and boutiques that use our services. The organization calms me. Everything has its place here. Including me.

The back door chime rings, and I look up to see Valerie stepping inside. Her long, normally straight, blonde hair is windblown from the morning breeze. She's wearing her usual, jeans and a graphic t-shirt, this one advertising some indie band I've never heard of and a thin sweater. It stays pretty cool in here all year round. She balances two cups from the coffee shop down the street in her hands.

"Sorry I'm late," she says, despite the wall clock showing 9:30. Which is opening time, anyway.

I smile. "You're not late."

"I brought reinforcements." She sets one of the cups beside my half-empty mug of coffee. "You look like you could use the good stuff. I thought I was going to be late anyway, so I grabbed your favorite and asked for an extra shot of espresso this time."

I don't ask how she can tell. Valerie has an uncanny ability to read my moods, to see past the mask I carefully construct each morning. She doesn't push, doesn't pry, but she notices.

"Thanks." I take a sip of the fancy latte, appreciating the creamy sweetness. She really does remember exactly how I like it. "How was your night?"

She shrugs, hanging her sweater on the hook behind the counter. "Boring. Fell asleep watching that documentary series I told you about. The one with the cults?"

"Did you finish it?" I ask.

"Nope. Conked out halfway through episode three." She pulls her hair back into a long ponytail. "Oh, Mia's visiting family today. She won't be in."

I nod, feeling a small pang of disappointment. "I'll miss her shenanigans today." Mia is the third in our trio.

"She texted at like 5 AM. Something about her brother needing help moving back into town." Valerie moves behind the register, counting the till with practiced efficiency. "How far did you get in that book I lent you?"

The question catches me off guard. I'd nearly forgotten about the romantasy Valerie had pressed into my hands last week, insisting I'd love it. I did start it, but I haven't been able to finish it yet.

"About halfway," I say, not wanting to disappoint her. "It's good."

Valerie's arches an eyebrow, then continues. "Well, when you get to the part where Kalden dies, prepare yourself. I sobbed for like an hour."

My eyebrows shoot up. "Spoilers, Valerie!" I raise my voice a little, laughing at her. "Kalden dies? But he's your favorite character!"

"I know!" She leans against the counter, eyes bright with enthusiasm. "That's what makes it so good. The author doesn't pull punches. It feels real, you know? Not like those books where you know the main characters have plot armor."

"Damn, now I'm scared to keep reading." I'm not lying this time. I've grown attached to Kalden, the reluctant hero with a troubled past.

"You have to. It's worth the emotional trauma, I promise." She tosses me a knowing look. "Besides, you're the queen of dark romance. I figured you could handle a little fictional heartbreak."

I laugh, the sound surprising me with its authenticity. "Fair point. Dark romance is different, though. Even when it's tragic, there's usually some kind of... I don't know, redemption? Healing?"

"And fantasy can't have that?" She challenges, eyebrows raised.

"You just told me your favorite character dies!"

"Keep reading," she says with a mysterious smile. "That's all I'm saying."

The door chime interrupts us as our first customer of the day arrives, a harried-looking businessman needing copies of a contract. I slip into work mode, processing his order while Valerie helps another customer who enters shortly after.

The morning passes in a comfortable rhythm of customers, phone calls, and processing orders. Around noon, during a lull, Valerie and I eat lunch together at the small table in the back room.

"New book coming out today?" she asks through a mouthful of sandwich.

I nod, surprised she remembered. "How'd you know?"

"You've been checking the time every five minutes since we started lunch. You only do that when you're planning a bookstore run after work." She winks. "What's this one about? More brooding anti-heroes and morally gray hotties?"

"Something like that." I feel my cheeks warm. My taste in books is something Eli ridicules mercilessly, but Valerie never judges. "Want to hit the bookstore with me after work? We could grab dinner after."

Valerie looks genuinely regretful as she checks her phone. "I've got banking deposits to handle for the shop. End of month reconciliation and all that boring owner stuff." She makes a face. "Rain check?"

"Of course." I try not to let my disappointment show. Going to the bookstore alone isn't unusual for me, but having company would have been nice.

The afternoon rushes by in a blur of shipments and customer service. At exactly 6 PM, I log out of the system and grab my keys from my purse.

"Have fun at the bookstore," Valerie calls from where she's hunched over the accounting books at her desk. "Get something steamy enough to make your husband jealous."

I force a laugh, though the joke falls flat in my chest. If Eli knew half the things I read, he'd probably burn my entire collection. He already thinks my books are a waste of money and space. If he knew they were my escape hatch, he'd make sure they disappeared.

"See you tomorrow," I say instead, tucking a printed invoice into the top drawer of my desk for a customer I promised to call with a quote in the morning.

Back in my car, I sit for a moment and let the summer heat soak into my body. The bookstore on Sunset Boulevard is calling to me, promising new worlds, new escapes. For a few hours, I can lose myself in someone else's story, someone else's pain and triumph. I can pretend that happy

endings exist, that women like me get to walk away and
rebuild.

I start the engine and pull out of the parking lot, turning toward Sunset. I sway and dance behind the steering wheel, blaring one of my favorites, Victim by MeMy-
selv&Vi. The irony of my toxic marriage is not lost on me.
Maybe that makes me weak.

3

Anthony

T HE BOX CUTTER SLICES through tape with a satisfying rip, revealing stacks of books I haven't seen in months. I inhale the familiar scent of paper and binding glue, running my fingers over spines that feel like old friends. After living out of a duffel bag for so long, these books are the first things that make this place feel like mine. This townhouse with its bay view and empty rooms. A blank slate. A fresh start. No one knows me here yet.

"Jesus, Tony, how many books did you ship back?" Mia asks, peering over my shoulder. Her long black hair falls forward as she leans in, examining the titles. "You know e-readers exist for a reason."

"Had one. Got broken on my last mission." I don't elaborate. Don't tell her how the device shattered when I hurled it against a wall after failing to extract a victim before the corrupt local authorities arrived. Some details my sister doesn't need to know.

"Of course it did." She rolls her eyes, but there's affection there. Mia's always understood me better than most, even if she only sees the parts I let her see. "You're hell on electronics."

I straighten, surveying the living room. Boxes stacked in precise formation against the far wall. Furniture arranged exactly as I'd specified to the movers. The sliding glass door leading to the balcony offers a perfect view of Assateague Bay, waves lapping gently at the shore beneath the stilts that elevate the townhouse. I could watch those waves for hours.

"So this is home now?" Mia asks, breaking my trance. She's unpacking dishes in the kitchen, placing them in cabinets with no discernible system. I'll reorganize them later when she's gone.

"For now." I don't commit to permanence. Never have. But something about this place feels right. The isolation. The view. The proximity to family. "At least until the next mission."

"Which hopefully won't be for a while," she says pointedly. "You promised you'd stay local for a few months this time."

I grunt in acknowledgment, not making promises I might break. Instead, I focus on arranging my books alphabetically by author on the built-in shelves flanking the gas fireplace. Each spine aligned perfectly with the edge. The system bringing order to chaos.

"Did you hear me?" Mia presses, stepping into my line of sight. "You said you were taking a break from international work."

I look up at her, forcing a smile. "I am. GameStream needs attention," I don't tell her about the mysterious murdering uploader.

The gaming platform generates substantial revenue without much input from me, the perfect cover for my other activities.

Mia's face softens. "Good. I've missed having my big brother around."

"Missed you too."

We work in companionable silence for the next several hours. Periodically making small talk. I arrange my belongings with military precision while Mia flits from task to task, her organization system more intuitive than methodical. It should irritate me, but with Mia, I've learned to let go of control. Mostly.

"Pizza should be here soon," she announces, checking her phone. "I ordered from that place on Coastal Highway you liked last time you visited."

"The one with the garlic knots?"

"Is there any other worth ordering from?" She grins, collapsing dramatically onto my new couch. "God, this thing is comfortable. Much better than that torture device you had in your last place."

"That was a perfectly functional sofa," I argue, joining her on the cushions. She's right though, this one is better. I researched for weeks before purchasing, reading every review, considering every angle. The perfect blend of comfort and support. A place where someone could sit for hours, feel at ease enough to let their guard down.

The doorbell interrupts my thoughts. Mia jumps up, waving away my wallet. "My treat. Housewarming gift."

While she pays for the pizza, I grab two plates from the kitchen, white ceramic, simple and sturdy. No unnecessary decoration. The wine glasses I unpack next are similarly utilitarian, but high quality. I pour us each a glass of cabernet, not too much for Mia since she's driving, even if it is only a few blocks.

"This view is incredible," Mia says when she returns, setting the pizza box on the coffee table. She moves to the sliding glass door, staring out at the bay. The sun still high in the summer sky, making the water glimmer in white and gold flowing patterns. "How did you get this place? I didn't know it was for sale."

Her own townhouse doesn't face the bay, but she still has community access to the water.

"Patience," I answer simply. What I don't say: I've had my eye on this townhouse for months. Monitored the market, waited for the price to drop, arranged for the previous owners to receive a too-good-to-refuse job offer out of state. Some things require a little time.

We settle on the couch with our pizza and wine. The first bite tastes like heaven after months of bland military rations and questionable local cuisine in countries where clean water is a luxury.

"So," Mia says between bites, "you're officially on business duty now? The GameStream offices missed their fearless leader."

I shake my head. "I'll check in tomorrow, but everything's running smoothly. The management team handled things well while I was gone." Another truth with convenient omissions. The platform practically runs itself, though some things have gone under the radar for too long.

"And the search and rescue work? Taking a real break from that too?"

I take a long sip of wine before answering. "For now. The last mission was... difficult." Images flash unbidden. Terrified eyes, blood-stained concrete, the scent of fear so thick you could choke on it. "Sometimes you can't save everyone."

Mia reaches over and squeezes my hand. "You can't carry the weight of the world, Tony. You've done more than most people ever will."

If only she knew the real weight I carry.

"Enough about *my* work," I deflect. "How's the print shop?"

Her face lights up, and I feel a genuine surge of pride. My little sister, the business owner. Building something real while I've been playing savior in countries whose names most Americans can't pronounce.

"By the Bay is doing amazing," she gushes. "We just landed the contract for all the resort's printing needs, brochures, menus, event flyers, the works. It's going to boost our revenue by at least thirty percent."

"That's fantastic, Mia." I raise my glass in toast. "I'm so proud of you for owning your own business. Really. You've built something special."

She beams at the praise, tucking her hair behind her ear, a gesture she's done since childhood. "I couldn't have done it without the loan you gave me for the down payment."

I wave away her gratitude. "Best investment I ever made. You paid it back in record time."

"Still." She takes another slice of pizza. "Speaking of the shop, you should stop by sometime. Meet my friends. They practically run the place with me."

Something in her tone catches my attention. The slight emphasis on "friends," the casual way she drops it into conversation. My sister is many things, but subtle isn't one of them.

"Trying to set me up again, Mia?" I ask, raising an eyebrow.

She laughs, not denying it. "Maybe. You've been gone so long, and you're not getting any younger. Thirty-two and still married to your work."

"I'm not looking for a relationship," I say firmly.

"You don't have to marry them," she persists. "Just meet them. My friends are amazing. Smart, funny, hardworking. And one is single, by the way."

"I need to get settled first," I demur. "Maybe next week. Besides, I need to visit the bookstore and grab some new books since my e-reader is broken."

Mia perks up at this, leaning forward eagerly. "Oh! You should definitely talk to my friends then. They're both avid readers."

"What kind of books?" I ask casually.

"One's into dark romance mostly, the darker the better. The other reads everything, but she's been on a fantasy kick lately." Mia grabs another slice of pizza. "They might even read similar stuff to you. What are you into these days? Still those psychological thrillers?"

I nod, mind racing. Dark romance. Darkness calling to darkness. "Among other things. I've been branching out."

"Well, if you're heading to the bookstore anyway, you might run into one of them. They're there all the time."

Mia says this offhandedly, unaware of how the information electrifies me. "One has this amazing book collection at home, an entire library room. Her husband is always giving her shit about it. Even though she told me all he does is play and stream brain rot games all day when he's home."

"He sounds like a winner," I say sarcastically, masking the surge of interest. "And your other friend?"

"She co-owns the print shop with me. She's amazing, completely independent, takes no shit from anyone." Mia gestures with her wineglass. "You'd like her."

Mia purposely leaving out their names. I know it's because she wants me to come check out her business.

I make an appropriately interested noise, but my mind is elsewhere. Cataloging the new information. The dark romance reader. Married to an asshole who streams video games. Does he use GameStream? I'll need to check our user database. A library room full of books. Bookstore on Sunset Boulevard.

"What about you?" I ask, redirecting. "Still reading those self-help books?"

Mia groans, rolling her eyes. "Don't make fun. They've helped me a lot."

"I'm not making fun," I say sincerely. "They've helped you be more self-awareness, to grow and succeed. That's what matters."

She studies me suspiciously, then relaxes when she sees I'm not mocking her. "Yeah, well, not everyone can read dense Russian literature for fun like you."

"Dostoevsky understood the human condition better than most modern writers," I shrug, finishing my wine. "Crime and Punishment is essentially the original psychological thriller."

"If you say so, Professor Literature," she teases, checking her watch. "I should probably head out soon. Early day tomorrow."

I nod, standing to clear our plates. "Thanks for helping me unpack. And for the pizza."

"That's what sisters are for." She rises, gathering her purse and keys. "Think about what I said, okay? About stopping by the shop. No pressure, but it would be nice to introduce you to the important people in my life."

"I will," I promise.

At the door, Mia hugs me tightly. "I'm glad you're home, Tony. For however long it lasts."

I return the embrace, breathing in the familiar scent of her shampoo. "Me too,"

After she leaves, I stand at the sliding glass door, taking in my the view of my new home. I wonder about the unnamed woman and can't answer my own questions. Why is this person so fascinating to me when I know nothing about her? Not a name, a face, anything.

I turn back to the half-unpacked living room, my eyes falling on my laptop bag. There's research to be done now. GameStream users nearby to find. A bookstore on Sunset Boulevard to visit.

4

Lila

T HE BOOKSTORE SITS LIKE a beacon at the end of Sunset Boulevard, its windows glowing with warm light against the early evening shadows. I pull into the parking lot, my heart already lifting at the thought of losing myself among the shelves. It's my sanctuary, the one place where Eli's voice doesn't follow me, where I can breathe without feeling his eyes tracking every expansion of my lungs. I grab my purse and practically skip to the entrance, the smell of paper and possibility greeting me as I step inside.

The bell above the door jingles, announcing my arrival, but no one looks up. That's what I love about this place. Everyone is too absorbed in their own literary worlds to care who comes or goes. I nod to the older woman behind the counter, a silent greeting we've exchanged dozens of times, and make a beeline for the romance section in the back corner of the store.

My hands tremble with excitement as I scan the new releases, running a fingertip down their spines. And there it is, the book I've been waiting for, its cover adorned with dark colors and the silhouette of a man. The latest from my favorite author. I clutch it to my chest like it's a precious artifact, already imagining the hours I'll spend curled in my library, lost in someone else's love story.

But one book isn't enough. Who knows when I'll be able to visit again? I need a stockpile, a fortress of fiction, to shield me from the silence of the house. I move methodically through the shelves, pulling out anything that catches my eye, a historical romance with a defiant-looking woman on the cover, a paranormal love story with a wolf-man whose eyes seem to follow me. My collection grows in my arms. Each book another night, I won't have to think about my own life.

"Those are some good choices."

The deep voice startles me so badly I nearly drop my precious stack. I turn, finding myself face to face with a man I've never seen before. He's tall, taller than Eli, with broad shoulders encased in worn leather. A motorcycle jacket, heavy boots, dark riding leather pants. His helmet dangles from one hand while the other holds a small stack of books.

I stare at him, unsure how to respond to a stranger starting a conversation. This doesn't happen to me. I'm not conventionally attractive at all. I'm the weird redhead girl.

"You're gorgeous, by the way," he adds, his eyes, a striking hazel I can see even in the dim corner lighting, fixed on mine.

My breath catches. Is he talking to me? I look around, certain there must be someone else, someone who actually deserves that word. But there's only the empty aisle and shelves of romance novels witnessing my confusion.

"Excuse me?" I finally manage, my voice flustered and shaky. "Who are you talking to?"

"You," he lightly chuckles. "You're gorgeous," he says, his eyes locked on mine.

"You're calling *me* gorgeous?" The words tumble out before I can stop them, disbelief making me blunt.

He smiles, and it transforms his face from merely handsome to something that makes my stomach flip. "I call it like I see it."

"You don't know me," I say, clutching my books tighter, as if they might shield me from this strange interaction. "And I'm married." I don't know why I add that last part, some ingrained loyalty to Eli that persists despite everything, or maybe just a reflex, a warning to myself as much as to him.

"Are you even buying those books, or are you just trying to pick up random women?" I ask, nodding at the small stack in his hand, trying to regain some control over this situation.

He holds up his selection, a couple of fantasy novels with dragons and skulls on their covers, and at the bottom, peeking out, the corner of what is unmistakably a dark romance novel, its cover featuring a masked man.

I laugh, not at his selection, but at the absurdity of the situation. A smoking hot man, in a bookstore, calling me gorgeous, reading the same kinds of books I do. It feels like a scene from one of my novels, not my actual life.

"What's funny?" he asks, but he's smiling too, like he's in on the joke.

"Nothing," I say, shaking my head. "I just... I need to check out."

I turn abruptly, walking toward the front of the store, my heart pounding in a way that has nothing to do with anxiety for once. Behind me, I hear his boots on the hardwood floor, following at a respectful distance.

One of my books, the paranormal romance, slips from my precarious stack and falls to the floor with a soft thud. Before I can bend to retrieve it, he's there, picking it up.

"You dropped something," he says, holding it out to me.

Our fingers brush as I take it, and the contact sends an electric current up my arm. I jerk back, nearly dropping the book again. "Thanks," I mutter, quickly adding it back to my pile.

At the counter, I place my stack down, avoiding the curious look the clerk gives me and the unnamed man, who's now standing a few feet behind me, waiting his turn. I focus on digging through my purse for my wallet, pulling out my debit card with slightly trembling fingers.

The clerk scans each book, the beep of the register a steady rhythm that helps calm my racing heart. "That'll be $87.45," she says, and I slide my card through the reader.

The machine beeps, an angry sound that's different from the scanner. "I'm sorry," the clerk says, her voice dropping to that sympathetic tone retail workers perfect. "It's declined."

Heat floods my face. "That's impossible. Can you try again?"

She does, her movements more careful this time, like she's trying to be extra gentle with the machine. Another angry beep. "I'm sorry," she repeats.

I can feel his presence behind me, witness to my humiliation. The air in the store suddenly feels too thick to breathe. "I... I need to make a call," I stammer, stepping away from the counter, leaving my precious books behind.

Stumbling toward the front door, pushing it open and gulping in the cooler outside air. My hands shake as I pull out my phone and dial the bank's number, already knowing what they'll say but needing to hear it, anyway.

After navigating the automated system, a customer service representative confirms my worst fear. "I'm showing that you called earlier today and notified us that your card was lost or stolen. You also added your husband as the account primary. We sent a notification earlier, 'If this was not a mistake, please ignore.' We didn't receive a response. So, we went ahead with the changes."

The timing isn't lost on me. I had just gotten to work and forgot about the bank notification. That wasn't even 10 minutes after I left the house and I told him I was coming here. My throat tightens as I thank the representative and hang up, then immediately dial Eli's number.

He answers on the second ring. "What?"

Just that one word, dripping with annoyance, makes me shrink. "My bank card is called in as missing... by me this morning." I say, trying to keep my voice steady.

"Yeah, I know," he says, and I can hear the smirk in his voice. "I told you no more books."

"It's my money," I say, but the words come out weak, lacking conviction because we both know it isn't true. Not really. Not in any way that matters.

"It's my money now," he says, "and I'm sick of you wasting it on that shit. You've got enough to last you a lifetime."

"They're not shit, they're-"

"They're garbage, Lila. Mindless garbage for bored housewives who don't appreciate what they have. Which apparently includes you."

My eyes burn with unshed tears. "I need to buy dinner and groceries, Eli. I can't do that now."

"Use my credit card. That's still open to you. Consider it a lesson in listening to me the first time I tell you something." He hangs up before I can respond.

I stand there with the phone pressed to my ear, listening to the silence, feeling the humiliation wash over me in waves. My vision blurs as tears finally spill over. I wipe them away furiously, hating that he can do this to me from miles away, hating that I still let him.

I need to get to my car before I completely fall apart. No one here needs to see me cry. I shove my phone back into my purse and start walking, head down, toward the parking lot.

Once inside my SUV, I let the tears come freely, hot tracks down my cheeks that I don't bother wiping away. I grip the steering wheel, resting my forehead against it, trying to breathe through the tightness in my chest.

A knock on my window makes me jump. I look up to see the man standing there, my stack of books in his arms, his expression concerned. For a wild moment, I consider ignoring him, driving away, pretending this humiliating evening never happened.

Instead, I roll down my window just enough to speak. "Yes?"

"Your books," he says, holding them up. "Your card went through on the third try."

I stare at him, knowing it's a lie. "I don't like liars," I say, my voice raspy from crying.

He has the grace to look sheepish. "Okay, I bought them. But they're yours. You looked like you really wanted them."

The gesture is so unexpected, so kind, that fresh tears spring to my eyes. "I can't accept that," I say, shaking my head. "I'm not a charity case."

"It's not charity," he insists. "Think of it as... an investment. In your happiness."

"You don't know me," I repeat my earlier words, feeling a little more frantic than the last time I spoke them.

"I'd like to," he says simply.

I look at him, really look at him, trying to find the angle, the hidden motive. Men like him don't notice women like me, and they certainly don't buy them books. "Why?"

He shifts the books in his arms, considering his answer. "Because you look like someone who deserves better than what you got tonight. Because I've never seen anyone's face light up the way yours did when you found that book. Because I'm curious about a woman who reads romance but flinches when someone calls her gorgeous."

His honesty disarms me, but I still shake my head. "Just leave me alone."

With that, he turns and walks away. I watch in my side-view mirror as he approaches a sleek black motorcycle parked near the entrance, placing the books in a removable compartment and making a phone call. I half wonder what it's about, and half don't care at all. After a few minutes, he slides his helmet on and swings his leg over the seat. The engine roars to life, a deep, throaty sound that vibrates in my chest.

The ride home stretches before me, a journey back to reality after this strange interlude. I start the engine but don't pull away immediately, instead sitting in the quiet darkness of my car, thinking about a stranger who called me gorgeous and the husband waiting at home who never has.

5

Anthony

S HE LOOKS REALLY UPSET. I'm not sure why that makes my heart ache so much; I don't know her at all. But now, I want to. I want to learn everything about her. There were six books in the pile she left behind. I bought them and tried to give them to her. She told me to leave her alone. So, now I'm carrying them back to my bike along with my own and stow them in a small pack I'd brought just for today's trip. I just need to figure out how to sneak the books she left into her house. I bet that would be romantic. But I'm no hacker; I can't connect to her phone and pull any information. However, I do have someone on my payroll who can.

Dialing his number, he usually picks up on the first ring whether he's busy or not, but this time it takes a few moments. "Hey, man. What's up?" Cainen asks on the other end.

"Let me start by saying, please don't judge me," I say.

"Never," he replies sincerely.

"I need you to help me hack this woman's phone. I saw her crying in the bookstore; turns out her husband financially abuses her. I want her. Catch my drift?"

"Well okay. I've got a few things to do first; I'll send you the basics now and some more in-depth methods later when I've got time to explain."

"Oh, thank fuck! I thought you were going to turn me down." A sigh of relief escapes me.

"Hey, there is one thing I need from you. You still got that guy on the police force?"

"Dillian? Sure do. What do you need?"

"No judgment, remember? Let me tell you the whole story first." He hesitates at first.

"Oh-kay? What is it?"

"Remember that uploader we keep trying to track down? The one making all those murder videos? Then disappearing."

"Yeah?"

"Well, I've been following this girl for a few days and she met up with a man who tried to assault her. She got away, but then I found him still in their hotel room," he says.

"Oh, no! Did you kill him?"

"Dude, wait until I'm done," he replies.

"Sorry! Please continue."

"I wasn't going to kill him until I went through his phone," he says. "He works for that guy; he's a bounty hunter. I accessed the private forums on his phone."

"Holy shit! This is our break; we can take them down!"

"I'll send you all the information I've got from him so far, but if there are men placing orders for specific women. Not just by appearance. We need to get this done," he says.

"I need him to look into Micheal Vanderburg and see if anyone is going to miss him."

"I'll forward it to Dillian. Can you come here, back to Maryland?"

"No way; she's on their list. I can't leave her until she knows."

"I guess you're going to be doing a little reconnaissance of your own, huh?"

"Yeah. Well, maybe this way I'll get to take down some more bounty hunters."

"Just be careful and let me know if you need me to get the police off your back."

"Will do, Batman." He hangs up before I can tell him not to call me that.

About five minutes later, he sends me the basics he promised. Enough for me to connect with her phone through Wi-Fi without notifying her. A list of visited locations pops up, but that's about it for now; nothing else is accessible yet. What other types of surveillance has Cainen been conducting? This is fantastic! I just need to swing by my townhouse and grab a jammer.

She's still sitting in her SUV and looks like she's crying. He must really be an asshole. A location labeled "Home" appears; she lives on a strip of land between the bay and ocean, those homes are very expensive in that area. Who is her husband?

I make my way there on my motorcycle, hoping that I'll be able to get in and out before she arrives home and hopefully no one else is home either.

6

Lila

B Y THE TIME I pull into the garage, I'm seething. So
embarrassed that my stomach is rolling, and I could
purge on the floor. I'll be the one cleaning it up if I don't
hold it in.

I slam the pizza on the counter before storming up
the stairs. If I hadn't already ordered the stupid pizza, I
wouldn't have brought any at all.

Throwing the office door open, startling Eli.

"What the hell!?" he yells, once again closing a mul-
titude of browser windows in a hurry, all some sort of
pornography.

"How did you get into my account!" I say louder than I
intended, but I don't feel bad about it. He deserves this.

"Didn't I tell you to knock?" He yells back, "and watch
how you talk to me."

"You don't knock when you snoop around my library,"
I reply. "And you'd better watch how you talk to me. I don't
have to take it either!"

"This is *my* house, and you will respect me in it. I already told you not to get any more books."

"Since when do you get to dictate whether I can get a book with my own money? You're my husband, *not* my master, and this is my house, too."

"Your name isn't on this house. Since you do nothing, you don't do anything to earn it."

He can't be serious... But he is, and here we go again, this cycle of me defending myself and my individuality.

"I do nothing?" I ask, wondering if he really doesn't notice. "What do you consider something? I cook, I clean—"

"Barely," he cuts in, "You've been using MY money to hire a cleaning crew."

"*You* told me I could because I was going back to work." I reply. "If that's such a big deal, then stay out of my account and I'll use my own money."

"If you quit that job, I'll take care of it all. You can go back to having an allowance and credit card in my name," he says.

He's trying to trap me. I can't agree with that and he knows it. He knows I won't, but he's taunting me, anyway.

"You know my answer. I won't do it," I reply, backing out of the door.

"Then I'll drain your accounts and you'll have to start over."

"You can't do that!" I seethe.

"I can, marital assets and no prenup, post-nup. I can and will take it all." He says, standing from his chair and slowly walking toward me.

Slamming the office door, he catches it before it latches and swings it back open. He walks through it, his dirty blonde hair falling over his eyes. At least he's showering regularly and doesn't smell like mold and rotten cheese much anymore.

I know that look, I need to get out of here right now. I've managed to avoid his assaults for the past few months. Today, having this lapse of judgment is going to get me into trouble. I've gotten too comfortable. That's why he picks these fights with me, to get me wound up and confrontational, so he can beat the shit out of me and rape me in front of his camera... then blame me later when he gives me his fake-ass apologies.

Heart already racing, I turn away and run down the stairs, into my library, quickly flipping the light on. I put all my weight against the door and flip the lock as fast as I can. Then, I shove a throw blanket under the door. The friction of the carpet and the blanket between the door should make it harder to open, even if the lock fails. Hurrying to move my chair against the door too. Relieved that I decided to keep it on this side of the room, just for this reason and never put it back.

He bangs on the door, trying to push it open. Maybe he realizes I've barricaded the door again. He stops.

"You can't stay in there forever, Lila." One last bang on the door.

"Leave me alone Eli, or I'll call the police!"

"Do it," he taunts.

I know he doesn't mean it because I can hear him walking away. I'm not stupid enough to open this door for the next few hours. He'll just come straight back for me.

Instead, I grab my phone from my back pocket and sink low into my chair. I've gotten surprisingly quick at moving this huge chair around. A lavender-purple, and the size of a twin bed.

In my library, the bookshelves are floor to ceiling. After today, I'll probably have sleep in here from now on. He could easily surprise me or taken advantage of me while I'm asleep. Or has he already, and I didn't realize it? It didn't physically feel like it.

Failing to find some lighthearted funny videos as I scroll online, I suddenly have a strange feeling that something is out of place. I look up and notice on the table next to the window, there is a pile of books I know I didn't put there. Maybe Eli got them and that's why he locked my card? No, not after that whole display just now. He hasn't attempted to get me anything or even spend time with me in a very long time.

I walk over to the table and pick one up, and it is definitely one in the pile I had planned to buy earlier today. Opening the first pages to see if there are any clues, a small, folded paper falls onto the floor. I pick it up and hold it in my hand.

What the fuck?

My heart pounds so hard, I can feel it in my ears. Who got in here? Are they still here? Should I even open this? Eli would have seen whoever it was on the camera, right? He would have said something to me when I got home and not waited in his office. Actually, he would have seen I was close with the GPS on my phone, but he didn't. He had no idea I was home at all until I opened the door.

Slowly, I look around to see if there is any movement. This room couldn't hide a person with the way I have it set up, but there is a closet and a bathroom. I walk over and cautiously open the bathroom door, turning on the light and checking behind the stand-up shower curtain. Nothing. Then, I pull open the closet door. Still nothing.

Moving over to the lone window on the other side, it has a small view of the bay with some dune grass just before the beach. It is also locked and hasn't been opened.

I'm just going to take my chances and go into the living room, since now I feel my only space has been invaded and I'm more than a little creeped out. The living room is rarely used anymore, anyway. White everywhere, except the couches, large and gaudy red velvet. It feels tight in here, and sad.

Phone in hand, I open the camera app and swipe through the many angles Eli has set up to watch me. No saved footage from my library, or from the outside cameras. I do see that Eli's car is gone. I guess he just left when he couldn't get to me. Good, I don't want him here, anyway. Maybe I'll be a little more safe looking around while he's gone, but how safe can you be with a stranger creeping around inside your house in the dark? Standing out here probably isn't the best idea, so I walk back into my library and lock the door behind me.

Slowly, I unfold the note and it says:

> Lila, huh?
>
> What a beautiful name. Anyway, I saw how upset you were and thought I would give you these books anyway. I hope you like them. Don't worry, I'm not still in your house. But I will be seeing you soon.

What does that even mean? He'll see me soon? Looking around quickly. He didn't sign a name either. Chills traveling up and down my spine and a cold sweat forming around my face and neck as I try not to panic, for the second or third time today.

I look back at the cameras again. All open so I can see each view, both inside and out. I know I was in the parking lot for a while trying to calm down before I left. He had time to get here and out. But how the hell did he with Eli being home? Unless Eli had his headphones on after I called. Still, nothing. Suddenly all views go to static and I can't see anything at all. Maybe they're broken? They can't be.

My heart, still pounding, drops into my stomach and bile creeps up my throat. How is this possible? There is no proof anyone was in here. If I call the police, there's nothing they can do. Even if they can, Eli wouldn't let them inside. There would be hell to pay if I let them in. And if I tell him, he'll accuse me of cheating. He does that whenever there's another man simply in the same place as me. Even though I know what *he's* been doing. It just isn't worth opening my mouth about it.

I block the door again and turn all the lights out, then double check the window. There is someone standing in the dune grass. If I hadn't turned the lights off before I checked the window, I wouldn't have seen him. But he could see me the whole time.

He's tall and broad, wearing a mask with dim L.E.D. lights on the front for fuck's sake. A dull green X on each eye, with the cheeks coming down to his jawline, leaving only his mouth exposed..

A cold chill runs down my spine and arms, causing me to shake violently as I pull up my phone. I start to dial 911 and stop. Flipping through the camera app again... still static. It vibrates while I'm still entranced by the sight.

Unknown Number: Don't call the police. I'm not going to hurt you.

Looking back through the window, he's gone. Just fucking gone. What the hell? What would happen if I called and there was no stalker? Would they take a statement or would they just leave?

Taking the books off of one of my least filled shelves and putting them into the cart where all the new books are. I pull the shelf out and jam it down into the window, even though the window is still locked. I don't want to take any chances.

Then, I call the police. Paying hell doesn't seem too bad right now. I'll deal with Eli's consequences when the time comes.

7

Anthony

THROUGH THE WINDOW, I can see Lila bolting into her library, her movements frantic and desperate as she shoves that lavender chair against the door. After a few minutes, a bright red BMW peels down the driveway, tires spinning on the pavement, the engine growling like an angry beast. Her fear is a physical thing, radiating through the glass. I step deeper into the shadows of the dune grass, my mask still covering most of my face, watching as she sinks into her chair. Not long after, she notices the stack of books I left by the window. The books that weren't supposed to scare her, but clearly have. I didn't think this through.

I can still picture the moment I discovered the key earlier, a poor hiding spot under the welcome mat. I almost laughed when my fingers brushed against it. Most people think they're clever, hiding keys in fake rocks or under flowerpots. Not Lila and her husband. They went with the most obvious spot in the world.

The lock had turned easily. I'd expected an alarm to blare, but nothing happened. Just silence greeting me as I stepped inside. The house felt empty, hollow, like those model homes they stage for open houses, beautiful but unlived in. I moved through it like a ghost, careful to avoid creaking floorboards, holding my breath at every sound.

Somewhere in the house, a shower was running. Her husband, I assumed. I didn't have much time.

The library was easy to find. First floor, in the front of the house. Right off the living room. The door stood slightly ajar, and I pushed it open, holding my breath. The smell hit me first, honeysuckle and vanilla, but underneath that, the unmistakable scent of books. Hundreds of them, lined on shelves from floor to ceiling. A sanctuary. Her sanctuary.

That chair by the door, massive and lavender, the size of a twin bed, it seemed out of place, facing the window instead of one of the bookshelves. But I understood when I saw the throw blanket and small pillow. She sleeps here. Not with him. That told me everything I needed to know.

I placed the books on the small table near the window, arranging them carefully, then scribbled the note on a piece of paper I'd torn from a small notebook nearby. The words seemed fine then, friendly, non-threatening. I wanted her to know I wasn't some random creep, that I'd seen her distress at the bookstore and wanted to help.

Now, watching her through the window, I realize how badly I've fucked up.

Backing away from the table, with my note in her hand, she looks around frantically. Checking in her bathroom. Her closet. Around her window, then walks into her living room and then back into the library. The fear in her is palpable, and I caused it. I never meant to scare her. Fuck, I only wanted to be romantic.

She's looking at the note now, her hands trembling as she unfolds the paper. I should have signed it. Should have explained better. The words I wrote seemed fine at the time, but now, watching her panic, I realize how threatening they must sound. "I will be seeing you soon." What the hell was I thinking?

Pulling out her phone now, scrolling through the cameras. But with the basics Cainen sent and the jammer I picked up from my townhouse, they should all be static now. I look down at my jammer and realize I hadn't turned it on. So, I switch it on and suddenly her face looks more worried than before.

The lights go out and I can barely see her as she looks through the window. I try to duck, not wanting her to see me yet. But she does see me, she looks directly at me. With my mask on, standing in the shadows like some horror movie villain. Her face goes pale, eyes widening as she spots me in the dune grass. I freeze, not daring to move again. Our eyes lock for a heartbeat that seems to stretch into eternity.

I pull out my phone, blocking my number before typing quickly.

> **Unknown number:** Don't call the police. I'm not going to hurt you.

I hit send, watching as her phone lights up in her hand. She reads the message, looks back toward the window, but I've already shifted position, hidden from view behind a tall clump of grass.

Through the window, I can see her dialing anyway. Three numbers before she places the phone to her ear.

"Fuck," I hiss, pulling out my phone again. I hit Dillian's number, not his personal line, but the direct line to his desk at the police station. He picks up on the second ring.

"Maryland State Police, Officer Reynolds speaking."

"Dillian, it's me," I say, keeping my voice low. "I need a favor. Big one."

There's a pause, then his voice drops. "Tony? What the hell, man? I'm on someone else's clock right now."

"I know. That's why I'm calling. There's going to be a 911 call coming in any second from a woman named Lila Fischer. I need you to take it."

"What? Why? What did you do?" His voice is sharp, suspicious.

"Nothing bad, I swear. Look, short version, her husband's an ass. I left her some books as a gift, and she freaked out. Now she's calling the cops on me."

"Books? Where did you leave the books, Tony?" The disbelief in his voice is clear.

"In her house." I reply.

"Have you lost your goddamn mind!?"

"Just take the call, please. Take a cruiser and go yourself. Talk to her, calm her down, but don't look for me. I'm not going to hurt her. I'm trying to help."

Another pause. I can practically hear the gears turning in his head.

"This better not be what it sounds like, Tony," he says finally.

"It's not. I swear."

"Fine. But you owe me an explanation. A real one, not this cryptic bullshit."

"Thank you."

I hang up, relief washing over me. Dillian will handle it. He always does. We've been through too much together for him to let me down now. Still, I owe him big time for this one.

I move further back into the dunes, finding a spot where I can watch the driveway without being seen. A police cruiser pulls through the open gate about fifteen minutes later. Dillian steps out, tall and solid in his uniform, his movements precise as he approaches the front door. Always the professional.

Lila answers after the second knock, her body language screaming anxiety—arms wrapped around herself, shoulders hunched forward. Even from this distance, I can see she's been crying. Was this because of me or her husband?

"Mrs. Fischer?" Dillian's voice carries on the evening air. "I'm Officer Reynolds. We received your 911 call about an intruder?"

She nods, glancing nervously over her shoulder. "Someone broke into my house. Left books and a note in my library. I saw him outside, in the dunes."

Dillian makes a show of looking around, even shines his flashlight toward where I was standing earlier. "I don't see anyone now, ma'am. May I come in and take a look at these books and the note?"

She hesitates, then steps aside. Dillian follows her in, and I lose sight of them. I edge closer to the house, careful to stay hidden, until I can hardly hear their voices through the closed window of the library.

"—a way to get in?" Dillian is asking.

"I don't know," Lila's voice trembles. "The alarm didn't go off. My husband was home earlier, but he left right after we had a fight."

"A fight? About what, if you don't mind me asking?"

Another pause. "Nothing important."

"Mrs. Fischer, I need to ask. Does your husband ever hurt you?"

The silence that follows is so heavy I can feel it pressing against my chest.

"No," she says finally, but the word sounds hollow, practiced. "Why would you ask that?"

"Just routine questions, ma'am. You mentioned a fight, and sometimes domestic situations can escalate."

"It wasn't like that."

Dillian doesn't push it. "What about this note? May I see it?"

There's a rustling of paper. "He says he'll be seeing me soon. What does that mean? Is he going to come back?"

"It could be nothing, ma'am. Some people leave notes like this, thinking they're being romantic, not realizing how threatening it can come across."

"Romantic?" Her voice rises slightly. "Breaking into someone's house isn't romantic!"

"No, it's not," Dillian agrees. "But the books and the note. Maybe the man is just a plain ole idiot?"

Gee, thanks. Dillian.

"Still, I don't want anyone in here without me knowing who they are." Lila says.

"Look, I recommend you carry some pepper spray, keep your doors and windows locked, and maybe consider staying with a friend for a few days if you're concerned."

"I can't leave," she says, so quietly I almost miss it.

"Ma'am?"

"Nothing. Never mind. Will you file a report?"

"Of course. I'll need to take these books as evidence."

"No!" The force in her voice surprises me. "I mean—they're not evidence of a crime, are they? He paid for them. For me."

Dillian pauses. I can picture his face—the slight furrow between his eyebrows when he's thinking. "I suppose not. But the note—"

"I'll keep it, in case anything else happens."

They talk for a few more minutes. Dillian takes down her information, promises to increase patrols in the area, and suggests she call if anything else happens. Standard procedure. I owe him.

The cruiser pulls away about twenty minutes later. I wait another ten before pulling out my phone again.

Dillian answers on the first ring. "You're lucky I caught that call before dispatch routed it. What the hell are you playing at, Tony?"

"Did you see her? Did you see how scared she was? And not just of me."

"Yeah, I saw," he admits reluctantly. "But breaking into her house? Leaving notes? That's crazy, Tony."

"She wouldn't talk to me in the bookstore. I just wanted to get to know her."

"By scaring the shit out of her? Great plan."

I run a hand through my hair, frustrated. "I didn't think it through. I just wanted to do something nice after what happened at the bookstore."

"What happened at the bookstore?" There's suspicion in his voice now.

"Long story. Look, I just need you to trust me on this one. Her husband's bad news. I feel it in my gut. Something isn't right."

"And then what? She falls into your arms, grateful for her knight in shining armor?" The sarcasm is thick.

"It's not like that."

"Isn't it?" He sighs heavily. "Look, just be careful. And for God's sake, stop breaking into her house. That's not helping anyone. This is not how we operate."

"Thanks for taking the call."

"Yeah, well, don't make it a habit. And Tony? We're having a beer soon, and you're going to tell me what this is really about."

"Deal."

I hang up, as I slide my phone into my pocket, it pings again. An email notification. Cainen's software package, right on time. I open it, scanning the instructions. Simple enough—a program that will clone her phone when installed, giving me access to her texts, calls, photos, everything. All I need is five minutes alone with her phone.

I settle in to wait, watching as Lila moves through the house. She keeps checking the windows, the doors. The security cameras are still down, thanks to the jammer. Eventually, she returns to the library, barricades the door again, and turns off all the lights, except a dim one on a table closest to her chair. But I know she's not sleeping. Not yet. The fear is too fresh.

Hours pass. The temperature drops to its nightly low for mid-June. I should leave, come back later, but I can't make myself go. Not until I know she's safe. Not until I can fix what I've done.

Around four in the morning, the dim light in the library finally goes dark. I wait another thirty minutes, watching for any movement, any sign she's still awake. Nothing.

I retrieve the key from under the mat again, turning it slowly in the lock. The door opens silently, and I step inside, holding my breath. The house is quiet, dark. I move through it like a shadow, making my way to the library.

I silently pick the door lock and push gently on the door, wincing at the slight creak of the hinges. The door isn't barricaded anymore. She must have moved the chair at some point.

Lila is asleep in the lavender chair, curled up under a thick throw blanket, her red hair spilling across the pillow. Her face is finally peaceful, the worry lines smoothed away by sleep. Beautiful. So fucking beautiful it makes my chest ache.

Her phone sits on the small table, just past where the door stops, charging. Perfect.

I move silently into the room, careful not to wake her. The installation takes less than five minutes. Cainen's program is efficient. A small green checkmark appears on the screen, confirming the software is installed and running.

I should leave now. I've done what I came to do. But I can't help standing there for a moment longer, watching her sleep. In this moment, she looks so vulnerable, so trusting. Despite the fear that drove her to barricade herself in this room earlier.

"I'm going to make you mine," I whisper, so softly the words barely disturb the air. "I promise."

She stirs slightly, a small frown crossing her face, and I freeze. But she doesn't wake, just shifts under the blanket, settling deeper into sleep.

Slowly, I back away, careful not to make a sound. At the door, I pause for one last look, committing the image to memory. Lila, peaceful in sleep, surrounded by her books. The one place in this house where she feels safe.

I relock the door and pull it closed behind me with a soft click, then make my way back through the silent house. Outside, the night's breeze is cool against my face as I remove my mask. The sky is just beginning to lighten with the first hints of dawn.

As I walk back to my motorcycle hidden in the dunes, I know I'm crossing lines that shouldn't be crossed. Breaking laws. Violating her privacy. But I've seen the fear in her eyes, not just of me, but of him. Of her husband. And I can't walk away from that. I won't.

Tomorrow, I'll start learning everything I can about Lila Fischer and the man who's made her so afraid. And then I'll figure out how to get her away from him.

For now, though, I just need to get home and sleep. I've done enough damage for one night.

8
Lila

I STARE AT THE grain of the wooden floor, tracing the lines and little gouges with my eyes. The house is too quiet. I can hear Eli in his office, the chair creaking under his weight, the faint thump of his desk against the wall when he slams his fist or pounds his keyboard. The walls between our rooms aren't thick enough. I can always hear when he's angry.

My hands tremble when I try to fold the laundry, so I give up and just stuff the shirts into the basket. I want to go back to the library, my safe room, but I have to pass his office to get there. The thought makes my stomach clench. I hover at the end of the hallway, basket pressed to my ribs, and listen.

He's yelling, but not at me. Not yet. I recognize the words, the kind of language he uses when he's online—"fuckin' lag," "bullshit RNG," "goddamn stream snipers." It's comforting, in a way, to know he's distracted. The moment I think that, the words stop, and the silence falls so hard it hurts my ears.

"Lila!" His voice slices through the house. "Get in here."

Oh, god. He must have lost his match.

I don't move. Maybe if I wait, he'll just forget and do something else. But then I hear the slam of his hand on the desk, the scrape of his chair. "Now!" *he shouts.*

I count to five, like I always do, and then shuffle forward. The hallway carpet muffles my steps, but I know he can hear me. He's always listening.

His door is half open, the blackout curtain drawn over the window so the room feels like a cave. It stinks in here. Sweat, old cheese, that sharp sourness that comes from leaving a wet towel to rot in the laundry. The monitors cast a blue glow over everything, turning Eli's face into something waxy and corpse-like. He doesn't look at me at first, just keeps clicking his mouse. Porn, it looks like. He's got the headphones on, so I can't hear what he's watching, but I see the flicker of pale bodies on the screen. I don't like it, so my eyes don't linger.

He glances at me, then yanks the headphones off his head and lets them hang around his neck. "Get over here," *he says, voice flat, like he's bored already.*

I hug the basket tighter. "I was just doing laundry."

"Drop it. Get on your knees."

My mouth is full of dry cotton. "Eli—"

"Did I stutter?" *His eyes are so pale they look white in the light from the monitor.* "I said get on your fucking knees."

I set the basket on the floor and kneel, like I'm at church. My legs are stiff and my knees hurt, but I kneel anyway. I stare at the threadbare carpet.

He spins his chair so he's facing me. He's already hard, the bulge straining through the mesh shorts he never bothers to change out of. "You know what to do," *he says.*

My tongue sticks to the roof of my mouth. "I don't want to."

He leans back, folds his arms, and smirks. "You don't want to?" He repeats it, mocking. "That's not my fucking problem, is it?"

I shake my head no, but my body moves on its own. It's easier to let it happen, to stop fighting. My hands find his thighs, the thin hair slick with sweat. I close my eyes.

He grabs the back of my head and forces me closer, the smell of him so strong I almost gag. He pulls his cock out and slaps it against my cheek, then my lips, smearing pre-cum on my mouth. "C'mon. Don't be fucking useless. Do your marital duties, you fucking fat whore."

I keep my mouth shut.

He wraps his fingers tighter in my hair. It hurts, but I don't make a sound. He jerks my head back and forth, rubbing himself against my lips and nose. I try to pull away, but he yanks hard, and a few strands of hair tear free.

He pushes the head of his cock against my mouth. "Open the fuck up. You want me to get mad?"

I shake my head again. My jaw aches already from clenching it shut, but I won't open it. I can't.

He lets out a sigh, like I'm an inconvenience. Then he slams the side of my head into the edge of the desk. The world goes white and then red. I taste blood, iron and salt.

I gasp, and he takes the opportunity to shove his dirty dick inside my mouth. It's too big, too dry, and he hits the back of my throat in an instant. I choke, sputter, and tears stream down my cheeks. He uses both hands now, one tangled in my hair, the other gripping my jaw so hard I feel the bones grind. He pumps my head back and forth, fucking my mouth like I'm just an object, not a person.

He's breathing heavy now, short little grunts. His eyes are fixed on the monitor, watching the porn even as he uses me. I try to push against his thighs to get away. My knees are numb, everything is numb except the pain in my scalp and the ache in my neck.

He keeps going for what feels like forever. I try not to think, try not to be present. I picture myself floating above, like a balloon, looking down at the mess on the floor. I hear myself making little whimpering sounds, like a puppy, but I don't remember doing it.

He groans, slams my face all the way down to the base, and holds me there. My nose is mashed against his skin, the hair on his dirty balls tickling my chin. I can't breathe. Hot, thick come floods my throat. I gag, but he won't let me pull away. He holds me there until I swallow, until it's all gone, and only then does he let go.

Collapsing backward, gasping. Snot and spit drip down my chin. My face is burning and my mouth tastes like old pennies and something rotten.

He wipes his cock on my hair and tucks himself back in his shorts. "See? It wasn't that fucking hard," he says, already turning back to the screen.

I scramble to my feet, legs shaking, and stumble out of the office. The hallway tilts and I almost fall. I make it to the ensuite bathroom in our bedroom and slam the door.

Dropping to my knees, I get sick in the toilet. My throat is raw, my eyes sting. I heave painfully until there's nothing left.

When I'm done, I sit on the cold tile and hug my knees to my chest. The house is quiet again, except for the distant sounds of Eli's game, and the quiet, rhythmic thumps of his foot bouncing against the floor.

I just sit and count the minutes and try to remember how to breathe.

9
Lila

'*GET THE FUCK OUT of bed, bitch go*'. My alarm repeats the techno beat over and over, jarring me out of a nightmare. I'm grateful. Being trapped in a nightmare of a terrible memory is not something I would wish on my worst enemy. My face and pillow are wet. I must have been crying in my sleep.

Realizing I have just enough time to get in the shower and make myself breakfast. I quickly check the cameras before I leave my library, all clear. I opt for some pop-tarts, a small cup of coffee, just to make it in without falling asleep on the drive. Then I fill my tumbler with ice water.

When I arrive, Valerie greets me as soon as I come into the rear door. "Hey, girl. I hope you didn't already have too much coffee? I brought one for you. Just the way you like." She got here before me today.

"I will always accept more coffee." I laugh.

I move to sit next to her at my own desk and organize all my things, then open up orders for print.

"Which books did you grab at the bookstore yesterday?"

Oh god, yesterday. I'm so exhausted and more than just physically, so much happened that I can't even imagine it all being just one day.

"I actually didn't get anything. Eli got into my account and locked it. I guess I should call the bank and close that account."

"Are you fucking serious right now, Lila?" She asks, and I can tell she's angry on my behalf. "I thought he was leaving you alone?"

"I guess not," I reply. Rubbing my temples. "He chased me into my library and I had to block the door." Leaving out the fiasco about the stalker, I must have a magnet somewhere on my body for unhinged men.

She looks speechless for a moment. A thousand thoughts running through her head. Advice she wants to give but doesn't know which first.

"Lila, you need to leave him before he kills you. You said he's hit you before. Men like that don't just stop. They may get distracted by other things, but it always gets worse."

The bell chimes and one of our regulars walks in with a pickup order. Leaving as soon as it's picked up.

"I'm never going to be okay with this Lila," she says. "Go call the bank and get everything fixed. I want you to start calling or even text me a code word when you get home on work nights. If I don't hear from you, I'm showing up at your house."

"Maybe a code word would be best. How about fluffy?"

She laughs and shakes her head, "Sure, fluffy is good."

The bell chimes again. This time it's Mia, late and rushing as usual. Late or not, she always lightens any mood when she's around. Her laugh is infectious.

"Hey there, my beautiful bitches!" She nearly yells. "You get me a coffee too, Valerie?"

"I sure did. It's in the microwave. Grab it and get out here."

She goes and gets her coffee and I fill her in on the details of yesterday, again leaving out my stalker. She agrees with Valerie, both offering me a place to stay for however long I want.

If I do decide to leave Eli, I can't stay here or anywhere nearby. I'd have to go into hiding. He's said before, I'm either his, or no one's. And that was definitely meant to be a threat. He would come find me.

On break I walk into the back room and make that dreaded call to the bank. The teller answers the phone and after telling her my details and she pulls up my account, she starts apologizing profusely.

"It's okay," I lie.

"Ma'am, we had no idea it wasn't you on the phone, whoever called in, we thought it was you. She had all your information," she says.

Eli must have used a voice changer. The lengths he goes to for control is insane.

She continues, "I put a highlight on your account. No one is to access it but you, in person, from here on out. We've already changed your account information and will be mailing you the details. You can also pull it up with the app."

"Don't mail them. I don't have access to anything that comes through the mail. Can we just change my address?" I ask.

"We can. In light of the situation. Would you be able to come in later today and confirm the changes in person for us?"

"Yes, right after work."

Once I clock out for the day, I head straight to the bank. We go through the motions and I decide to have my banking mail set to Mia's house. Signing what I need to sign to make sure this doesn't happen again.

That was easier than I thought it would be. But that means I'll have to change my direct deposit numbers tomorrow when I get to the shop. They're sending me a new debit card to Mia's house. But now, I can't spend money on anything big or Eli will know my account is back under my control.

Fuck my life. I wish I had known he would be like this before I married him. Showering me with gifts, opening doors, being a complete gentleman... into whatever this is as soon as we left the courthouse. Every time I would try to leave, he would shower me with gifts all over again and apologize. 'It will never happen again' he would say.

Even after hitting me. He would stop, but only for a short time. This has been the longest era of faux peace, three months before yesterday. If peace is what I should even call it, that just came to an abrupt end last night had me fearing the worst. He would have hurt me if he'd caught me before I locked myself away. Now I fear going home.

I'll have to make it a point to check the cameras before I get home to make sure his car isn't there. If he's home, I can try staying gone until he's asleep or just rush straight into my library like before. What a way to live! Usually, when he gets wound up like that, he leaves for anywhere from 3 days to a week or even two. God knows where he goes.

Chapter header

10

Lila

THE WORDS ON THE page blur as I sink deeper into my lavender chair. This horror novel should terrify me, but compared to what's been happening, fictional monsters seem almost comforting. My library wraps around me like a cocoon. The one place in this house where I can breathe. Eli's been gone for a few days now, disappeared after our fight, just like I predicted. A few days of blessed silence, of sleeping without one eye open. But as I turn the page, a flicker of movement outside my window catches my eye, and every muscle in my body tenses at once.

I freeze, book forgotten in my lap. The dune grass outside my window sways in the evening breeze, backlit by moonlight. Nothing there. Maybe it was just....

There. A shadow shifts, too solid to be grass, too deliberate to be wind. I squint, leaning forward in my oversized chair. The silhouette of a man emerges from the darkness, standing perfectly still among the tall grass. My heart hammers against my ribs. It's him. The masked man.

He doesn't move, doesn't try to hide. Just stands there, watching. Even from this distance, I can make out the dull green X's over his eyes, the exposed lower half of his face. The mask that haunts my dreams now. A small blue glow illuminates the bottom edge of his face, his phone screen. My breath catches in my throat.

Is he... is he watching me through the cameras? The same cameras Eli uses to control me?

I grab my phone from the side table, fingers trembling as I open the security app. The feed is crystal clear. No static this time. From the camera angle, I can see myself sitting in my chair, book open, hair falling wild and all over the place. I look small. Vulnerable.

The realization hits me like a punch to the gut. He's hacked into our system. He's watching me through Eli's cameras. I check the other angles: living room, kitchen, upstairs hallway, all functioning perfectly. Has he been watching me all this time? While I sleep? While I shower?

I should call the police. But what would I tell them? That a man is standing in the dunes on the outskirts of my property? That someone might have hacked my security system? Last time they came, they found nothing. Told me to call if "*anything else happens.*"

My mouth goes dry. I know this isn't normal, isn't right. But there's something about the way he stands there, so patient, so still. Not trying to break in, not threatening me directly. Just... watching. As if he's content just to see me.

God, I must be losing my mind. This is exactly how women in horror movies end up dead.

I set my book aside and stand, my legs unsteady beneath me. The smart thing would be to block the window again, hide in the darkness. But I'm tired of hiding, tired of being afraid. If Eli has taught me anything, it's that showing fear only makes things worse. I mean, I like it. But not Eli's variety. He actually hurts me and won't stop, no matter how many times I tell him to.

The kitchen is dark when I enter, moonlight spilling across the marble island. I move toward the butcher block, fingers wrapping around the largest knife. The one with the black handle and a blade that gleams even in the darkness. The weight of it is reassuring in my palm.

I glance at the nearest camera, mounted in the corner above the refrigerator. Its dim red light blinks steadily. Watching. Recording. I lift the knife so it catches the moonlight, making sure it's visible to the camera. I want him to see it. To know I'm not defenseless.

"I'm not afraid of you," I whisper, the words sounding hollow even to my own ears.

I wave the knife slowly in front of the camera, a clear message. Then I turn and walk back to my library, knife clutched tightly in my fist. My heart still pounds, but there's something else mixed with the fear now, a strange, electric thrill. For once, I'm the one making someone else nervous. I'm the one with power.

Back in my library, I approach the window cautiously. He's still there, still watching. The moon highlights the strong line of his shoulders, the breadth of his chest. I can see the slight tilt of his head as he studies me. Does he know I can see him too? Does he want me to?

I reach for the lamp beside my chair and switch it off. The room plunges into total darkness, my eyes taking a moment to adjust. But now I can see him more clearly without the glare of interior lights on the window. He hasn't moved, but his posture has changed somehow. More alert, more intrigued.

We stand like that, separated by glass and distance, watching each other in the darkness. Minutes stretch like hours. My arm grows tired from gripping the knife so tightly, but I refuse to set it down. If he makes one move toward my window, I'll—what? Scream? Attack? Run?

His shoulders move slightly, a silent laugh. As if he finds this little standoff amusing. As if he knows exactly what I'm thinking. The blue glow of his phone lights up again, illuminating the bottom half of his face. I catch the hint of a smile and a dimple in his chin.

My phone buzzes on the chair where I left it. Without taking my eyes off him, I reach back with my free hand and grab it.

> **Unknown Number:** You're beautiful when you're angry.

The words send a chill down my spine. I glance back up, and he's holding his phone, watching for my reaction. I should be terrified. I should be calling the police right now. Instead, I feel something unfamiliar unfurling in my chest. A dark, hungry curiosity.

My fingers hover over the keyboard, trembling slightly. Before I can talk myself out of it, I type:

> **Me:** Who are you?

I watch him read the message, watch his shoulders rise and fall with a deep breath. He types something, then pauses, then deletes it. Types again.

Unknown Number: Someone who sees you. And not just through your window.

The simplicity of it, the truth in it, hits harder than any threat could. When was the last time anyone truly saw me? Not as property, not as a responsibility, but as a person? I type back:

Me: You're stalking me. That's creepy as hell.

Unknown Number: I'm protecting you.

Me: From what exactly?

There's a long pause. The moonlight catches on something slightly reflective at his side, is that a helmet? My grip tightens on the knife.

Unknown Number: From him.

Eli, he means. The thought that this stranger may know more about us than even my closest friends makes my skin crawl. Yet there's something almost comforting in not being alone with this secret anymore. Even if he only knows because he's a fucking stalker. I can easily see myself losing my goddamn mind.

Me: You don't know me.

Unknown Number: I know enough.

Another pause, then:

Unknown Number: Sleep well, Lila. I'll be watching.

With that, he steps backward, melting into the shadows of the dune grass. I move closer to the window, straining to see where he's gone. Nothing. Just darkness and wind-swept grass.

I stay by the window, knife in hand, scanning the darkness for any sign of movement. My phone remains silent. The security cameras continue their steady surveillance, revealing nothing but empty rooms and the occasional shadow cast by passing clouds.

My legs grow tired, but I don't sit. What if he comes back? What if he decides watching isn't enough anymore? The adrenaline that kept me alert begins to fade, leaving exhaustion in its wake. How long has it been since I've truly slept? Not just dozed fitfully with one ear listening for Eli's footsteps, but actually slept?

Minutes tick by. My eyelids grow heavy. I should move the chair to block the door again, just in case. Should check that all the windows are locked. Should do something about the cameras he's somehow hacked into.

Instead, I sink back into my lavender chair, knife still clutched in my hand. Just for a moment, I tell myself. Just need to rest my eyes.

The last thing I see before sleep claims me is the blinking of that dim red light on the camera in the corner of my library, watching. Always watching.

And for the first time in years, that thought doesn't terrify me quite as much as it should.

11

Anthony

WHEN I MAKE IT back to my bike, I hope a short ride will settle me down. My dick and balls are crushed between me and the seat and since I can't stop thinking about her, the fucker won't go back down. It would be better if I just made my way home and either took an ice bath, or rubbed one out. I want her to be mine and feel safe, to enjoy the experience with me. If she feels safe, she'll let me do whatever I want to her.

I imagine chasing her down and catching her, fucking her hard and then caring for her tenderly. Just the way I know she would like. There are no journals in her room, no writings that were personal anywhere, but her books have a ton of highlighted sex scenes and chapters. I took pictures and saved some on my phone.

She has no idea how often I sneak in when no one is home, just so I can learn more about her. I even watch her while she sleeps, and she is a deep, deep sleeper. I bet she thinks she isn't. She hasn't woken up before her alarm the entire time I've been sneaking inside. Not even tonight's visit, after she'd thought I'd left. I went rummaging upstairs first and stole a pair of her lacy panties. That whole stunt with the knife didn't change my mind at all, but it did seem to make her feel better.

Pulling up to my townhouse, a nice view of the bay here. I hadn't realized how close I lived to her until Cainen sent me that software.

Leaving my bike in the garage, I head through the inner garage door, up the stairs into the kitchen. I put my keys on the counter. The only downside is there are three levels to this townhouse and the master suite is on the third floor. I dart up the stairs. These panties are burning a hole in my pocket while my dick is trying to drill through my pants. A cold shower isn't going to cure this ache.

Throwing all my clothes on the floor and climbing onto my bed, with my phone in one hand and her panties in the other, I bring up the camera from her library. She's sleeping soundly. What I wouldn't give to have her here.

Propping my phone up on the side table so I can watch her sleep, laying on my back with my head turned to her relaxed form. She's also on her back, with her copper hair splayed over her pillow, highlighting those beautiful blonde streaks on either side. One arm above her head, the other tucked into her night shorts.

I bring the panties up to my nose and inhale, imagining that she's touching herself for me, too. My cock twitches and I take it in my other hand. Stoking gently at first, wishing that it was her small hand gripping me.

Adding in some lube, hoping it will make it feel more like her pussy, I stroke harder and faster. My body tightens and loosens as the sensation of my orgasm builds at the base of my spine and works its way up my body. She stirs in her chair and lets out a sleepy sigh, almost like she knows.

I'm undone. I wrap Lila's panties around my cock and grip a little harder, stoking faster. Releasing ropes of cum all over them. Who knew that simply having her panties would make me come so much harder?

"Fuck, Lila." I growl as I throw my head back. Unable to keep my legs still until my climax is over. "Damn it, I've ruined your underwear," I sigh deeply at my phone screen. She's still sleeping peacefully. "Guess I'll have to try and take another pair before I leave for a week next month."

I don't care that the next pair aren't lace either. As long as they carry the scent of her velvet pussy.

Wanting this woman so badly; I don't understand it myself. I want her body, her mind, her very soul. She will be mine. I won't settle for anything else.

Good thing I got this little piece of her now, though. In case I can't get back in before next month. I have a mission and I need to be focused. Fortunately for her, if this goes on much longer, I'll be forced to come inside and love her whether she wants me to or not. Though, I have a strong feeling that she would be willing.

I'm starting to get hard thinking of her all over again. Maybe I should try a cold shower before I hurt myself.

12

Lila

HE STANDS OUTSIDE MY library window most nights, between the sections of dune grass. Even after I threatened him with a knife in the camera. It's been a couple of weeks and he hasn't made contact again. Nor has he left any more notes, assuming that he is the one who left it with the books before.

He just stands there and watches, like he's hoping for some sort of reaction. Eli told me I couldn't call the police again and if whoever it was wanted to kill me, they would have already. That is not comforting at all. Then again, it has been a very long time since he cared to comfort me, if he ever has.

After that last incident, Eli hasn't really spoken to me either. I prefer this over what was going on before. I'd rather coast along alone than be in the same house with Eli. He didn't come home after that night for over a week, yet still seemed to know that I'd called the police. He hasn't stayed more than a night or two since then either.

As I sit here in my little library, alone, thoughts move from past to present, as they usually do. My chair is facing the window but still in front of my door. I keep all the lights in this room off when it's dark outside so I can see him out there, wearing his strange mask with the dim lights. It's harder for him to see through the window. His silhouette is lit up by the moonlight when the moon is high in the sky, reflecting off of the bay. He stands there for hours. Watching me on his phone instead of through the window after I've turned all the lights off.

I can't help the thrill I feel that moves from the fear in my heart, to the heat between my legs. Before he started watching me, I don't remember the last time I felt that way. Thrill and not the terror Eli instills. I can't trust him, I *know* he will hurt me... he has before.

Of course, I'm not stupid enough to believe this man outside won't hurt me, either. What the hell am I hoping for, anyway? I'm married and I know if I try to leave, Eli will find me. I'm snared and can't get away, no matter how many times I've tried in the past.

This almost has to be the man from the bookstore. He's the only run in with a man that I've had. I haven't met anyone else, and he was way too friendly when we met and followed me to my car like a lost puppy. I can't believe he called me gorgeous in public. That and how the fuck he got into my house. I thought I'd been clear when I told him no.

These staring contests are the worst. I can't do anything else until I'm sure he's left. I can't read, I can't sleep. Though sometimes I pretend to sleep to see if he will get closer to the window, but he doesn't. Both he and Eli know how to manipulate the cameras. I never seem to catch Eli's activities or when this voyeur shows up and leaves.

Only when I see him walk away and outside cameras stop cycling, I assume he's gone. He could just be moving to watch me from somewhere I can't see. Giving me false security.

Is he getting gratification from watching me or is he fucking with me? There are a million women out there that are actually beautiful. Worth spending time with and doting on, versus watching me, an unhappily married woman, through the window. I haven't meant anything to my own husband for such a long time. So emotionally neglected that I accept attention from a lunatic.

What would it be like to be loved again, or was I ever? Geez, I am stupid. Letting my thoughts wander to a stalker romance instead of reality. This is unhealthy. I couldn't stray even if it were reality. I'm married, I can't be that kind of person. Even if Eli has broken his vows, I won't. But... Maybe I should. Would Eli even care?

I tried to tell Eli that I knew this person was hacking into our cameras, but he doesn't think anyone else can do it because they're not as smart as him. There are plenty of people in this world smarter than he is. He simply has a bigger ego and is high on himself most of the time.

I watch as he turns and picks something up off the ground, then steps back behind the grass.

He doesn't come back to the window once he walks away, so I've gotten comfortable falling asleep after. Though his watching is oddly comforting compared to the heavy feeling that comes from Eli's office, even when I know I'm here alone. That could be my own paranoia. These men have me on edge.

13
Anthony

W HEN THE SUN STARTS to set, turning the sky a brilliant shade of orange and pink, we've been up for hours, gathering information about the villagers and their children. We had dinner with the families and the extraction is planned for tomorrow morning.

The families here offer to pay us to retrieve their stolen daughters from a group of terrorist. They'd killed the bus driver and took the whole bus with twelve girls, we were told they were all under fifteen, still inside. Their government has all but given up.

These sorts of rescues we do for nothing, we ask only for room and board until the mission is over. This way we can figure out who we can trust and who we can't.

I use my income from GameStream to cover it all. Being the silent owner of the largest streaming company in the world has its perks. I'd say these rescues are the most important.

It's scorching hot here during the day and freezing cold at night. Even though I'm trained for this, I still complain. The locals don't seem to notice; they're either used to it or keep their gripes to themselves. When the sun sinks below the horizon, and it's different in the desert. There are no clouds for the light to bounce off—just an open sky where the moon and stars' true brilliance goes uninterrupted, casting a rippling glow across the salt flats. Nowhere else in the world is like this.

My thoughts drift to Lila at home, probably curled up in her oversized lounge chair, lost in one of the books I left her. She has no idea I'm away or anything about me, really. Yet she is the one person I want to see as soon as our flight home lands.

"Tony!" One of my team members calls out, pulling me back from my thoughts. It's Dillian.

"What?!"

"I've been calling your name for ten minutes! What's going on?" Dillian asks, his flat blue eyes piercing through the firelight.

"You already know, Dilly Boy. It's that woman he's stalking," Jonathan chimes in. He's the oldest among us still working extraction; almost all his hair is gray now.

"I'm not stalking her, dumbass. I'm just trying to get to know her," I retort.

"By watching her cameras all the damn time and leaving her little gifts?" Jonathan asks with a smirk as he leans back and pretends to stretch like an old man. "That's stalking, son."

"You didn't see how hurt she was when her husband cut her off. You'd be pissed, too."

"Not stalking pissed," Dillian replies. "Most normal guys don't just pick a random woman and stalk her."

"I don't know why I'm attached to her! When I figure it out, I'll let you know." I lean back against my camping chair and cross my arms and ankles. "I just have this strange feeling that she isn't safe. And for fuck's sake, stop using the word stalk."

"We've done this long enough together to trust our gut," Jonathan says while tossing small sticks into the fire he has been trying unsuccessfully to ignite for over an hour.

I trust my gut, I know her husband is worthless, and there is so much they don't understand about Lila that I haven't shared with them.

"Give that here, old man. I'll light it," Dillian says as he snatches sticks and lighter from Jonathan's hands and quickly starts a fire. "Losing your touch! Maybe it's time you retire," Dillian teases.

"And leave all the fun for you babies? No way! You'd get yourselves killed. Especially with Tony spacing out over there." Jonathan turns the focus back to me.

"You know Tony," Dillian says while raking his fingers through his dark blond hair, "my wife once told me about something she believes in."

"What's that?" I ask sarcastically but feigning interest.

"She reads those same types of books as Lila, she said you're welcome for those book recommendations."

Shaking my head dismissively, I roll my hand in encouragement for him to continue.

"Get to the point, Dilly Boy." Jonathan echoes my displeasure; he has never had much patience during conversations, anyway.

"She thinks humans have soul-ties," Dillian explains while avoiding eye contact with me. This guy is a genius with logic and science; does he actually believe this?

"What kind of fuckery is that?" Jonathan scoffs with amusement sparkling in his deep green eyes.

"It means when you see someone and feel a connection you can't explain, and they feel it too. Like when a mother hears her child calling out while they're apart or when a wife loses a spouse while away."

"Good God, boy! Go to sleep before I knock your head off. That's ridiculous. We have a long day tomorrow; things are going to be hellish. We don't want Tony distracted while we're getting shot at."

"Whatever, man," Dillian shrugs as he rises from his chair and heads toward our small hut. "I thought I'd bring it up since he doesn't understand himself."

"Maybe he has a point there, even if it's crazy," I say quietly as Dillian walks away. "I don't understand."

"I get it, but if you're not focused tomorrow, this could end badly." Jonathan points toward Dillian. "Now get your dirty ass some sleep, too."

"Fine! Goodnight Dad!"

"Fuck off!" Jonathan replies sharply.

It isn't even five in the morning and it's already hot enough to make the air hum; the dawn seeping into our borrowed hut. The first thing I do is drink from the warm canteen beside my cot, feeling the mineral tang in my mouth, before I walk out into the village and face the day's preliminary chaos. Roosters crow across the valley, and the breeze is filled with dust, incense smoke, prayers to their gods for the girls' safe return.

Our client, a middle-aged former politician with a voice that rattles when he speaks, is waiting for us outside, clutching a photo of his daughter and squeezing an effigy until his knuckles blanch. He bows his head and says nothing, just holds out a folded note with the latest ransom demand, which Jonathan takes with gentle hands. For twelve daughters, the terrorists want $100 for each girl. These people are used to losing things, governments, teachers, crops. But, when it comes to their children, they appeal to whatever god will answer quickest.

This time, it's us. I've brought enough to get the girls without a fight. But we will fight for them if we have to. No one should be trafficked or abused.

Inside, Dillian is already hunched over a laptop, blue light washing out the lack of sleep beneath his eyes. He's running comms with the nearest airfield and scouring foreign social channels for any sign of movement from the crew holding the girls. They run on generator power, so we've supplied batteries to keep things running smoothly with no flits and flickers. He glances up when I enter and gives a quick nod.

"You know how long they'll last in there," he says. "If they're still inside with the windows locked up, no air conditioning, they're not going to make it much longer."

I check the maps again, then my gear, then Jonathan's, then Dillian's, and double-count our supplies. Tape, fuel, injectables, commemorative cigarettes in case the job goes to hell. Jonathan is already suited up, sorting the small bundles of local currency and folding them into separate envelopes, one for each of the girls' ransom. He insists on doing these things himself.

At the edge of the village, we gather our things and step into the waiting pickup. A boy no older than the girls we're saving, waits to drive us. His eyes so dark they reflect the world.

The desert here isn't like the ones in movies; it's flat and white, with heat simmering just above the horizon and giving everything a mirage blur. The radio hisses in another language, cutting in and out. The plan is simple: Dillian will jam their cameras, Jonathan will negotiate the drop while I cover him, then we grab them and run before the rest of the enemies change their minds. Everyone expects it to go badly and it might, if they realize who we are and that we could pay more. I wouldn't put it past the greedy bastards to try.

The drive takes an hour, the sun climbing overhead, pounding the roof of the pickup. I swear I can hear sizzle. The closer we get, the more I start to think of the girls, how they might be huddled together in the bus, dehydrated, and how their throats must be raw from crying and their wrists bruised from ties. It reminds me of things I locked away a long time ago, people I couldn't save when I was new at this. Some mornings I wake up convinced those ghosts are sitting at the foot of my bed.

Dillian's phone buzzes a warning: We've reached the drop site. The pickup stops behind a spit of rock, and we walk the rest of the short distance on foot.

When we're in position, Jonathan takes a moment to kneel in the sand and say a prayer. He says he doesn't believe in God, but I've been doing this with him long enough to know better. Maybe it's for the girls, maybe it's for us, or maybe it's for the wife and daughter he hasn't seen in ten years. I don't ask.

I'm not sure when they realized it, but my worse fear is going down. They know who we are and are making more demands of Jonathan. They shot first, aiming for Dillian.

Then, the gun battle is exactly as expected, a short, brutal window of noise and dust and men screaming in four different languages. We're faster, better trained, and more desperate than they are, especially after Dillian's surprise cut to the bus's battery, which unlocks the doors and switches off the cameras. There's blood on my hands today, but thankfully, not innocent blood.

When it's over, we hustle the girls into the bed of the pickup, counting off twelve terrified faces, none of them older than thirteen. We tell the boy to drive fast, and he does. Back at the village, the parents don't hug them right away; they just stare, wide-eyed, as if the universe has played a trick on them by returning what was lost. We add security measures to the local villages so that this is less likely to happen again, at least in the near future.

After the debrief, when I am alone at sunset and can finally breathe, I find myself thinking not of the girls or the bullets, but of Lila, curled in her chair, reading the books I'd left her. She knows nothing about this side of me. She may not want to. Even so, she is the only thing that feels real when the adrenaline fades.

Now, I can't wait to get home. I can't wait to pay my girl a visit.

14

Lila

I'M NOT SURE HOW long I've been asleep, but when I wake up, it's still dark. Thirsty, I notice my water bottle is empty. I decide to head to the kitchen and fill it with filtered water from the refrigerator before going back to sleep.

Since I threatened him with the knife, I'd only seen him sporadically, when before I'd seen him nearly every night. I've lost track of how long it's been since I saw him. Which is good. Maybe he's forgotten about me. And after that day Eli chased me in my library, he's only been staying home for a night or two at a time before leaving again. I wish I knew exactly what he was doing, but I can't go into his office to investigate. He watches me from wherever he is. I also wouldn't be surprised if there was an alarm on that door.

As I turn away, I lean against the sink, taking a drink from my newly filled water bottle. That's when I see movement by the sliding door. My stalker stands there holding the handle, looking inside, staring right at me. The sight of him makes my heart pound. Swallowing the water in my mouth, it immediately goes dry, and pressure builds in my head.

I just stand here and stare at him, frozen in place. Then, the door slowly clicks shut and latches. That sound hits me hard, I realize he was just inside while I slept, and I forgot to check the cameras before leaving my library. I know better than to check the cameras now; there won't be anything to see. They will be cycling and there would be no evidence. They've both been gone so long that I keep forgetting to check and Eli must be gone if he's this close. He backs carefully away from the door toward the steps, and that's when my body kicks back into gear.

Grabbing a knife from the butcher's block, I stomp toward the door as he steps down onto the patio below. Throwing it open so hard that it slams against the frame as I rush through it and toward the same steps. My foot lands on the first tread when I remember it rained earlier, and I'm barefoot. I slip, and thankfully, the knife clatters on the deck behind me instead of under me as I slide down a few treads.

Fuck, fuck, fuck.

It takes me a moment to register that he stands in front of me, his mask still on. He must have turned back when I fell. I can't see his face, only his mouth, where a small dimple rests in his chin. His head tilts down at my sheer white tank and thin black night shorts. Suddenly, he rushes me, pinning my wrists above my head. The weight of him presses down on me as he slides a knee up between my legs and spreads them apart. A gasp escapes my lips. Heat radiates from my wrists down between my legs, and my face burns.

"I won't hurt you," he whispers in my ear, his hot breath caressing my neck, sending a warm thrill coursing through my body, straight to my core.

He moves one hand from my wrists to caress the side of my face, then slowly trails it down over my breast and hard nipple; I shudder at the contact as he continues down to my waist. I can feel his hard length straining against his pants as he starts to grind over my now throbbing clit. My body ignites with desire; a soft moan slips from me, and I hear him groan in response.

"I've missed you," he says.

I am ruined, absolutely ruined. My stalker grinds into me, and I let him do it. I must be sick in the head, but god, I love it. If this is what depravity feels like, then I embrace it fully. The edges of his mask lightly scratch against my skin while he kisses and nips gently at my neck and jaw. He moves against me. The friction builds toward an orgasm while I sigh and gasp. I know I'm soaked; I can feel it between my legs, knowing I'll leave that evidence on his pants.

He slides his hand up into my shirt between my breasts, massaging that space tenderly as he growls low in my ear, "No bra? Naughty girl."

Then he cups my breast and palms my nipple while continuing to kiss the sensitive skin of my neck and cheek. At that moment, I come apart, sparks fly before my eyes, and no one has ever given me an orgasm before. God, what have I been missing?

I can't believe I just came like this. He didn't even need to touch the tender skin under my shorts with his hands. Have I really been so touch starved that this does it for me?

Once the spasms subside, he pulls his hand from under my shirt and hooks a finger into the crotch of my shorts, nuzzling gently against my throbbing flesh. The touch makes me let out a light, breathy moan.

"So wet for me," he groans in response. "Gorgeous."

Realization crashes over me, I recognize his voice; it IS the man from the bookstore, and even though part of me wants more, another part knows and that word escapes me anyway: softly spoken yet barely audible to myself. He hears it; suddenly his weight disappears from atop me and I miss the warmth immediately.

I scramble trying to get on my feet, hoping not to slip again I end up climbing back up the steps on my hands and feet, I quickly reach down and grab the knife before rushing through the door behind me, locking it tight after flipping the door latch closed, and tossing the knife into the sink as panic floods through me while looking out through the window down towards the driveway leading to the main road of our community: he's gone.

What just happened? What have I done? Embarrassment washes over me like fire while terror grips tightly around my heart. I can't shake off thoughts of Eli seeing any of this on camera; if he does... I'm dead.

Yanking my water bottle off the counter and quickly making my way back inside my library. I am utterly confused now. I grab my phone and pull up the camera feeds just to check; they had been cycling earlier without even revealing that stalker was here at all. The cameras remain clear for now, thank goodness.

Thoughts race uncontrollably: Am I a horrible person? Was that cheating? Did I just cheat on Eli? Why do I care so much? Bringing my left hand up slowly reveals naked ring finger, no wedding band since the last time Eli forced himself on me, not like tonight. He'd really hurt me, leaving physical scars on my body and in my mind.

Sliding my chair back against the library door, I crawl under one of my throw blankets, feeling safer there until noticing something new resting atop the nightstand. Another book! I must have woken up because he was in the room, then tried to leave unnoticed when I came into the kitchen... I lay awake, fantasizing about what would have happened if I'd let him continue. Simultaneously berating myself for both telling him to stop and letting him go as far as he did.

15

Anthony

I HEAR HER WHISPER "stop" in my ear, and I do. I don't want to stop at all; I crave her so intensely that my entire body aches. It's not worth breaking her trust. I pull back, distancing myself from her. The front of my pants is slick with her arousal, and I let out a groan as I hurry around the house toward the dunes where my bike is hidden. She scrambles back up the steps, and I hear the knife softly clatter as she picks it up again. Then the sliding door slams shut. None of this was part of the plan.

All I wanted was to leave her another book. She woke up and caught me off guard. After that last mission, I couldn't wait to see her. Tonight was the perfect night since Eli wasn't home. She hid the key somewhere else, so I had to pick the back lock and disable her alarm. Maybe I made too much noise? Maybe I lingered too long; perhaps her body sensed my presence and stirred her awake. I wanted to apologize to her for this, but that would make things worse.

If she hadn't fallen down those steps, I wouldn't have turned around, and she might have gone back inside. Did I take it too far? I was so close to losing control that it terrified me. Jesus Christ, that would have been better than this insatiable ache within me. In my 32 years of life, I've never felt so turned on before.

Once I'm back at my bike, I watch her house from a distance. All the lights switch off again, and I can picture her settling back into her chair, blocking the door as she used to do, not long ago. Tonight I was surprised to find her library door unlocked. I'm not sure if it was a fluke, she just forgot, or if she was becoming comfortable again.

Since that night I put the surveillance software on her phone, I've watched her for hours while we were away. Even as she worked with Mia. I watched from their security cameras and I watched from her phone camera as she scrolled while having lunch. She's had almost no interaction with Eli at all. Hopefully, his intent isn't to make her comfortable, then try to hurt her. I want him to stay as far away from her as possible.

Starting my bike here isn't an option; the noise would draw attention and I've already caused enough trouble tonight. So, I walk it down the street a bit before hopping on and heading home. It starts to rain again. Thankfully, I don't have far to go.

My townhouse sits on the other side of the bay from Lila's place, conveniently near my little sister Mia's house, but I've never seen Lila visit there herself. Is that because of Eli? He probably accuses her of cheating if she doesn't come straight home after work or errands. Is that why she escapes into those fantasy novels so often?

After I arrive home, I put my bike in its own mini plastic cubical. Perfect for a matte black beauty. Ascending the stairs from the garage into the kitchen, the only noise inside is the faint hum from the refrigerator. Taking a beer from it, I chug it hoping the cold will cool me off after my experience. It does nothing. Maybe a cold shower will?

My master suite is at the top, so I head up there and undress, placing all my wet clothes in the hamper. Except for the jeans with Lila's scent, I toss those on my bed.

Sleep is going to be impossible tonight. I lean forward, pressing my palms against the cool tile, breathing heavily. Trying to think of something else, anything, but all I can picture is Lila on the stairs, her cheeks flushed a deep red, her tank top clinging to her skin, eyes wide and alive. I can't shake her from my mind. I squeeze my eyes shut and let the water wash over my face, hoping it will drown out thoughts of her. It doesn't work. I feel her thighs pressed around me as I rub against her. I think of how she shudders when I hold her wrists above her head. The desire to taste her makes my teeth ache.

I replay the sound she made when I moved against her. Her breath hitching in a way I've never heard before, as if she's never been touched like that. With some conditioner in my hand, I grip myself tightly and stroke quickly, wishing for a swift release so I can finally rest. I envision the curve of Lila's backside as she hurries up the stairs and recall the first time I'd seen her at the bookstore. She tries to shrink away from me, her hair bright against that black shirt, chin tucked down as she avoids meeting my gaze.

I imagine kneeling between her legs in that library of hers, pushing apart those soft thighs and licking until she forgets every word she's ever read; so she can live those

scenes instead of pretending they are just stories. As I
pump my hand faster, muffled noises escape me. The
image that keeps returning is Lila gasping for air, eyes
rolling back in bliss as pleasure courses through her body;
how that thin tank top fabric reveals every detail beneath.

I want to ruin Lila for every other man, to make her
scream my name and then hold her close as she comes
down from that high. Thoughts drift to seeing her on her
knees in my shower; water cascading down those shoulders while hair clings to her face. I'd guide those hands to
my thighs and let her decide how far she'd go, not forcing
but not stopping either, as she'd let me take control.

Pleasure builds within me; legs tremble under pressure while locking my knees into place to keep going.
That's when it hits hard enough that everything around
me fades for a moment. I lean back with each pulse releasing itself from me with low grunts escaping my lips. Even
after finishing, an ache remains, a hollow feeling inside
that only Lila can fill.

After rinsing off and turning off the water, I dry myself
quickly before padding naked into my bedroom where
earlier-worn jeans lie on the bed; pressing them briefly
to my face inhaling any last traces of her scent brings
a strange guilt creeping in, a sense of crossing an irre-
versible line.

The longing consumes me. It scares me more than anything else because it isn't just about sex; it's about wanting
every piece of who she is. Wanting access to all parts of
Lila's life. Collapsing onto the mattress pushes aside these
thoughts for only a few minutes before rolling over to grab
my phone instead, I open up the app checking camera feeds
scanning for any sign of familiarity among shadows within

Lila's home's angles until one realization strikes: there are no cameras inside Eli's office.

I wonder what he's trying to hide. Maybe I should dig a little deeper and find out. Something feels off. He has all these cameras to watch Lila, but none for her to watch him.

She is in her library, and it seems like she's already asleep. I hope this means she will trust me. Halloween is around the corner, and it's hard to believe I've been following her for four months, yet this is the closest we've come in contact. It's October now.

There's a masquerade party at the club by the board-walk; I wonder if I can cleverly ask Mia to persuade Lila to come without her finding out my secret. Our brief encounter might have given her some confidence.

After closing the app I've been using to watch her, I send Cainen a text message asking if he thinks there's a way to tap into Eli's office or even track his car. I really do wonder where he goes during these long absences, especially with someone like Lila at home.

16

Lila

MY TECHNO ALARM BLASTING repeatedly again, forcing me back to consciousness after what feels like mere minutes of sleep. My body feels different this morning, there's a lingering warmth where his hands touched me, phantom pressure where his weight held me down. I stretch and wince at the slight soreness in my wrists, faint bruises already forming like bracelets. What happened last night was real. Not a dream, not a fantasy pulled from one of my books. And I'm going to have to face Valerie and Mia with this secret written all over my face.

I go through my morning routine on autopilot. Shower, coffee, clothes. I pull on a long-sleeved shirt desperate to hide the dull marks circling my wrists. In the bathroom mirror, I spot a faint pink mark on my neck where he kissed me. I dab concealer over it, hands trembling slightly before covering it with a towel again. What am I doing? Hiding evidence like some criminal?

The drive to work is a blur. My head buzzes with replays of last night, each memory sending fresh waves of heat through my body. I should be horrified. I should be calling the police. Instead, I'm pressing my thighs together at stoplights, reliving the pressure of him against me.

When I pull into the print shop parking lot, I catch myself smiling in the rearview mirror. A real smile, not the practiced one I've worn for years. I quickly school my expression into something more neutral, but it keeps creeping back. God, I'm a mess.

The bell chimes as I come through the back door. Valerie and Mia are already there, both hovering near the counter with coffee cups in hand.

"Well, look what the cat dragged in! You're later than usual," Valerie says, but her teasing tone falls away as she studies my face. "Holy shit, what happened to you?"

I freeze halfway to my desk. "What do you mean?"

Mia steps closer, her eyes narrowing. "You're... glowing. And smiling. At 9:30 AM on a Tuesday." She presses the back of her hand to my forehead. "Are you sick? Did you win the lottery? Did Eli finally get hit by a bus?"

A nervous laugh bubbles out of me before I can stop it. "No, nothing like that." I set my purse down and busy myself with arranging things on my desk, avoiding their eyes.

"Spill it," Valerie demands, blocking my path when I try to move toward the microwave to grab Val's daily gift of morning coffee. "You haven't looked like this since... actually, I don't think I've ever seen you look like this."

I hesitate, suddenly aware of how crazy this will sound. My two best friends are staring at me with matching expressions of curiosity and concern. I trust them more than anyone else in my life. If I can't tell them, who can I tell?

"I had an... encounter last night," I begin, my voice dropping to a whisper even though we're alone in the shop.

Mia's eyebrows shoot up. "An encounter? Like, with a person? A male person?"

I nod, my face burning.

"Oh my god," Valerie breathes. "You cheated on Eli?"

"No!" I say quickly, then backtrack. "Well, sort of. Not really. Nothing happened. I mean, something happened, but not... that."

"You're not making any sense," Mia says, pulling me toward the back room. "Come on, we need privacy for this conversation."

They usher me into the small break room and close the door. Valerie leans against it like she's worried I might bolt, while Mia perches on the edge of the table, both of them staring expectantly.

I take a deep breath. "Remember how I told you about that guy at the bookstore? The one who tried to buy me those books?"

They nod in unison.

"And remember how I mentioned someone watching the house? Standing in the dune grass?"

More nods, more intense now.

"Well, it's the same person. And last night, I caught him. Or he caught me. It's complicated."

I explain how I woke up thirsty, went to the kitchen, and saw him at the door. I tell them about grabbing the knife, about slipping on the steps, about him pinning me down. My body betraying me, where I let him touch me, where I came apart under his hands.

"And then I recognized his voice, it was the book-store guy. I said 'stop,' and he just... left. Disappeared into the night." I twist my hands in my lap, the sleeve of my shirt riding up slightly to reveal the edge of a dull bruise.

Valerie grabs my wrist before I can pull it back, pushing the sleeve higher. "Jesus, Lila," she hisses. "He did this to you?"

I snatch my hand back. "It's not what you think. He didn't hurt me."

"Those are fucking handprints," Mia says, her voice rising. "He held you down. That's assault!"

"No, it wasn't like that," I insist, though I know how it sounds. How do I explain that those bruises came from pleasure, not pain? That I didn't fight him because I didn't want to?

"Then what was it like?" Valerie asks, her tone softer now, concerned rather than accusatory.

I stare at the linoleum floor, tracing patterns with my eyes. "He stopped when I asked. He could have hurt me. I was alone, Eli wasn't home, he had me pinned, but he didn't. He just... left."

"That doesn't make him a good guy," Mia says. "That makes him, bare minimum, not being a rapist."

I flinch at the word. "I know how it sounds. I know I'm probably crazy. But for a moment there, I felt..." I trail off, unable to articulate the mix of fear and excitement and desire that still courses through me when I think of him.

"You felt what?" Valerie prompts.

"Alive," I whisper. "I felt alive. For the first time in years."

The room falls silent. I don't dare look up, afraid of what I'll see in their faces. Judgment, disgust, pity—all reactions I deserve.

"Lila," Valerie says finally, her voice gentle. "You know this isn't normal, right? A stranger watching your house, breaking in, putting his hands on you. That's not romantic, it's dangerous."

"I know," I say, though part of me rebels against the words. "But nothing about my life is normal. My husband locks me out of my own bank accounts and chases me around the house. I sleep with furniture against my door. I have a safe word with my friends in case I need rescuing. Is it really that crazy that something abnormal would make me feel good for once?"

Mia sighs and slides off the table, coming to sit beside me. "We're not judging you," she says, though I can tell she absolutely is. "We're worried. Men like this, they seem exciting at first. Different. But they all turn out the same in the end."

"He's not like Eli," I say, a hint of defiance in my voice.

"You don't know what he's like," Valerie counters. "You've only even been close enough to actually touch him once, let alone speak to him. That's not exactly a solid character assessment."

I bite my lip, knowing she's right but hating to admit it. "I'm not saying I'm going to run away with him or anything. I'm just... I don't know. Processing, I guess."

"Just promise us you'll be careful," Valerie says. "And remember, if anything, anything, feels wrong, text us 'fluffy' and we'll be there in ten minutes or less."

"With baseball bats," Mia adds, a fierce glint in her eye.

I laugh despite myself. "I promise. And thank you, for not thinking I'm completely insane."

"Oh, we definitely think you're insane," Mia says, but she's smiling now. "But we love you anyway."

The conversation shifts as customers begin to arrive, though I catch Valerie and Mia exchanging worried glances throughout the morning. I throw myself into work, grateful for the distraction from my swirling thoughts. We print labels for a local bakery, package up a rush order of business cards, and sort through the day's mail drop-offs.

By lunchtime, the tension has eased. We eat sandwiches in the back room, and Mia starts telling us about a disastrous date she went on over the weekend. It's comforting, this return to normalcy, even if everything beneath the surface has shifted.

"Oh!" Mia says suddenly, mid-story. "I almost forgot. The club is doing a Halloween Masquerade next weekend. We should go!"

"I don't know. It's been a long time since I've done anything like that." I say.

"Oh, come on. The point is, it's a masquerade. Masks, dancing, drinks. We're going." Mia adds.

My heart skips at the word "masks." Images of green X's and a dimpled chin flash through my mind. "I don't know," I hedge. "Eli might be home."

"Has he said anything about a trip?" Valerie asks.

I shake my head. "No, I never know when he's going to be home or when he'll be leaving again. I do know that once he does leave, I have at least three days."

"Well, if he's gone, you're coming," Mia declares. "No excuses. You need a night out that doesn't involve being stalked or manhandled."

I feel a blush creeping up my neck and hope they don't notice. "Fine, if he's gone, I'll come."

Valerie nods approvingly. "Good. And if anything happens with your 'admirer' before then, you tell us immediately. No keeping secrets just because you think we'll judge you."

"I won't," I promise, though I'm already wondering what I'll say if he comes back tonight. If he touches me again. If I let him.

The rest of the day passes in a whirl of customers and orders. By closing time, I'm exhausted but strangely light. Sharing my secret, most of it, anyway, has lifted some of the weight from my shoulders. My friends might think I'm making a mistake, but they're still here, still on my side.

As I drive home, I find myself scanning the dune grass, looking for his silhouette. Part of me hopes he's there. A larger part hopes he isn't. Because despite what I told Valerie and Mia, despite the thrill that runs through me at the memory of his touch, I know they're right. This isn't normal. This isn't safe.

But then, neither is going home to Eli. And at least with my masked man, I have a choice.

17

Lila

I CHECK MY PHONE for the fifth time in twenty minutes, scanning for any notifications from the home security system. Eli left this morning for another "business trip," his BMW roaring down the driveway before I'd even finished my coffee. His absence should feel like freedom, but instead, my chest tightens with the knowledge that someone might be watching now. I tuck the phone back into my purse and push open the door to Akira Sushi. Valerie and Mia are already seated at our usual corner table, heads bent together in conversation, and the sight of them loosens something inside me.

"There she is!" Valerie waves, her blonde hair catching the light. "We were about to send out a search party."

I slide into the booth across from them, my body sinking gratefully into the cushioned seat. "Sorry. Traffic was bad near the boardwalk."

"Sure it was," Mia says with a knowing smile. "It definitely wasn't you standing in front of your closet for thirty minutes deciding what to wear."

Heat creeps up my neck as I glance down at my outfit. Dark jeans and a loose emerald blouse that Valerie once said brings out the blue in my eyes. I did spend longer than usual getting ready, though I'm not sure why. It's just dinner with friends, not a date. But this is the only time I really get to dress up.

"I see you ordered without me," I nod toward their half-empty glasses of plum wine.

"First round only," Valerie pushes a menu toward me. "We were thirsty."

A waitress appears at our table, notebook in hand. I order a pot of green tea rather than wine, still feeling the need to keep my senses sharp. Habits from living with Eli, I suppose. Never let your guard down completely.

"So," Mia leans forward, her dark eyes sparkling with mischief. "Any updates on your masked admirer?"

I nearly knock over my water glass. "What? No. Nothing."

"Mmm-hmm," Valerie hums, clearly not convinced. "That flush on your face says otherwise."

"It's warm in here," I protest weakly.

"Sure it is," Mia grins. "Just like traffic was bad."

The waitress returns with my tea and takes our sushi orders. I pour myself a cup, letting the steam rise to my face, grateful for an excuse for my flushed cheeks. I haven't seen him since that night on the steps. Haven't felt that electric current running through my body, haven't woken up gasping from dreams of his hands on me. But I've thought about him. God, I've thought about him.

"Let's talk about something else," I say, desperate to change the subject. "How's the new graphics design project going, Val?"

Valerie accepts the diversion, launching into a story about a difficult client who keeps changing his mind about logo colors. Mia interjects with commentary, and I let their chatter wash over me, slowly unwinding the knot of tension between my shoulders.

Our food arrives, colorful plates of sushi rolls, each more elaborate than the last. Mia's choice is covered in tempura flakes and drizzled with three different sauces. Valerie's is wrapped in cucumber instead of rice. Mine is simple, tuna, avocado, nothing fancy.

"I still don't understand how you can eat that," Mia points to my plate with her chopsticks. "It's so... boring."

I shrug, popping a piece into my mouth. "I like knowing exactly what I'm getting."

"That's your whole problem right there," Valerie says, jabbing her chopsticks for emphasis. "You play it too safe. In food, in books, in life."

"In books?" I raise an eyebrow. "Have you seen what I read? Dark romance isn't exactly 'safe.'"

Mia snorts. "Please. You read the same kind of story over and over. Tortured bad boy meets innocent girl, they fight, they fuck, happily ever after."

"That is not—" I start to protest, then stop, because she's not entirely wrong. "Okay, but at least my books have a plot. Not like those self-help manifestation books you read."

"Hey!" Mia places a hand over her heart in mock offense. "Those books saved my life. Well, my mental health at least."

"And what about Valerie's fantasy romances?" I turn to our blonde friend. "Dragons and magic and people with unpronounceable names having sex while setting shit on fire? Don't get me wrong, I love them, too,"

"Romantasy," Valerie corrects primly. "There's nothing wrong with a little escapism."

"I think that's what we all want from our books," Mia says thoughtfully, twirling her wine glass. "Different kinds of escape."

I consider this, thinking about the stacks of novels in my library. The heroines who face down monsters, both supernatural and human, and emerge stronger. The dark, dangerous men and women who are tamed by love. "I guess I like reading about women who survive terrible things," I admit. "Who find their way to something better."

A loaded silence falls over the table. I know what they're thinking, that I'm one of those women, trapped in a nightmare marriage, looking for an escape. But unlike in my books, there's no brooding hero waiting to save me. There's just me, too afraid to leave, too broken to start over.

"What about you, Val?" I ask, eager to move the spotlight off myself. "Why romantasy in general?"

Valerie leans back, considering. "I like the idea that there's more to the world than what we see. Magic hiding in plain sight. Secret worlds just beyond our reach." She shrugs. "Plus, who doesn't want to bang a hot Fae king?"

We laugh, and just like that, the tension dissipates. Mia launches into a defense of her self-help books, explaining how they taught her to set boundaries and value herself after a string of toxic relationships.

"It's not just about positive thinking," she insists, waving a piece of sushi for emphasis. "It's about recognizing your own worth, figuring out what you really want."

"And what do you want?" Valerie asks, sipping her wine.

Mia's eyes gleam. "A man who can handle me. All of me. The good, the bad, the crazy."

"You'll be waiting a long time," I tease. "That's a tall order."

"Speaking of tall," Valerie nods toward the entrance. "Check out the eye candy that just walked in."

I turn, following her gaze, and my heart stutters in my chest. Two men stand by the hostess station, one tall and broad-shouldered with dark hair, the other slightly shorter with a lean build and blonde hair. It's the taller one that catches my eye, something about the set of his shoulders, the way he stands, sending a jolt of recognition through me.

"That's my brother," Mia says, sounding surprised. "Anthony. And his friend Dillian."

I whip my head back to her. "Your brother?"

"Yeah," she nods, waving to catch their attention. "He just moved back to town a few months ago. I had no idea he was coming here tonight."

Anthony. The name settles in my stomach like a stone. Could it be him? The man from the bookstore? My masked man? I study him from across the room, the breadth of his shoulders, the confident stance, the dimple in his chin when he smiles at something Dillian says. It could be him. It could definitely be him. I recognize Dillian too, Officer Reynolds. Good God.

"Should we go say hi?" Valerie asks, already gathering her purse as if the decision has been made.

"Yes!" Mia stands. "I want to introduce you guys. Anthony's been away for a few years, he hardly knows anyone in town anymore."

I remain frozen in my seat, mind racing. If it is him, if the man who's been watching my house, who pinned me to the stairs and made me come apart with just his touch, is Mia's brother—what does that mean? How much does he know about me from Mia? How much does she know about what he's been doing?

"Lila? You coming?" Valerie looks back at me, brow furrowed.

"Yeah," I say, my voice sounding far away to my own ears. "Of course."

I follow them across the restaurant, my legs moving on their own. Anthony and Dillian have been seated at a high-top near the bar, a pitcher of beer between them. As we approach, Anthony looks up, and our eyes lock.

Something flickers across his face, recognition, surprise, something else I can't name. In that moment, I know. It's him. The masked man who's been haunting my dreams is Mia's brother.

"Anthony!" Mia exclaims, throwing her arms around him. "What are you doing here?"

He hugs her back, his eyes never leaving mine. "Dillian and I were in the neighborhood. Thought we'd grab a beer."

"What a coincidence," she says, pulling back. "Let me introduce you to my friends. This is Valerie, my business partner, and this is Lila, our colleague and resident dark romance addict."

Valerie shakes his hand first, then steps aside, leaving me face to face with him. He's even more imposing when I'm not lying on my back, over a foot taller than me, with hazel eyes that seem to see right through me. He extends his hand, and I take it before I can think better of it.

The moment our skin touches, electricity shoots up my arm. His hand engulfs mine, warm and calloused, and he holds on a fraction too long, his thumb brushing over my knuckles in a gesture that could be accidental but isn't.

"Lila," he says, my name rolling off his tongue like he's tasted it before. "It's nice to meet you."

His voice, that voice, confirms what I already knew. It's the same one that whispered in my ear on the steps, that called me gorgeous in the bookstore. I should pull away. Should make an excuse and leave. Should tell Mia exactly what her brother has been doing.

Instead, I stare at him, caught in his gaze like a deer in headlights. "Nice to meet you, too."

Dillian clears his throat, breaking the spell. "And I'm chopped liver, apparently."

Mia laughs, making introductions all around. I shake Dillian's hand too, barely registering the contact. My mind is spinning, trying to reconcile this normal social interaction with what I know about Anthony. With what he's done.

"Pull up some chairs," Dillian offers. "Join us for a beer."

"We were just finishing up," Valerie says, glancing at her watch. "Actually, we should probably get going. Early day tomorrow."

"Right," Mia nods, though she looks reluctant to leave her brother. "But we should all get together soon. Anthony, you should come to dinner at my place soon. I'll invite the girls."

Anthony smiles, and there's that dimple again, the one I glimpsed beneath his mask. "Sounds great. I'd love to get to know your friends better."

His eyes find mine again, and the double meaning in his words isn't lost on me. I feel exposed, like he's seeing every thought racing through my head, every memory of that night on the steps.

"We should go," I manage, touching Valerie's arm lightly. "I've got that... thing in the morning."

Valerie gives me a strange look, but nods. "Right, the thing. Can't be late for that."

We say our goodbyes, and I make it through without betraying the turmoil inside me. As we walk away, I feel Anthony's eyes on my back, tracking my movement through the restaurant. It takes everything in me not to look back.

Outside, the night air is cool against my flushed skin. I take a deep breath, trying to calm my racing heart.

"You okay?" Valerie asks, studying my face. "You look like you've seen a ghost."

"I'm fine," I lie. "Just tired. And I've got a headache coming on."

"Well, text us when you get home safe," Mia says, hugging me goodbye.

We part ways in the parking lot, them toward Valerie's car, me toward my SUV parked at the far end. With each step, my thoughts tumble over each other. It's him. It's been him all along. Mia's brother. Watching my house, breaking in, leaving books, pinning me to the stairs, making me—

I stop short, keys in hand, as I reach my car. Through the window, I can see something on the driver's seat—a book, its dark cover gleaming in the overhead lot lights. My breath catches in my throat.

With trembling hands, I unlock the door and slide inside, picking up the book. It's a romance novel, one I've never seen before. The cover shows a man in a mask standing behind a woman, his arms wrapped around her, her head tilted back in ecstasy.

I flip open the cover, unable to help myself, and gasp. There on the title page, is a handwritten inscription:

"For my gorgeous Lila."

Heat floods my body, pooling low in my belly. I snap the book shut, clutching it to my chest as I glance around the parking lot. He must have put it here while we were inside. While we were sitting just feet apart, acting like strangers. While I shook his hand and pretended I didn't know the feel of his body against mine.

I should be terrified. Should be calling the police, or at least telling Mia what her brother has been doing. Instead, I find myself running my fingers over the cover of the book, imagining his hands doing the same. Wondering what he has in mind?

"What is wrong with me?" I whisper to the empty car, but I already know the answer. I'm drawn to him, to the danger he represents, to the way he makes me feel. Alive. Wanted. Seen.

As I start the engine, I catch a glimpse of movement near the restaurant entrance. Anthony stands there, watching me, that same intense look on his face. Our eyes lock across the parking lot, and he raises a hand in silent acknowledgment.

I should look away. Should pretend I don't see him. Instead, I find myself raising my own hand in response before pulling out of the parking space, the book still clutched to my chest like a secret.

18

Anthony

I STAND IN FRONT of the entrance of Akira Sushi, watching Lila's SUV pull away, satisfaction spreading through me like wildfire. She found my gift. She saw me watching her. And instead of fear or disgust, she raised her hand in acknowledgment, a small gesture that sends my heart racing. The book I left on her seat wasn't just any romance novel. It was carefully chosen, a story about a masked man who becomes obsessed with a woman. Just like us. I can't stop the grin that spreads across my face.

Fuck, that went even better than I expected. The shock on her face when she realized who I was, priceless. I watch her car until it's completely out of sight, savoring the moment. There is no way she doesn't know it's me now. And she didn't run screaming. She didn't tell Mia. She just waved at me, like we share a secret.

The night air is cool against my skin as I head back into the restaurant, the warmth and noise washing over me as soon as I step inside. Dillian's still at our high-top, nursing his beer, a knowing look spreading across his face as I approach.

"So," he says, pushing a fresh pint toward me. "That was interesting."

I slide onto the stool across from him, unable to wipe the smirk off my face. "You could say that."

"Lila. The woman whose house you broke into and I had to cover for you?" He keeps his voice low, though there's no one close enough to hear us over the restaurant noise.

"Yep." I take a long pull from my beer. "Lila Fischer. My sister's friend."

Dillian shakes his head, a mix of amusement and disbelief on his face. "Jesus Christ, Anthony. Of all the women in Maryland, you had to fixate on your sister's best friend?"

"I didn't plan it that way," I shrug, remembering that first moment in the bookstore when I saw Lila, something electric passing between us. "I didn't know they knew each other for sure until I started following her."

"And you didn't think that was a sign to back off? To find someone else to stalk?"

"I'm not stalking her," I protest, though the denial sounds weak even to my own ears. "I'm watching her. There's definitely a difference."

Dillian snorts. "Right. That's why you broke into her house. That's why you left a book on her seat before we came inside. That's why you stand outside her window at night like a fucking creep." He leans forward, his voice dropping even lower. "That's why I had to answer a 911 call at her house, because you scared the shit out of her."

The mention of that night hits differently, now that I've seen her face to face again, now that she knows who I am. "She didn't look scared tonight," I point out.

"She looked like a deer in headlights," Dillian counters, but there's less conviction in his voice. He saw it too, the way Lila looked at me, the recognition in her eyes that wasn't just fear.

Our server arrives with two plates of sushi, setting them down with a practiced smile before disappearing again. I grab a piece of spicy tuna roll, popping it into my mouth to buy time before responding.

"You remember that 911 call," I say finally, meeting Dillian's gaze. "You saw her that night. Did she seem like a woman living a happy, healthy life?"

His expression shifts, a flicker of concern passing over his features. "No," he admits reluctantly. "She seemed... tense. Jumpy. Said she'd had a fight with her husband right before she saw the intruder."

"Eli," I practically spit the name. "The guy's a piece of shit. Tries to control her money, watches her on cameras, disappears for days at a time. Who knows where he goes or when he'll come back."

"And you know all this because...?" Dillian raises an eyebrow.

"I've been *watching*," I admit. "But not just her. Him too. There's something off about him, Dilllian. He installs cameras all over their house but conveniently has none in his own office. Takes these long 'business trips' but doesn't seem to actually work much."

"So what, you're investigating him now? Playing detective?" There's skepticism in Dillian's voice, but also curiosity. The cop in him can't resist a potential case.

"I'm figuring him out," I say, reaching for another piece of sushi. "And in the meantime, I'm making sure Lila knows she has options."

"Options," Dillian repeats flatly. "Like the option to fuck her stalker instead of her husband?"

I feel a flare of anger at his words. "It's not like that."

"Isn't it?" He challenges, leaning back in his chair, arms crossed. "Because I've known you a long time, Anthony. I know that look in your eye. You want her."

"Of course I want her," I admit, lowering my voice. "Have you seen her? Those eyes, that hair, the way she moves... But it's more than that."

"Enlighten me," Dillian says, his tone softening slightly. Despite his skepticism, he's giving me the chance to explain.

I take a breath, trying to put into words what I've been feeling since that first encounter in the bookstore. "It's like... I knew her before I met her. Like there's a connection that doesn't make any fucking sense but is there anyway." I shake my head, frustrated at how stupid it sounds out loud. "You're the one who was talking soul-ties. She's trapped, Dillian. With a man who doesn't appreciate her, doesn't deserve her. And she's scared to leave."

"I know, man, but this is real life. My wife talked about it, I'm not sure how much I believe that. And you're what, her knight in shining armor? Going to rescue the damsel in distress?" There's a hint of sympathy in his voice, but also something else, understanding, maybe.

"If that's what she needs," I say simply.

Dillian studies me for a long moment, then sighs. "The 911 call," he says finally. "You asked me to take it. Said you left books in her house and she freaked out."

I nod, remembering that night clearly, how scared she'd looked through the window, how quickly she'd called the police. How relieved I'd been when Dillian answered.

"She was terrified," Dillian continues. "Shaking. Said she saw someone in a mask outside her window, right after finding books in her library that hadn't been there before. I searched the property, didn't find anyone." He gives me a pointed look. "Because you were hiding in the dunes like the creepy bastard you are."

I can't help but grin. "Guilty."

"But," Dillian says, his expression turning serious, "when I asked if her husband had ever hurt her, she got this look on her face. Like she was closing a door. Said 'no' but wouldn't meet my eyes."

My grip tightens on my beer glass. "He has," I say with certainty. "Maybe not recently, but he has. She sleeps in her library. Pushes a chair against the door. Who does that if they're not afraid of someone in their home?"

Dillian nods slowly. "I had the same thought. Domestic violence cases are the worst, victims often refuse to press charges, go back to their abusers." He takes a thoughtful sip of his beer. "But that doesn't mean what you're doing is right, Anthony. Breaking into her house, watching her, leaving gifts... That's not how you help someone."

"It's working, though," I insist. "You saw how she looked at me tonight. She knows it's me, the man in the mask, the one from the bookstore. And she didn't run. Didn't scream. She's curious."

"Or terrified," Dillian counters. "Maybe she's just trying not to piss off another man who might hurt her."

The thought hits me like a punch to the gut. Could that be it? Could Lila just be playing along out of fear? I think of that night on the steps, how she responded to my touch, the way she came apart beneath me. That wasn't fear. That was desire, raw and real. But doubt creeps in anyway.

"I'd never hurt her," I say, my voice low and fierce. "Never."

"I believe you," Dillian says, and I can tell he means it. "But does she know that? All she sees is a man who breaks into her house."

I wince at his blunt assessment. "It wasn't like that. She came at me with a knife. I was just trying to stop her from hurting herself when she slipped."

Dillian's eyebrows shoot up. "A knife? Jesus, Anthony. You didn't mention that part before." He shakes his head. "This is getting out of hand. What if she'd stabbed you? What if her husband had been home?"

"But he wasn't," I say stubbornly. "And she didn't stab me. And now she knows who I am."

"Does she, though? She knows you're Mia's brother. Does she know you're the one who's been watching her?"

I think back to the look on Lila's face when our eyes met across the restaurant, the recognition that flashed there. "She knows now, she has to," I say with certainty. "The way she looked at me... And she found the book I left in her car. I don't see how she wouldn't know."

"And Mia?" Dillian asks, his voice gentler now. "Does she know what her brother's been up to?"

I shake my head. "No. And I'd like to keep it that way, at least for now."

"You don't think she deserves to know that you're stalking her friend?"

"I'm not—" I start to protest again, then stop, sighing. "Look, it's complicated. Mia would freak out if she knew.

She'd tell her, I need Lila to trust me first, to understand that I'm not the enemy."

Dillian studies me, his cop instincts clearly at war with his loyalty as my friend. "This is a dangerous game you're playing," he says finally. "For both of you."

"I know," I admit. "But I can't stop now. Not when I'm so close."

"Close to what, exactly?" Dillian asks, genuine curiosity in his voice.

I lean back, considering the question. What am I trying to accomplish here? What's the endgame? "I want her to leave him," I say finally. "I want her to be free. And then..." I trail off, the possibilities stretching out before me like a banquet.

"And then you want her for yourself," Dillian finishes for me, no judgment in his voice now, just understanding.

"Yeah," I admit. "I do."

"Well," Dillian says, raising his glass. "At least you're honest about it." He takes a drink, then sets the glass down with a thunk. "So what's your next move? Now that she more or less knows who you are?"

I grin, already formulating a plan. "The Halloween masquerade at the club. Mia's already invited Lila and Valerie. I'll be there too."

"Wearing your mask?" Dillian guesses.

"Of course," I nod. "One last dance with the mysterious stranger before she fully connects the dots. Before we drop the pretense and see what happens next."

"You're enjoying this," Dillian observes, something like wonder in his voice. "The cat and mouse of it all."

"I am," I confess, not bothering to hide my excitement. "And I think she is too. You should have seen her face when she found that book tonight. Shock, sure, but also... intrigue. Like she's as curious about where this leads as I am."

"Just be careful," Dillian warns, the concern of a friend overtaking the professional skepticism of the cop. "With Eli, especially. If he's as controlling as you say, if he has hurt her before... men like that don't like having their possessions taken away."

"Let him try something," I say, a cold edge entering my voice. "I'm not exactly easy to intimidate."

Dillian chuckles at that. "No, you're not. But still, watch your back. And hers."

"Always," I promise, raising my glass in a toast.

We finish our meal. The conversation shifting to lighter topics, the motorcycle parts I've been waiting on, Mia's plans to expand the print shop. But my mind keeps drifting back to Lila, to the way her breath caught when our eyes met, to how she clutched the book to her chest as she drove away.

As we pay the bill and head out to the parking lot, Dillian claps a hand on my shoulder. "For what it's worth," he says, "she did look at you differently. Not just scared. Something else."

A grin spreads across my face. "I told you."

"Just do it right," he warns, but there's a smile playing at the corners of his mouth. "And maybe try approaching her like a normal person next time. Ask her out for coffee or something, instead of breaking and entering."

I laugh, the sound echoing in the night air. "Where's the fun in that?"

Dillian shakes his head, already walking toward his car. "You're a lunatic, you know that?"

"Takes one to know one!" I call after him, still grinning as I head toward my bike.

As I swing my leg over the seat, I can't help but glance in the direction Lila's SUV disappeared. She's out there somewhere, maybe already home, maybe sitting in her library reading the book I left her. Thinking about me. About us. About what happens next.

The anticipation is almost as sweet as having her will be.

19

Anthony

T HE SEA OATS SWAY around me, a perfect natural blind on this moonless night. I've been crouched in these dune grasses for nearly an hour, the salt air clinging to my skin while I watch Eli's house. My muscles ache from stillness, but I don't shift position. It's much easier to stand still like this when I'm watching my girl. Headlights finally sweep across the darkened windows of Lila's prison, I check my watch: 11:42 PM.

Eli's red BMW gleams under the moonlight as he pulls into the driveway. The car is too flashy, too attention-seeking, just like him. I watch him climb out, his movements jerky with the kind of tension that comes from a day of hiding who you really are. He fumbles with his keys at the front door, disappears inside. Lights flip on, first the entryway, then the kitchen. Through the window, I can see his shadow moving, probably heading upstairs to the bedroom Lila no longer sleeps in. She's safely tucked into her library.

I count to one hundred, giving him time to settle. Then I move.

The soft sand gives way to the pavement as I cross the street, keeping to the shadows. My dark clothes blend with the night. The garage door is still open. Eli always leaves it up for a few minutes when he gets home, like he's too important to wait the extra seconds it takes to close. Arrogant fuck.

I slip inside, ducking below the windows of the house. The space smells like Eli's expensive cologne, sickly sweet and some type of cleaner, bleach maybe? His car sits there, cooling with soft ticks. I crouch by the rear bumper, retrieving the small magnetic tracker from my pocket. It's no bigger than a quarter, matte black and virtually undetectable unless you're looking for it. I slide beneath the car and reach up, feeling for the perfect spot along the frame. My fingers find the metal ridge I'm looking for, and I press the tracker firmly into place.

Ten seconds in and out. I'm back in the shadows before the garage door starts to descend, probably triggered by Eli finally remembering to hit the remote inside.

As I retreat across the driveway to the dunes, my heart isn't racing. This isn't adrenaline—it's purpose. Every move I make is calculated, designed to protect her. To watch over what's mine, even if she doesn't know it yet.

The wind shifts, bringing the scent of the ocean stronger now. I take one last look at the house. Inside, Lila is living with a monster who doesn't deserve to breathe the same air as her. I've seen the fear in her eyes when she thinks no one is watching. The way she flinches at sudden movements. The way she's become a ghost in her own home.

I melt back into the darkness, heading toward my motorcycle parked three blocks away. No one notices me. No one ever does. Invisible to most, I'm just a shadow with more money than a God and enough resources to dismantle a man like Eli piece by piece.

And that's exactly what I intend to do.

Three days later, I'm standing in my townhouse overlooking Assateague Bay, a steaming cup of black coffee in my hand. The morning light bounces off the water, creating a gentle shimmer that does nothing to calm my mood. My phone sits on the marble countertop, the tracking app open and active.

The small red dot that represents Eli's car hasn't moved in eighteen hours. It's parked in an enclosed garage about sixty miles north, at a private residence that belongs to someone who doesn't exist on paper. I've had Dillian run the property records. The owner is a shell company that traces back to another shell company. Classic move for someone with something to hide.

I set an alert that will notify me the moment Eli's car moves again. There's no reason for him to leave his precious BMW in a garage when he could drive straight to GameStream headquarters. That's where he told Lila he was going, another business trip to meet with the executives. Another lie.

I've never introduced myself to Lila's husband. He was never on my radar until I saw her. Though I've watched him from a distance for months now. He doesn't know that the company he claims to visit regularly for "work" belongs to me. He knows that GameStream only hosts executive events four times a year, and that the last one was two months ago. But my company still seems to be what he uses to lie to his wife.

I remember spotting him there, in the corner of the hotel bar, his hand resting possessively on the lower back of a woman who wasn't Lila. Her dress was expensive, her laugh practiced. I recognized the signs immediately, the way she leaned in at precisely the right moments, the calculated touches, a professional. Though, warmth never reached her eyes.

My suspicions were enough to have Dillian look into it. As a police officer with access to resources I technically shouldn't have, he's invaluable. It didn't take him long to confirm what I already knew: the woman was a high-end escort using an alias. According to Dillian's investigation, she specializes in multi-day appointments, fly-away weekends with wealthy men willing to pay for her time and discretion.

I pick up my phone and dial Cainen. He answers on the first ring.

"Thought you might call," he says, his voice slightly distorted by poor reception. "I'm in the middle of nowhere, West Virginia. Signal's shit."

"You still following her?" I ask, though I already know the answer. Cainen doesn't do anything halfway.

"We're heading to Texas next," he says. "She's camping at some state park tonight. Set up her little trailer right by a lake. She posted some pictures to her personal social media. She definitely doesn't know that the wrong people can still see them."

I can hear the possessiveness in his voice when he talks about Maeve. It mirrors something in me, something I recognize but don't bother to analyze. We're cut from the same cloth, Cainen and I.

"Eli's car has been stationary for almost a day," I tell him, getting to the point. "He told Lila he's at GameStream headquarters for meetings."

"And we both know that's bullshit," Cainen finishes for me.

"The car's in a private garage registered to a ghost. He's with someone, the same pattern as before. Goes away for a few days, comes back like nothing happened."

There's silence on the line for a moment, just the sound of wind whipping past Cainen's microphone.

"You sure you're not biased because he's Lila's husband?" Cainen finally asks. It's a fair question. One I've asked myself.

"I trust my gut," I reply, watching a heron glide low over the bay water outside my window. "Something isn't right with him. Dillian's investigation confirmed the escort last time. The patterns match. He's cheating on her."

"Definitely," Cainen repeats, and I know he's thinking what I'm thinking. Men who control and abuse their wives rarely stop at infidelity. "And you're sure about the GameStream angle? No chance he could actually be there on legitimate business with another streamer?"

"I own the fucking company," I remind him. "There are no executive meetings scheduled. He's lying to her, and not even bothering to make it convincing."

Cainen makes a sound of understanding. If anyone gets this, it's him. His obsession with Maeve mirrors my fixation on Lila, though our methods differ. Where he's chosen to follow his target across state lines, I've opted to dismantle the threat to mine.

"The Masquerade Halloween party is in two days," I say, thinking out loud. "Based on his previous patterns, he won't be back for at least three days. Gives me time to do some more digging."

"You still planning to approach her at the party?" Cainen asks.

"Yes."

"Be careful," he warns, but there's no judgment in his voice. "These things can get complicated fast."

"Says the man stalking a woman in a camper across the country," I reply dryly.

He laughs, a short, sharp sound. "Touché. At least I know what I am."

"So do I," I assure him.

"Did Dillian find anything on Micheal Vanderburg?" Cainen asks.

"No, actually. Only some small stuff. Possession of marijuana. These guys cover their tracks."

"That's surprising, since he was such an idiot in person. He must have someone else higher up."

"We've got eyes on that forum now, thanks to you. It's been a while since he went missing and no one has come forward."

He lets out a sigh of relief. He's never killed anyone before. Since he'd decided to take this guy out, he had to have seen more than just what was on his phone in Micheal's eyes.

After we hang up, I turn back to the bay window. The water is calm today, deceptively peaceful. I check the tracker app one more time. Still no movement. Eli is where he wants to be, with who he wants to be with, telling whatever lies makes his life easier.

I set my phone down and move to my desk, opening my laptop to the security footage from outside Lila's house. The cameras Eli placed outside angles a the deck give me perfect visibility of her favorite places to sit outside. I watch as she emerges onto the porch with a book in her hand, another romance novel, from the look of the cover. She settles into a chair facing the ocean with a warm blanket, pulls her knees up to her chest, and begins to read.

Even from here, I can see the relief in her posture. Eli is gone, and she can breathe again. For now.

20

Lila

I STARE AT MY reflection in Mia's full-length mirror, barely recognizing the woman looking back at me. The emerald green baby doll dress hugs my curves in all the right places, making me look softer, more alive than I've felt in years. The matching mask frames my eyes, turning them into mysterious pools that hide the nervousness flickering behind them. I adjust the delicate gold filigree along the edge of the mask, my fingers trembling slightly. Tonight feels different, dangerous, like I'm stepping into one of my book worlds instead of just reading about it.

"Holy shit, you look hot," Valerie says, appearing behind me in the mirror. Her red dress matches the style of mine, the same cut but different color, her blonde hair cascading over her shoulders in loose waves.

"You think?" I ask, smoothing the fabric over my hips. "I feel like I'm playing dress-up."

"That's the whole point," Mia calls from the bathroom where she's putting the finishing touches on her makeup.

Her dress is a sparkling sapphire blue, matching beautifully with her black hair. "Tonight, we can be whoever the
fuck we want."

Whoever I want. The thought sends a thrill down my
spine. Eli left yesterday morning, another "business trip"
that he refused to explain. His absence feels like freedom,
and I hope he's gone for longer. Usually his shorter trips
are three days, but I never know for sure. Sometimes he's
gone for over a week.

"Here," Valerie says, handing me a shot glass filled with
amber fluid. "Liquid courage."

I down it in one go, wincing at the burn. "Jesus, what is
that?"

"Tequila," she grins. "The good stuff."

Mia emerges from the bathroom, her mask already
in place, a stunning blue creation that makes her eyes
look even more striking. "I called the Uber. Five minutes,
ladies."

We take selfies while we wait, posing with exaggerated
pouts and sultry stares that make us collapse into giggles.
It feels good to laugh, to be silly with my friends without
constantly checking the time, calculating when I need to
be home before Eli gets angry.

"I can't remember the last time we did this," I say as
we pile into the back of the Uber, a cloud of perfume and
excitement filling the small space.

"That's because it's been too fucking long," Valerie
says, squeezing my knee. "Tonight, we're making up for
lost time."

The club is already packed when we arrive, a line
stretching down the block. But Mia knows someone at the
door, she always does. Then we're ushered inside without

waiting. The bass hits me immediately, vibrating through my chest as if my heart has synced to its rhythm. Lights flash across the dance floor, turning masked faces into flickering apparitions.

"Drinks first?" Mia shouts over the music, already heading toward the bar.

We follow, weaving through bodies pressed close together. The bartender slides three colorful cocktails our way, and we clink glasses before taking long sips through thin black straws. The alcohol warms my insides, loosening the knot of tension that's lived between my shoulder blades for years.

"Come on," Valerie grabs my hand, pulling me toward the dance floor. "I love this song!"

I let her lead me into the crowd, Mia following close behind. We form a small circle, moving to the beat, our hips swaying in sync. The masks create a strange sense of anonymity even among friends, I feel bolder, less self-conscious than usual. I raise my arms above my head and let the music take over, closing my eyes briefly.

When I open them again, I catch a flash of something familiar across the room. A dull green X on each eye of a mask, the lower portion cut to expose the mouth. My heart stutters, then races. It's him. My stalker. My masked man.

"You okay?" Mia asks, noticing my sudden stillness.

I nod, not trusting my voice. My eyes scan the crowd again, but he's gone. Was he ever really there, or am I seeing what I want to see?

We dance for what feels like hours, pausing only to get more drinks. Several men approach, asking for dances, but we decline them all with polite smiles and firm nos.

Tonight is for us, at least that's what I tell myself as I continue to search the crowd for him.

As the night wears on, I begin to think I imagined him. The disappointment sits heavy in my stomach, souring the sweetness of the night. But then the music changes, shifting to a slower, more hypnotic beat. A voice cuts through the melody, "Stalker" by Stevie Howie. I freeze, the lyrics washing over me like a premonition.

And that's when I feel it, a presence behind me, the subtle shift in the air that raises the hair on my arms. I turn slowly, already knowing who I'll find.

He stands there in a perfectly tailored black suit, the mask with its green X's covering the upper half of his face. His mouth, that mouth I've thought about for weeks, curves into a slight smile.

"May I have a word?" he asks, his voice carrying that same tone I remember from the bookstore, from my back steps, and the sushi bar. He gestures toward the stairs leading to the VIP section.

Mia grabs my arm, her fingers digging in slightly. "Lila," she says, her voice low and urgent. "Is that...?"

I nod, unable to tear my eyes away from him.

"You don't have to go," Valerie says, stepping between us like a shield. "We can leave right now."

"Did you request this song?" I ask him, ignoring my friends for the moment.

His smile widens slightly. "Yes."

Something warm unfurls in my chest, a strange mixture of fear and flattery and desire.

"I'll be fine," I tell Mia and Valerie, finally turning to face them. "He can't murder me here. Too many witnesses."

"That's not fucking funny," Mia hisses, but I can see the curiosity in her eyes, too. The part of her that wants to see how this plays out.

"Go," Valerie says finally, surprising me. "But we're checking on you in twenty minutes. And remember—"

"Fluffy," I mouth to her, our code word. "I know. I'll be fine."

I turn back to him, taking a deep breath. "Lead the way."

He offers his arm, a surprisingly gentlemanly gesture from someone who's been watching me through windows for months. I take it, feeling the solid muscle beneath his suit jacket. We climb the stairs together, his hand coming to rest on the small of my back as he guides me toward a door at the end of a dimly lit hallway.

The VIP room is smaller than I expected, just a black couch positioned along the back wall facing the door. The music is still audible but muted enough that we can hear each other without shouting. Through a large window, we can see the dance floor below, a swirling mass of bodies and lights.

"Your friends are protective," he says, closing the door but not locking it. "That's good. You should have people looking out for you."

"Are you?" I ask, remaining standing even as he gestures for me to sit. "Looking out for me?"

He tilts his head, studying me. "In my way, yes."

"Most people would call what you're doing stalking, not protection."

"Most people aren't married to Eli Fischer."

The sound of my husband's name from his lips makes me flinch. "How do you know about Eli?"

"I know a lot of things about Eli," he says, his voice hardening slightly. "Things you should know, too."

I cross my arms, suddenly feeling vulnerable despite the crowded club just beyond the door. "Like what?"

He reaches into his jacket and pulls out a small envelope. "Like the fact that he's been cheating on you. Regularly. With paid companions."

I stare at the envelope full of photographs and receipts, but don't take it. "Prostitutes," I say flatly. It's not a question, I've suspected for a while now.

"Yes."

"How do you know?" I ask.

"I've been watching him too," he admits. "Following his movements when he leaves you alone in that house."

I should be horrified by this, by all of this. But all I feel is a strange sense of validation. Someone has been paying attention. Someone has been seeing what I've been afraid to look at directly.

"Why?" I ask, the question that's been burning in me since that day in the bookstore. "Why me? Why all of this?"

He takes a step closer, close enough that I can smell his cologne, something lightly floral, cedar and linen. "Because from the moment I saw you, I knew you deserved better. Because something in me recognized something in you."

It sounds insane. It probably is insane. But standing here, in this small room with the man who's been haunting my thoughts for months, it feels like the most honest thing I've ever heard.

"Fuck it," I whisper, and then I'm moving toward him, closing the distance between us.

I pull him down to my level by the lapels of his jacket and kiss him, hard. He makes a surprised sound against my mouth before his arms wrap around me, pulling me flush against his body. The hard edges of his mask press into my skin, but I don't care. All I care about is the heat of his mouth, the taste of him, butterscotch bourbon and something woodsy, rugged.

When we break apart, we're both breathing hard. His eyes behind the mask are dark with desire.

"I want this," I tell him, surprising myself with my boldness. "But no penetration. Not until I'm divorced."

He nods, his hands sliding down to my hips. "Whatever you want. However you want it."

I step back, creating space between us. "I want to see you. Take your shirt off, keep the mask on. I want to see what you've been hiding under that suit." I say, feeling emboldened behind my own mask.

Even if I know who he is, I don't want to see his face just yet. As if he would disappear as soon as I find out.

His smile turns predatory as he shrugs out of his jacket, letting it fall to the floor. His shirt follows, revealing a torso mapped with muscle and scattered with scars, evidence of a life I know nothing about. My mouth goes dry at the sight of his cock pressing desperately against his pants.

"Your turn," he says, his voice rough.

I look at him warily, eyes wide. I hate my body and I hadn't thought this far ahead.

I shakily reach for the hem of my dress, but he stops me with a gentle hand. As if sensing my reluctance.

"It's okay, leave it on," he says. "Just lift it for me."

Heat floods my face as I slowly gather the fabric in my hands, inching it up my thighs. His eyes follow the movement hungrily.

"Beautiful," he murmurs as the dress clears my hips, revealing the black lace underwear beneath. "So fucking beautiful."

He drops to his knees in front of me, placing one hand on mine over the fabric of my dress. "Higher," he instructs, and pushes the fabric the rest of the way up.

His hand slides up my thigh, his touch featherlight until he reaches the edge of my underwear. He looks up at me, seeking permission, and I nod. Beyond words now.

He hooks his fingers into the waistband and pulls them down slowly, helping me step out of them. Then his hands are on my inner thighs, gently urging them apart.

"I've dreamed of this," he says, his breath hot against my skin. "Of tasting you."

The first touch of his mouth sends electricity through my body. I gasp, my head falling back as he licks a long, slow swipe over my slit. My free hand finds his shoulder, needing something to anchor me as he explores me with his tongue.

He's methodical, almost reverent, learning what makes me shudder and gasp. When he finds my clit, circling it with the tip of his tongue, my knees nearly buckle. His hands grip my thighs tighter, supporting me as he doubles his efforts.

"Oh, fuck," I breathe, heat building low in my belly.

He hums against me; the vibration adding another layer of sensation. One of his hands leaves my thigh, and then I feel a finger tracing where his tongue has been, teasing my entrance without pushing inside, respecting my bound-aries.

The combination of his tongue on my clit and his finger circling my opening pushes me closer to the edge. I rock against his face, chasing the pleasure building inside me. My hand moves from his shoulder to the back of his head, holding him where I need him most.

"Fuck," my voice breaking on the word.

He responds by sucking my clit into his mouth, ap-plying just the right amount of pressure, and that's all it takes. The orgasm crashes over me in waves, my body shaking with the force of it. I cry out, not caring who might hear through the door.

He works me through it, gentling his touch as the aftershocks ripple through me. When I finally push at his shoulder, oversensitive, he pulls back, looking up at me with undisguised hunger.

"You taste even better than I imagined," he says, wiping his mouth with his thumb and middle finger.

I let my dress fall back into place, suddenly shy de-spite what we've just done. But as I look at him, still on his knees, chest heaving, the obvious bulge in his pants, the shyness fades, replaced by a different kind of desire.

"Stand up," I tell him, and he does, watching me curiously.

I reach for his belt, undoing it with fingers that only tremble slightly. The button of his pants follows, then the zipper. I push the fabric down just enough to free him, wrapping my hand around his hard length.

"You don't have to—"" he starts, but I silence him with a look.

"I want to," I say, beginning to stroke him. "I want to hear you come apart for me."

His head falls back slightly, a groan escaping him as I find my rhythm. I watch his face, fascinated by the play of expressions visible beneath the mask, pleasure, vulnerability, hunger.

"Please," he whispers, his hips jerking forward into my touch. "Fuck, Lila, please."

Hearing my name on his lips sends a fresh wave of heat through me. I tighten my grip slightly, speeding up my strokes. With my free hand, I reach up to touch his face, tracing the edge of his mask.

"Come for me," I urge him, my voice barely above a whisper. "Let me see what I do to you."

His breathing grows ragged, his hands gripping my shoulders. I can tell he's fighting to stay quiet, to maintain some semblance of control. I want none of that.

"That's it," I tell him, looking up into his mask as I work his cock in my hand. "I want to hear you."

That seems to break something in him. His hips buck forward, his breath catching on a whimper that turns into a guttural groan as he comes, spilling over my hand and onto the floor between us. The sound, so vulnerable, so raw, sends a thrill through me unlike anything I've ever felt.

I stroke, gentling my touch as he shudders with aftershocks. When he finally stills, I step back, looking for something to clean my hand with, not caring about the floor. He pulls a handkerchief from his discarded jacket, offering it to me with a slightly sheepish smile.

"Always prepared," I comment as I wipe my hand clean.

"Not for you," he admits, tucking himself away and fixing his clothes. "You keep surprising me."

I smooth down my dress, suddenly aware of the passage of time. "My friends will be coming to check on me soon. Will I see you again?" I ask, hating how exposed the question makes me feel.

He pauses, buttoning his shirt, looking at me with an intensity I can feel even through the mask. "You know you will."

"And if I asked you to stay away?"

"Then I would," he says simply. "Whatever you want, Lila."

I laugh, the sound sharp and disbelieving. "You've been watching me for months without my permission."

"Yes," he acknowledges. "And I'll apologize for that every day if you want me to. But from here, from this moment, it's your decision. I can disappear from your life tonight if that's what you truly want."

The thought makes my chest tight, panic fluttering beneath my ribs. I shake my head. "No. That's not what I want."

Relief flashes across his face, visible even with half of it covered. "Good."

We stand there looking at each other, the air between us charged with something I can't quite name. Then there's a knock at the door, and the moment breaks.

"Lila?" Valerie's voice calls. "You okay in there?"

"I'm fine," I call back, not taking my eyes off him. "Be right out."

He steps closer, pressing a soft kiss to the top of my head. "Go. Be with your friends. Enjoy the rest of your night." Then he leans down, picking my panties up from the floor and shoving them in his pocket.

"And then?"

He smiles, the expression transforming his face even behind the mask. "And then we'll see each other again. Soon."

21

Anthony

I STEP OUT OF the VIP room into the pulsing hallway, my body still humming with electricity from Lila's touch. Her taste lingers on my lips, sweet and intoxicating. I take a deep breath, steadying myself against the wall for a moment as the bass from the club pounds through my chest. What just happened in there was, it was pure instinct, pure need. And now that I've had a taste of her, I know I won't be able to stop. I'm in too deep. Ruined, completely ruined for anyone else.

Behind me, I hear the door open again. Lila emerges with Valerie, their masks glittering under the dim hallway lights. Lila's cheeks are flushed pink, her lips slightly swollen from our kisses. Our eyes lock briefly before she quickly looks away, but not before I catch the small smile playing at the corners of her mouth. It takes everything in me not to reach for her again.

Instead, I nod politely to Valerie, whose suspicious glare burns through her red mask. She doesn't trust me. Why should she?

"We should get back to Mia," Valerie says to Lila, her voice cool but not hostile. She's being careful, measuring her response because she saw something in Lila's face that told her to tread lightly. I'm grateful for that, at least.

"Yeah," Lila responds, her voice a little breathless. "Let's go."

I wait until they're a few steps ahead before following them down the stairs. I need distance, not for my sake, but for hers. The club is packed, bodies pressed together in a writhing mass under flashing lights. I hang back, watching as Lila and Valerie weave through the crowd toward Mia, who stands near one of the bars with an expression of anxious curiosity.

Lila leans in to say something to Mia, who immediately looks up, scanning the crowd until her eyes land on me. For a moment, I think I've miscalculated, that Lila has told them everything and now they're plotting my demise. But then I see the shift in Mia's expression, the slight widening of her eyes as they fix on my mask.

Fuck. She recognizes it.

Not just the mask, she recognizes me. Her brother. In the sea of costumed faces, my sister has picked me out with unnerving accuracy. The dimple in my chin maybe, or the set of my shoulders. We share enough features that even half a face is enough for her to know.

I freeze, waiting for her to out me. To point and yell and create a scene. To grab Lila and rush her away from the predator who's been stalking her for months. But Mia does none of these things. Instead, she gives me the tiniest nod, so small it could be mistaken for a twitch, before turning her attention back to Lila and Valerie.

She won't be causing a scene, not right now anyway.

Relief floods through me, followed immediately by shame. I should be the one to tell Lila who I am without the mask. She deserves that much after what we've shared. But not yet. Not until I can guarantee her safety from Eli. Not until I can offer her more than just another complicated man in her life.

I turn and push my way through the crowd toward the exit. The cool October air hits me like a slap, clearing some of the fog from my head. The bouncer nods as I pass, and I make my way to where I've parked my bike, behind the club near the service entrance.

My motorcycle waits for me like a faithful companion, its matte black finish nearly invisible in the darkness. I swing my leg over the seat, feeling the familiar leather beneath me. The key slides into the ignition, and the engine roars to life, vibrating between my thighs in a way that reminds me painfully of Lila's touch just minutes ago.

I zip up my jacket against the night chill and pull away from the curb, accelerating perhaps faster than I should. The wind tears at my clothes, and I realize I'm still wearing the mask. I reach up and pull it off, stuffing it into my jacket pocket. Without its protective barrier, the cold air stings my face, but I welcome the sensation. It helps clear my head, helps me focus on something other than the lingering scent of Lila on my skin.

The roads are nearly empty this late, and I open the throttle, letting the bike eat up the few miles between the club and my townhouse. The speedometer climbs, and for a few blissful moments, the only things that exist are the road, the bike, and the night sky above. No Eli, no complicated emotions, no lies of omission, just pure, simple speed.

But even the rush of adrenaline can't keep my thoughts from circling back to Lila. The way she looked at me in that VIP room, with desire and curiosity and a hint of defiance. The soft sounds she made as she came apart under my tongue. The feel of her hand wrapped around me, confident and demanding.

Jesus Christ, what am I doing?

I slow the bike as I approach the bridge that leads across a river to my condo. The water beneath glitters with reflected moonlight, beautiful and serene. So different from the chaos in my head right now.

By the time I pull into my garage, I've managed to regain some semblance of control. I park the bike in its designated spot, a small plastic cubicle that keeps it protected from the elements. The stairs up to my kitchen feel steeper than usual tonight, my legs still wobbly from what happened at the club.

Inside, the townhouse is quiet except for the low hum of the refrigerator. I flip on a single light in the kitchen, not wanting to dispel the darkness completely. It feels fitting somehow, this half-light. A mirror of my half-truths.

I grab a bottle of water from the fridge, downing half of it in one go. My throat is dry, my head beginning to pound from the combination of alcohol, adrenaline, and the persistent bass from the club that seems to have taken up residence in my skull.

Upstairs in my bedroom, I strip off my clothes, placing the mask on my nightstand. I should shower, I smell like alcohol and sweat and Lila, but I can't bring myself to wash her away just yet. Instead, I pull on a pair of clean boxers and head back downstairs.

I settle onto my sofa, leaning my head back against the cushions and staring out at the bay through the wall of windows that makes up the eastern side of my living room. The water is black and still, reflecting the lights from the houses on the opposite shore. Somewhere over there, Lila will be going home tonight. To an empty house, thankfully, not to Eli. But empty nonetheless.

I close my eyes, remembering how it felt to have her in my arms. How right it seemed, even with all the wrong surrounding it. I'm not supposed to want her like this. I'm supposed to be helping her, not complicating her life further.

My phone rings, jarring me from my thoughts. I glance at the screen and feel my stomach drop. Mia.

I consider letting it go to voicemail, but that would only delay the inevitable. Better to face this now.

"Hello?" I answer, trying to sound casual, as if this is just a normal late-night call from my sister.

"What the actual fuck, Tony?" Mia's voice comes through sharp and clear, anger evident in every syllable.

I sigh, pinching the bridge of my nose. "I can explain."

"You'd better. Do you have any idea how scared shitless I've been for Lila these past few weeks? Hearing about some creep watching her house, breaking in, leaving books? And it's been you the whole goddamn time?"

"Yes," I admit, no point in denying it now. "It's been me. I thought she knew after we ran into each other at Akira Sushi."

"Jesus Christ, Tony. What the hell are you thinking? This isn't some rescue mission in a foreign country. This is my best friend, if she thought it was my *brother*, she wouldn't say a word! Her life is way too hard to be dealing with this right now."

"I know," I say, more sharply than I intended. "That's the whole point. I know exactly who she is and what she's going through."

There's a pause on the other end of the line. When Mia speaks again, her voice is quieter but no less intense. "How long? How long have you been stalking her?"

"I wasn't stalking her," I protest, though I know that's exactly what it looks like. What it is, if I'm being honest with myself. "I was watching out for her. Making sure she was safe when that piece of shit husband of hers was gone."

"Answer the question, Tony."

I sigh again. "Since June. Since I saw her at the bookstore."

"The Dark Chapters Bookstore?" Mia asks, surprise in her voice. "That was you? The guy who tried to buy her those books?"

"Yes."

"Fuck, Tony. She told us about that. She was freaked out that you followed her to her car. And then when she started talking about someone watching the house..." Mia trails off, and I can picture her pacing in her living room, gesturing with her free hand the way she does when she's worked up. "Why didn't you just introduce yourself normally? Why all the cloak and dagger bullshit?"

It's a fair question. One I've asked myself more times than I can count.

"I didn't plan for it to happen this way. I tried to and she turned me down," then I pause, not ready to tell Mia everything yet. Not ready to explain the full truth of my interest in Lila. "I wanted to help her. I could see she was trapped, unhappy. And then I found out who her husband was."

"Eli Fischer," Mia says flatly. "The streamer."

"Yes, Eli Fischer. The abusive piece of shit who uses our platform to make money while he torments his wife and visits prostitutes on the side."

Another pause. "How do you know about the prostitutes?"

"I've been following him when he goes on his 'business trips.' I have proof, Mia. Photos, videos, receipts. Enough to bury him if Lila decides to divorce his sorry ass."

"So this is about taking down Eli? Not about Lila?"

"No, I didn't know who he was until after I saw her." I say. "There is still a lot about him we don't know yet. I just can't seem to connect those dots."

"But scaring the shit out of her was okay? Watching her through windows? Showing up at a club in a mask and taking her to a VIP room?" Mia's voice rises with each question. "Do you hear yourself, Tony? Do you understand how fucked up this sounds?"

I do. God help me, I do.

"I'm going to tell her about it all. About me, what I do, and GameStream. About what I found on Eli," I say. "I'm going to tell her everything. But not yet. Not until I know she's safe."

"Safe from what? Eli's not even home most of the time and she says he's been staying away on purpose."

"That may be when she's safest," I explain. "But when he comes back... Mia, you don't know what he's capable of. If he finds out she's planning to leave, if he suspects there's someone else..." I trail off, the possibilities too grim to voice.

Mia is quiet for a long moment. "So, what's your plan? Keep playing masked man until Eli is out of the picture?"

"Something like that," I say, though I know how inadequate it sounds. "I'm working on it, Mia. I promise."

"She's falling for you, you know," Mia says suddenly. "The mask, the mystery, the danger, it's like one of those dark romance books she reads. But this is real life, Tony. She's a real person with real trauma, not a character in a book."

Her words hit me like a punch to the gut because I know they're true. I've been so caught up in my own narrative, the hero rescuing the damsel, that I've lost sight of the real woman at the center of all this.

"I care about her," I say softly. "More than I should. More than makes sense given how little time we've spent together. I won't hurt her, Mia. I swear."

"You already are," she replies, but her tone has softened slightly. "Every day you keep lying to her, you're hurting her."

I close my eyes, the truth of her words settling heavy in my chest. "I know. I'll make it right. I just need a little more time."

"Time for what?"

"To make sure she has a way out. A clean break. Financial security, legal protection, all of it. I can't tell her who I am until I can offer her something real, something lasting."

Mia sighs, a sound I know well, exasperation mixed with reluctant understanding. "I won't tell her I know," she says finally. "But you have to. Soon. Before this goes any further."

"I will," I promise. "When the time is right."

"And in the meantime, you'll keep her safe? Make sure Eli doesn't hurt her?"

"With my life," I say, and I mean it more than I've meant anything in a long time.

There's a moment of silence, and then Mia says, "She's special, Tony. Not just because of whatever this is between you two. She's been through hell with Eli, and somehow she's still... still Lila. Still kind and funny and stronger than she knows. Don't break her."

"I won't," I whisper. "I promise."

After we hang up, I sit in the darkness for a long time, replaying the conversation in my head. Mia's right, I'm hurting Lila by not being honest with her. But telling her everything now could put her in even more danger. If Eli found out... if he suspected...

No. I made the right call. I'll keep watching, keep protecting her from the shadows until I can bring her fully into the light. Until I can give her the freedom she deserves.

I pick up my phone again and open the security app, checking the cameras at Lila's house. All clear. No sign of Eli returning early from his "trip." Lila isn't inside, I check her GPS on her phone and it looks like she's at Mia's, Only a few doors down.

Leaning back against the sofa, I realize how tired I am. The night's events, the club, Lila, the confrontation with Mia, have drained me completely. But underneath the exhaustion is a current of something else. Hope, maybe. Or determination.

One way or another, I'm going to free Lila from Eli. I just hope that when that moment comes, she'll be able to forgive me for the deception. That she'll understand why I had to do it this way.

Because the alternative, losing her before I've even truly had her, is unthinkable.

22

Lila

THE UBER RIDE TO Mia's place feels surreal, like I'm floating slightly above the backseat. My skin still burns where he touched me, my lips still tingle from his kiss. Valerie and Mia flank me on either side, shooting glances at each other over my head when they think I'm not looking. They're dying to ask questions, I can tell, but the Uber driver's presence keeps them quiet for now. I press my forehead against the cool window and watch the streets blur past, wondering what the hell I'm doing with my life and why it suddenly feels more right than it has in years.

"You good?" Valerie whispers, nudging me gently with her elbow.

I nod without turning from the window. I'm better than good.

When we pull up to Mia's townhouse, we stumble out in a giggling heap, our heels dangling from our fingers. The night air is cool against my flushed skin, and I tilt my face up to feel the breeze. Above us, stars punch through the darkness, witnessing everything.

"Come on, princess," Mia says, tugging me toward the door. "Save the stargazing for when we're inside with wine."

Her place is exactly what you'd expect. Stylish but comfortable, with photographs on every wall and throw pillows in shades of blue and gray. I've been here a couple of times, but tonight it feels different. Safer. Like a sanctuary.

"Alright, pajama time," Valerie announces, heading for Mia's bedroom. "I call the pink set!"

We change out of our dresses, wiping away makeup and pulling our hair into messy buns. I borrow a pair of Mia's sleep shorts and an oversized t-shirt with a faded logo. The fabric smells like her laundry detergent. It's comforting.

Back in the living room, Mia uncorks a bottle of red wine while Valerie arranges crackers, cheese, and grapes on a wooden board. I sink into the corner of the couch, tucking my feet beneath me. Everything feels soft-edged and warm, nothing like the sharp corners and cold silence of my house with Eli.

"Here," Mia hands me a glass of wine, then settles cross-legged on the floor opposite me. "Now, spill it."

I take a long sip, the wine smooth and rich on my tongue. "Spill what?"

Valerie snorts, dropping onto the couch beside me. "Don't play dumb. What happened in that VIP room with Mr. Mysterious Mask?"

My cheeks flush hot at the memory. "Nothing much."

"Bullshit," Mia says, leaning forward. "You went in there looking nervous and came out looking like you'd been thoroughly kissed. Maybe more."

I bite my lip, unsure how much to share. These are my best friends, but some things feel too private, too precious to voice aloud.

"Fine," I sigh. "We talked. He told me some things about Eli that I already suspected. We... got close. That's it."

"Define *close*," Valerie presses, nudging my knee with hers.

I roll my eyes. "We kissed. It was nice. That's all you're getting."

It's not the whole truth, but it's all I'm willing to share. The rest, his mouth between my thighs, my hand wrapped around him, the sounds he made when he came, that's mine alone.

"And what did he tell you about Eli?" Mia asks, her tone shifting from playful to serious.

I swirl the wine in my glass, watching it catch the light. "That he's been cheating. With prostitutes."

"I fucking knew it!" Mia shouts, slamming her palm against the floor. "That slimy piece of shit. I knew he was screwing around."

Valerie's face darkens, her lips pressing into a thin line. "Are you sure the mask guy is telling the truth? How would he even know that?"

"He's been following Eli," I admit. "Watching him, like he's been watching me. He had photos and receipts."

"Jesus, Lila," Valerie whispers. "This is so fucked up."

"I know," I say, but there's no real conviction in my voice. "But it makes sense. The 'business trips,' he doesn't want to touch me anymore-not that that is a bad thing. He locks himself in his office for hours... I've suspected for a while." I keep some of that a secret because they don't know anything about the sexual assaults I've endured.

"That bastard," Valerie seethes. "After everything else he's put you through? The control, the isolation, the fucking mind games? And now this?"

I nod, surprised by how little pain I feel. Maybe I've been numb to Eli for longer than I realized. Or maybe tonight, with the masked man, something fundamental shifted inside me.

"Val's right," Mia says, her dark eyes flashing with anger. "Eli has always been garbage, but this is next level. You need to leave him, Lila. For real this time."

The words hang in the air between us. I've talked about leaving before, in whispers and hypotheticals. But it's always seemed impossible, where would I go? How would I survive without access to our joint accounts? What would Eli do when he found me?

"I know," I say finally, my voice stronger than I expected. "I'm going to."

Valerie's eyes widen. "For real? You're not just saying that?"

"For real," I confirm, and as the words leave my mouth, I feel their truth settle into my bones. "I can't do this anymore. I can't keep living like a ghost in my own life."

Mia springs to her feet, nearly spilling her wine in her excitement. "Holy shit, yes! Finally!"

"It won't be easy," Valerie warns, always the practical one. "Eli won't just let you go."

"I know," I say again, because I do. Eli sees me as a possession, not a person. "But I have to try."

"Stay here," Mia says immediately. "My guest room is yours for as long as you need it."

Tears prick at my eyes, unexpected and unwelcome. I blink them away. "Are you sure? It could be a while before I get on my feet."

"Positive," Mia says firmly. "My house is your house. Always has been."

"When do you want to do this?" Valerie asks, already shifting into planning mode. "We should be strategic."

I take another sip of wine, thinking. "He's away until Tuesday. So maybe Monday? That gives us three days to plan."

"Perfect," Valerie nods. "We'll need to be quick. In and out. Only take what you absolutely need."

"Clothes," I list off. "My laptop. Important documents."

"Your books," Mia adds with a small smile. "At least some of them."

The thought of my library, my sanctuary in that cold house, makes my chest tighten. "I can't take them all."

"We'll get you new ones," Valerie promises. "A whole new collection."

"And we'll need to think about legal stuff," Mia says, her brow furrowing. "Divorce papers, restraining orders if necessary."

The word 'divorce' sends a shock through me, though it shouldn't. That's what this is, what I'm planning. The end of my marriage. The thought brings both terror and relief.

"We'll figure it out," Valerie says firmly. "Between the three of us, we have enough to keep you afloat until we can sort out the finances."

Mia nods in agreement. "And you can pick up more hours at the print shop if you want. Or we can pay you more. Whatever you need."

Their generosity overwhelms me. These women, who have stood by me through years of Eli's abuse, who have watched me shrink and fade and still refused to give up on me. I don't deserve them.

"Thank you," I whisper, my voice thick with emotion. "Both of you."

"Don't thank us," Mia scoffs. "Just promise you won't back out this time."

I think about the masked man, about Anthony, if that's really his name. About how he made me feel tonight. Wanted. Desired. Seen. I think about Eli and his cold eyes, his cruel words, his indifference to my happiness. The choice seems so clear now.

"I promise," I say, and I mean it more than I've ever meant anything. "I'm done with Eli. For good."

Valerie raises her glass. "To Lila's freedom."

"To freedom," Mia echoes, lifting her own glass.

I clink my glass against theirs, the sound ringing out like a bell. "To freedom."

We spend the next hour planning the details, what time to go to the house, what to prioritize packing, how to ensure Eli doesn't track me down afterward. I'll need to change my phone number, close any accounts he has access to, be careful about my routine. It's exhausting to think about, but necessary.

"What about your parents?" Mia asks as we start to wind down, the wine nearly gone. "Will you tell them?"

I haven't spoken to my adoptive parents in ten years, not since I eloped with Eli against their wishes. They told me they wouldn't speak to me until I left him. Pride and shame have kept me from reaching out all this time.

"Maybe," I say, not ready to think about that yet. "One step at a time."

Valerie yawns, stretching her arms above her head. "We should sleep. Tomorrow we can make a proper list, figure out exactly what we need to do."

We make up the guest bed together, Mia finding extra pillows while Valerie hunts down a spare toothbrush for me. It's nearly four in the morning by the time we say goodnight, all of us exhausted but buzzing with a strange energy.

Alone in the guest room, I sit on the edge of the bed and check my phone for the first time in hours. No texts from Eli, which isn't surprising. He rarely checks in during his "trips." One missed call from a spam number, but no voicemails.

I set my phone on the nightstand and lie back on the bed, staring at the ceiling. For the first time in years, I feel a flutter of hope in my chest. Three days from now, I'll be free. Free from Eli, free from fear, free to discover who I am without his voice in my head telling me I'm worthless.

And maybe, just maybe, free to explore whatever this thing is with the masked man. Anthony. The thought of him sends a shiver through me. Is he thinking of me right now, the way I'm thinking of him? Is he lying awake somewhere, replaying our encounter the way I keep doing?

I close my eyes and let myself drift toward sleep, the ghost of his touch still lingering on my skin. For the first time in ten years, I'm not dreading tomorrow. I'm looking forward to it.

23

Anthony

I JOLT AWAKE TO the sound of my phone buzzing against the coffee table. Sunlight streams through the windows, hitting my face at just the right angle to make my eyes water. I blink, disoriented, trying to piece together where I am. My living room. The couch. I must have passed out while watching Lila's phone cameras. The clock on my phone reads 9:27 AM. Shit. I've slept longer than I meant to. Dillian's name flashes on the screen, and something in my gut tells me this isn't a casual check-in.

"Yeah?" My voice comes out rough with sleep.

"Morning, sunshine. Hope I didn't wake you from your beauty rest." Dillian's tone is light, but there's an edge to it that has me sitting up straight.

"What's up?" I rub a hand over my face, trying to clear the fog from my brain.

There's a pause on the other end of the line. "We need to talk about your *friend* Eli."

My stomach tightens. "Please don't use that word. Sarcastic or not." I say. "What about him?"

"Remember that escort from the quarterly meeting? The one you pointed out to me a few months back when we started tracking his movements?"

I do remember. Tall, blonde, looked expensive. Eli had his hand on the small of her back as they walked into the hotel bar. I was there for a GameStream executive meeting, one of the rare ones I actually attend as the silent owner, and he didn't know who I was. Just another suit in a room full of suits.

"Yeah, what about her?"

"Her name is Amanda Finley. And she's missing."

The last traces of sleep evaporate from my mind. "What do you mean, missing?"

"Family filed a report three days ago. She didn't come home, didn't call, nothing. Her roommate said she went out for a job and never came back, that was months ago."

I stand up, suddenly unable to sit still. "And you think Eli had something to do with it?"

"I'm not saying that. Not exactly." Dillian sighs, and I can picture him at his desk, phone pressed to his ear, making sure no one else at the station can hear him. "But there's a witness who saw a woman matching her description talking to a man on a street corner the night she disappeared. Said the guy grabbed her by the arm and practically dragged her into a car. Witness couldn't get a good look at the man or the vehicle."

"Fuck." I pace to the window, looking out at the bay. The water is calm today, deceptively peaceful. "Do you have any leads?"

"That's the thing. Since you asked me to look into everyone connected to Eli, I've had one of our guys keeping tabs on him when possible. Not officially, of course. Just as a favor to me."

"And?"

"And your boy is paranoid as hell. He knows he's being watched."

Something cold settles in my chest. "How can you tell?"

"The way he moves. He's careful. Too careful. He parks that red BMW of his in this row of garages off Route 1. The garages are owned by shell companies. It took some digging to figure that out. He goes in, waits a while, then comes out and gets into a rented sedan. Different one each time."

"He's switching cars to throw off tails," I mutter, more to myself than to Dillian.

"Exactly. And he's good at it. My guy lost him three times in the last month alone."

I'd been so focused on where he was going that I hadn't paid enough attention to how he was getting there. Amateur mistake.

"What about the other night? When he left town?" I ask, thinking of Lila at the club, in my arms, her lips on mine while her husband was supposedly away on business.

"That's another thing. He did the car switch, then drove to Baltimore. Checked into a hotel under a fake name, but my guy recognized him. Then Eli spotted him in the lobby and lost him. Stared right at him, smiled, and walked out. My guy followed, but Eli had vanished. Just... gone."

"Shit." I run a hand through my hair, tugging at the ends in frustration. "So we have no idea where he went after that?"

"None. And here's the kicker—he hasn't used his credit cards, his phone is off, and his car is still in that garage. It's like he's deliberately dropped off the grid."

My mind races, connecting dots I don't want to connect. An escort missing. Eli going dark. The timing of it all.

"You think he did something to her? To Amanda?"

Dillian is quiet for a moment. "I think it's a hell of a coincidence that a woman he's been seen with goes missing right around the time he decides to play ghost. But I don't have anything concrete yet. Just... watch your girl, Tony. If Eli's involved in something bad and he thinks someone's closing in on him, he might get desperate. And desperate men do desperate things."

I glance at my phone, pulling up the security app to check on Lila's house. The feeds are clear, no movement. According to her phone's GPS, she's still at Mia's house. Safe, for now.

"I'm on it," I tell Dillian. "What about Amanda? What are you doing to find her?"

"Everything I can without raising flags. It's tricky. Officially, she's just another missing persons case. But prostitution complicates things—some of the guys aren't exactly rushing to find a hooker, you know? But I've got a few people I trust looking into it. Checking hotel records, traffic cams, that sort of thing."

"Let me know if you find anything. And Dillian... thanks. I know you're sticking your neck out here."

He snorts. "Yeah, well, you'd do the same for me. Have done, actually. Multiple times. Besides, if this guy is hurting women, I want him off the streets. Badge or no badge."

After we hang up, I throw a pair of sweatpants on and head to the kitchen to make a pot of coffee to go with my breakfast, my mind churning. I need to be smart about this. If Eli knows he's being watched, he'll be more careful than ever. And if he's somehow involved in Amanda's disappearance, he's more dangerous than I thought.

I pull out my laptop and log into GameStream's secure server. As the owner, I have access to everything, including the personal information of our top streamers. Eli's profile comes up, showing his streaming schedule, subscriber count, and payment history. Nothing unusual there. But when I dig deeper, looking at his login locations over the past few months, I notice something odd. There are gaps, periods where he doesn't stream at all, doesn't even log in to check his account. And these gaps line up perfectly with his "business trips."

What kind of streamer doesn't stream for days at a time? Doesn't check his metrics, his subscriber count, his revenue? Unless streaming isn't his real business at all, but a cover for something else.

I cross-reference the dates of his absences with news reports, police blotters, missing persons cases. Nothing jumps out immediately, but that doesn't mean there's nothing there. I just need to dig deeper.

My phone pings with a notification from the security app. Movement at Lila's house. I switch screens quickly, heart rate spiking until I see it's just Lila herself, coming home from Mia's and she's alone. She moves through the house with purpose, heading straight to the bedroom she shared with Eli. I watch as she pulls a suitcase from the closet and begins filling it with clothes.

Is she leaving? Running away? Does she know something about Eli that I don't?

I grab my phone and am about to call Mia when another notification pops up. A car pulling into Lila's driveway. Not Eli's red BMW, but a black sedan I don't recognize. The driver's door opens, and Eli steps out.

Fuck. He's back early.

I watch, helpless, as Eli enters the house. Lila doesn't hear him over the sound of drawers opening and closing. He stands in the doorway of the bedroom, watching her pack, his face eerily calm. When he finally speaks, I can't hear what he says, the cameras aren't picking up audio. But I see Lila freeze, her whole body going rigid before she turns to face him.

I'm already moving, grabbing my keys and helmet, rushing down to the garage where my bike waits. But I know, even as I fire up the engine and tear out onto the street, that I'm too far away. It'll take me at least fifteen minutes to get to her house, even pushing the bike to its limits.

Fifteen minutes is a long time when you're alone with a man who might have made a woman disappear.

As I weave through traffic, ignoring speed limits and the angry honks of other drivers, my mind races with possibilities, none of them good. I try to call Lila's phone, but it goes straight to voicemail. Same with Mia and Valerie. I call Dillian next.

"I need a patrol car at Lila's address, now," I say as soon as he picks up. "Eli's back, and she was packing a suitcase when he walked in. Something's wrong."

"Shit. I'll make it happen. But Tony, stay away. If you show up there masked or unmasked, it's only going to make things worse."

"I can't just do nothing!"

"You can and you will," Dillian snaps. "Let us handle this. I'll call in a domestic disturbance check. We'll be there in fifteen minutes or less."

I want to argue, but he's right. Showing up now would only escalate the situation, possibly putting Lila in more danger. "Fine. But I'm staying close. If those officers don't show up—"

"They will. I promise. Now hang up and let me make the call."

I pull over to the side of the road, a couple of miles from Lila's house. Close enough to get there quickly if needed, but far enough away that Eli won't spot me. I pull up the security app again, watching as Lila and Eli face each other in the bedroom. He's gesturing at the suitcase, his movements sharp and angry. She's backed against the wall, her posture defensive. But she's not cowering. There's a defiance in the way she holds herself that makes pride swell in my chest even as fear claws at my throat.

The minutes crawl by like hours. Where are those fucking cops? I check the time, only five minutes since I called Dillian, but it feels like an eternity. On the screen, Eli takes a step toward Lila. She says something that makes him stop short. His hand twitches at his side, and I tense, ready to gun the engine and race to her regardless of the consequences.

24

Lila

I SIT AT MIA'S kitchen table, cradling a mug of coffee between my palms. The warmth seeps into my skin, a stark contrast to the cold determination settling in my chest. Valerie paces behind me, her footsteps marking time like a metronome while Mia scribbles furiously on a notepad, making lists of what we need to do. The morning light streams through the blinds, painting stripes across the table.

"I should go home today," I say, the words tumbling out before I can second-guess myself. "It's Sunday, Eli left Friday morning, he shouldn't be he back until Monday or Tuesday. I could pack a suitcase now, be done with it."

Valerie stops pacing, her body going rigid. "Absolutely not."

"That's a terrible idea," Mia agrees without looking up from her list. "We planned for Monday for a reason. We're going to chill today and make a plan. File for a restraining order and have an escort tomorrow."

I trace the rim of my mug with my finger, gathering my thoughts. "I know, but think about it. Eli never comes home early from his trips. Never. And this way, I can take my time, really think about what I need."

"And what if he decides to surprise you?" Valerie challenges, dropping into the chair across from me. "What then?"

"He won't," I insist. "He's probably too busy with his prostitutes."

The bitterness in my voice surprises even me. It's not jealousy. God, no. More like resentment for all the times he made me feel worthless and forced himself on me all while he was paying other women for what he claimed I couldn't give him.

Mia sets down her pen, finally looking up. "Lila, it's not worth the risk. We can all go together on Monday, like we planned."

"I need to do this," I say, meeting her eyes. "I need to walk into that house knowing I'm walking back out for good. I can't explain it, but it feels important."

Valerie and Mia exchange a look I've seen too many times, concern mixed with resignation. They know once I've made up my mind, there's little point in arguing.

"Fine," Valerie sighs. "But you're not going alone. We'll drop you off and wait outside."

"No," I shake my head. "I appreciate it, I do. But I need to do this part myself."

Another look passes between them.

"At least let us drive you," Mia tries.

"I'll take my car," I counter. "I'll text you when I get there and again when I'm leaving. If you don't hear from me within an hour, you can come breaking down the door."

"One hour," Valerie counters. "And you text us the second anything feels off. If you forget anything, we'll go back on Monday. No more exceptions."

I nod, feeling a strange mix of fear and exhilaration. "One hour."

The drive to my house… Eli's house, I correct myself, is surreal. The familiar streets look different somehow, as if the decision to leave has altered my perception of everything. I grip the steering wheel tightly, reminding myself to breathe. I've lived in fear for so long that this small act of defiance feels monumental.

I pull into the driveway and sit for a moment, staring at the house. It's beautiful from the outside, a modern two-story with large windows and a manicured lawn. The perfect facade hiding the ugliness within. Just like our marriage.

Me: At the house. All quiet. Starting the timer now.

Mia: One hour. Be careful.

The house is silent when I step inside, the kind of emptiness that feels heavy rather than peaceful. I stand in the foyer, listening for any sign that I'm not alone. Nothing. Just the faint hum of the refrigerator and the ticking of the grandfather clock in the living room.

I head upstairs, my footsteps echoing on the hardwood. Our bedroom… Eli's bedroom; is pristine, as always. He can't stand disorder. For years, I've lived with the constant anxiety of leaving something out of place, of facing his cold anger over a book left on the nightstand or a towel folded the wrong way.

Not anymore.

I pull a suitcase from the closet and toss it onto the bed. What do I take? What matters? Clothes, of course. Documents. My laptop. I start with the essentials, moving quickly but methodically through drawers and shelves.

My hands shake slightly as I fold shirts and pants into the suitcase. Each item feels like a declaration. I'm choosing what parts of this life to take with me, what parts to leave behind. It's terrifying and liberating all at once.

I move to my side of the closet, reaching for the few dark-colored dresses I actually like. Most of my wardrobe was chosen by Eli, clothes that fit his idea of what his wife should wear. I grab only what feels like me, leaving behind the designer pieces that never felt right.

As I reach for a hoodie on the top shelf, the hairs on the back of my neck stand up. That feeling. Someone is in here with me.

I turn slowly, heart hammering against my ribs.

Eli stands in the doorway.

His face is blank, that controlled emptiness more frightening than any display of rage. His eyes, those icy blue eyes that used to make me feel special, now look colorless and dead.

"Where the fuck were you last night?" His voice is calm, too calm.

My mouth goes dry. Words stick in my throat like tar. "I went out to dinner with my co-workers," I manage, the lie feeling flimsy even to my own ears.

"Try again." He steps into the room, closing the distance between us with measured steps. "The cameras never showed you come home and I couldn't see your location on your phone."

My mind races. He wasn't supposed to be here. How long has he been home? Did he see me leave with my dress yesterday?

"My phone died. I stayed at Mia's because I had too many drinks to drive," I say, clinging to at least part of the truth. "Girls' night."

His eyes flick to the suitcase on the bed, clothes spilling over the edges. "And this? Planning a trip I don't know about?"

The moment stretches between us like a wire pulled too tight. I could lie. Make up some story about visiting a friend, a weekend away that he'd never allow but might pretend to consider.

But I'm done lying. Done pretending. I do the dumbest thing you could ever do when leaving a domestic abuser. I tell him:

"I'm leaving you, Eli."

The words hang in the air, impossible to take back. For a moment, his face doesn't change. Then something shifts in his eyes, a flash of disbelief followed by a darkness that makes my blood run cold.

"No, you're not." He says it like he's correcting a simple misunderstanding, like I've made a mistake in basic arithmetic.

"Yes, I am." My voice shakes but doesn't break. "I'm done with this marriage. I'm done with you."

His movement is so sudden I don't have time to react. His hand shoots out, fingers tangling in my hair, yanking my head back with enough force that I cry out. Pain lances across my scalp, sharp and immediate.

"You ungrateful bitch," he hisses, his face inches from mine. "After everything I've done for you? Everything I've given you?"

"Let go," I gasp, my hands flying up to grab his wrist, trying to lessen the pressure on my scalp.

He drags me toward the door, my feet stumbling to keep up, my hands clawing at his arm. I don't recognize the sounds coming from my throat, half-words, half-animal noises of pain and fear.

"You think you can just walk away?" he asks, his voice oddly conversational despite the violence of his grip. "You think you can just decide you're done?"

We're at the top of the stairs now. I know what's coming even before he shoves me, but there's no time to brace myself. My body pitches forward, hands desperately reaching for the railing but finding only air.

The fall feels both impossibly slow and too fast to process. I'm aware of each impact. Shoulder, hip, elbow, ribs, as I tumble down the stairs, each point of contact a new explosion of pain. When I finally land at the bottom, sprawled on the hardwood floor, I can't breathe. The jarring contact has knocked the air out of me, and for a terrifying moment, I can't make my diaphragm work.

Eli descends the stairs methodically, each step deliberate. Through the haze of pain, I try to move, to crawl away, but my body won't cooperate. Something must be broken, everything hurts in a way that makes coherent thought nearly impossible.

"Look at you," he says, standing over me. "Pathetic. You can't even leave properly."

He grabs my shoulders and flips me onto my stomach. The sudden movement sends fresh pain shooting through my body, and I cry out. His knee presses into the small of my back, pinning me down.

"Maybe you need a reminder of who you belong to," he says, his hands going to the waistband of my pants.

Ice-cold terror cuts through the fog of pain. "No," I gasp, trying to buck him off. "Don't. Please."

He ignores me, yanking my pants down to my thighs with one brutal movement. I feel the heat of his body as he leans over me, hear the clink of his belt buckle.

"Stop," I plead, my voice breaking. "Eli, please stop."

"Shut up," he growls, one hand pressing my face against the floor. "You're my wife. This is what wives do."

I squeeze my eyes shut, preparing for the inevitable violation. Then a sound cuts through the horror, a sharp, insistent knocking at the front door. Eli freezes above me, his breathing heavy in my ear.

The knocking continues, growing louder, more urgent. Unrelenting.

"On of your little friends?" Eli asks, his weight still crushing me. "Did you tell them to come check on you?"

I don't answer, focused only on the knocking that hasn't stopped. It's my lifeline, my only hope.

The pressure on my back shifts as Eli stands. "Don't move," he orders, zipping his pants.

The moment his weight lifts, I drag myself forward, pants still tangled around my thighs. Every movement is agony, but terror is a powerful motivator. I claw my way across the floor as Eli moves toward the door, yelling for whoever it is to go away.

The library. I need to get to the library.

I pull my pants up with trembling hands and force my battered body to move faster. Behind me, I hear Eli yelling at the door, his voice rising in anger. I don't look back. I focus only on reaching the sanctuary of my library, on putting a locked door between me and the monster I married.

My legs finally cooperate enough to let me stand, though I nearly collapse with the first step. I stagger through the living room, one hand against the wall for support. The library door looms ahead, the only safe place in this house of horrors.

I stumble inside and slam the door shut, turning the lock with shaking fingers. It won't hold him for long if he really wants to get in, but it might buy me time. I shove a blanket under the door, unable to move the chair in my current state.

The banging on the front door hasn't stopped. If anything, it's grown more frantic. Through the window, I can see part of the driveway, Valerie's car parked haphazardly near the gate, and both she and Mia are there. They knew something was wrong. Then who was at the door?

When the pounding stops, I hear Eli's footsteps in the living room, heavy and purposeful. Then his fist pounding on the library door.

"Open this fucking door, Lila!" he shouts. "Now!"

The doorknob rattles violently. The lock breaks and the blanket is all that's keeping the door closed. It won't hold. I know it won't hold.

The window. It's my only chance.

I unlock it with fumbling fingers and push it open. It's a six-foot drop to the ground. Not ideal, but better than staying here. I swing one leg over the sill, then the other, lowering myself as far as I can before letting go.

The impact jars my already battered body, but I don't have time to acknowledge the pain. I hear the crash of the library door giving way behind me. Eli curses as he sees the open window. I run.

My legs are weak, unsteady, but adrenaline drives me forward. The driveway stretches ahead, the gate at its end both a barrier and my best hope for escape. Valerie and Mia are on the other side, calling and waving me forward.

I'm halfway down the driveway when I hear Eli behind me. His footsteps pound on the pavement, closing the distance between us with terrifying speed. I push harder, ignoring the screaming protest of my ribs and muscles.

Too slow. I'm too slow.

Eli's fist connects with my back, between my shoulder blades, with enough force to send me sprawling forward. My hands instinctively go out to break my fall, but the impact still scrapes my cheek against the rough pavement. I taste blood, feel the sting of torn skin.

"You don't get to leave," Eli pants, standing over me again. "You're mine. You've always been mine."

Behind him, at the gate, I see movement. Valerie and Mia, both clutching baseball bats, their faces twisted with rage and fear.

"Don't fucking touch her!" Valerie screams, rattling the gate. "Get away from her, you psycho!"

Eli turns, momentarily distracted by their yelling. It's the opening I need. I roll to the side, out of his immediate reach, and struggle to my feet.

"It's over, Eli," I say, the taste of blood sharp on my tongue. "We're over."

His face contorts with fury. "Nothing's over until I say it is."

He lunges for me again, but freezes at the sound of an engine revving. We both turn to see Mia in the driver's seat of Valerie's car, her face a mask of determination. Before either of us can react, she floors it.

The gate groans, then gives way with a screech of tearing metal as Valerie's car bursts through. Eli jumps back, narrowly avoiding being hit, as the car skids to a stop between us.

Valerie yanks open the back passenger door. "Get in!" she shouts.

I don't hesitate. I dive into the car, slamming the door shut just as Eli recovers enough to grab for me. His fist pounds on the window, his face a contorted mask of rage.

"Drive!" Valerie yells, and Mia stomps on the accelerator.

The car lurches forward, then stops with a jolt as flashing lights suddenly illuminate the driveway. Police cars, their sirens wailing, pour through the broken gate. Eli freezes, his eyes widening as officers emerge with weapons drawn.

"Police! Hands where we can see them!"

Eli raises his hands slowly, his face transforming in an instant from rage to confusion, as if he can't understand how this is happening to him.

An officer approaches our car, gesturing for Mia to roll down the window. "Are you the ones who called in the domestic disturbance?"

Valerie shakes her head, her hand gripping mine tightly. "No. But he was trying to kill her."

The officer's gaze shifts to me, taking in the blood on my face, the bruises already forming on my exposed skin. His expression hardens.

"We'll need statements from all of you," he says, then turns to watch as his colleagues handcuff Eli.

Through the windshield, I watch the man who has controlled my life for ten years being led to a police car, his head bowed in a performance of bewilderment and innocence that I've seen too many times before.

"It's over," Mia says, her voice soft but firm. "He can't hurt you anymore."

I lean back against the seat, exhaustion crashing over me in waves. My body is a map of pain, each bruise and scrape a landmark of what I've survived. But for the first time in years, I feel something beyond the pain, beyond the fear.

I feel free.

25

Anthony

I SLAM THE DOOR to my townhouse so hard the windows rattle. My hands won't stop shaking. The image of Lila's battered face on my security feed keeps flashing through my mind like some sick slideshow. If I hadn't started banging on that door when I did, if I hadn't called Dillian... Eli would have raped her right there on that floor. Maybe killed her after. The thought makes bile rise in my throat. I've failed her. All my watching, all my planning, and when she needed me most, I was too fucking far away to stop him.

I pace through the kitchen, unable to settle, the rage and guilt churning inside me like a storm. Eli had been waiting for her. It was a trap, and I didn't see it coming. His car never pinged on my tracking app because it never left that goddamn garage. He must have switched cars again, just like Dillian warned me. Drove home in something I wasn't tracking and waited like a spider in the corner of his web.

The realization hits me like a physical blow. "He planned it," I mutter to the empty room. "He knew she was going to try to leave."

But how? Did he see something on the cameras? Did he have access to her text messages? Is the entire house bugged? Suddenly, I don't trust any of my information. I grab my laptop and pull up the security feeds from Lila's house again. The police are still there, moving through the rooms with evidence markers. In one frame, I catch a glimpse of a small device being bagged; a camera, hidden in a smoke detector that I never detected in my sweeps.

"Fuck!" I slam my fist down on the counter. I'd been so focused on helping Lila escape that I missed the extra surveillance Eli had installed. I made a mistake, one that nearly cost Lila everything. If he's capable of this, then I need to tell Dillian to ask Eli about Amanda.

I need to move fast now. I grab my phone and call Dillian.

"It's over," he says when he picks up. "We've got him in custody."

"Listen to me," I say, cutting through his reassurance. "You need to question him about Amanda Finley before anyone else gets to him."

There's a pause on the other end. "That's not how this works, Tony. He's been arrested for domestic assault. The missing persons case is separate. If we do this the wrong way, if we start before his lawyer arrives, which he asked for one. He could walk. You wan't to risk that?"

"Don't give me that bullshit," I snap. "You know as well as I do that once the lawyers get there, we'll never get anything out of him. This might be our only chance."

Dillian sighs, and I can picture him rubbing his fore-head the way he does when he's torn between protocol and doing what's right. "What makes you so sure he's involved with Amanda's disappearance?"

"The timing. The car switching. The way he went completely dark when he realized he was being watched. And now this...he'd tried to kill Lila when she was leaving him. What do you think he'd do to a prostitute who might have threatened to expose him?"

"That's all circumstantial. If that's all we have to go on, I can't bring it up at all or I could compromise the case."

"Since when do you need a smoking gun to ask a few questions?" I challenge him. "Just get in there before he shuts down. Please."

Another sigh, longer this time. "I'll see what I can do."

"Thank you," I say, the words inadequate for what I'm asking him to risk.

After we hang up, I pull up Cainen's software on my laptop. He sent it to me months ago, a custom program designed to identify and neutralize spyware on mobile devices. I've been hesitant to use it, worried that Eli might notice if his surveillance suddenly went dark. This situation is partially my fault. I was the one who accidentally turned off Lila's location to Eli. But now there's no reason to hold back. She is safe, and he's going away, for a while at least.

I input Lila's phone information and connect remotely. Watching as the program searches for malicious code. The results make my stomach turn. Eli has installed multiple tracking apps, a keylogger that records every message she types, and software that forwards copies of all her texts and emails to his accounts. He's been reading everything, seeing everything. Including my blocked number. He knew she was at the club.

With a few keystrokes, I activate the cleansing protocol. Cainen's software systematically removes each piece of spyware, replacing it with dummy code that will continue to send fake data to Eli's accounts and wipe all the old information. He won't immediately realize it's been changed. In case he has others working for him. Sometimes men like him will enlist others to play in their sick games. Now he'll see only what I want him to see. Normal, mundane activity that won't give him any ammunition when she divorces him.

When the program finishes, I sit back and stare at the confirmation screen. Lila's phone is clean now. For the first time in probably years, her digital life is truly private. Except, of course, for my own surveillance. The irony isn't lost on me. I'm no better than Eli in some ways, watching her without permission. The difference, I tell myself, is intent. I've never used that information to hurt her and I've never read her private messages.

But intent only matters so much. Results matter more. And today, the result was Lila getting thrown down a flight of stairs while I watched helplessly from afar.

I pull up her contact on my phone. According to the hospital records I shouldn't have access to, she's being treated for a couple of broken ribs, contusions, a sprained wrist, and possible concussion. She'll be kept for at least two days for observation. My finger hovers over the screen as I try to find the right words.

Finally, I type:

Unknown Number: I'm sorry I couldn't protect you today. I should have been there sooner. I should have seen him coming. I've removed all of the spyware from your phone. No one can track you or read your messages anymore, including me. I want you to know that when your divorce is final, I'll show you who I am. No more masks, no more secrets. You deserve the truth, and I promise you'll have it. Until then, I'll be waiting for you.

I read it over three times before hitting send. It's more vulnerable than I've allowed myself to be with her, even during our most intimate moments. But after today, I owe her honesty.

I watch the screen, waiting for those three dots to appear that will tell me she's responding. One minute passes. Two. Five. Maybe she's asleep. Maybe she doesn't want to talk to me. Maybe she blames me for not being there when she needed me most.

Just as I'm about to set the phone down, the dots appear. My heart pounds as I wait for her reply.

Lila: I knew it was you who called the police. Thank you for that. I don't know how to feel about everything else right now. I need time.

It's not forgiveness, but it's not rejection either. She needs time. I can give her that.

Unknown Number: Take all the time you need... I'll be here when you're ready.

I set the phone down and walk to the window, looking out at the bay. The water is dark now, reflecting the lights from the houses on the opposite shore. Somewhere in that direction is the hospital where Lila is recovering. I imagine her lying in a sterile bed, bruised and scared but finally free of Eli.

My phone rings, and I answer without looking, expecting Dillian with news about the interrogation.

"Tony?" It's Mia's voice, tight with anger and concern.

"Hey," I say, suddenly exhausted. "How is she?"

"How do you think she is?" Mia snaps. "She's been thrown down a flight of stairs by her psycho husband. She's hurt and terrified and confused. And where the fuck were you?"

The accusation lands like a physical blow, all the more painful because it echoes my own thoughts.

"I was too far away," I admit, my voice hollow. "I didn't see him coming. He switched cars, like Dillian warned me he might. By the time I realized he was there, he'd already cornered her."

"You were supposed to be protecting her! That's the only reason I didn't tell her!" Mia's voice breaks on the last word, her anger giving way to the fear that must have gripped her when she realized her friend was in danger.

"I know," I say quietly. "I fucked up. I got cocky, thought I had all the angles covered. I was wrong."

The silence on the other end stretches for several seconds.

"At least you called the police," she finally says, some of the heat gone from her voice. "If they hadn't shown up when they did..."

"I know," I repeat. "Trust me, I know exactly what would have happened."

Another silence, this one less charged.

"I texted her," I tell Mia. "Told her I'd reveal myself after the divorce is final. No more games, no more masks."

"And?"

"She said she needs time. I'm giving it to her... and I'm pretty sure she knows it's me."

Mia sighs. "That's... actually decent of you. She probably does. She survived Eli because she's observant, not that intuitive, but observant. I don't know why she needed to go alone."

"Closure," I reply.

"Lila told us what happened at the club. About the VIP room," Mia replies and I imagine her rubbing her temple.

I tense, waiting for more recrimination, but Mia continues in a softer tone.

"She really cares about you, Tony. God knows why, but she does. Don't let her down again."

"I won't," I promise. "I'm done hiding. As soon as Eli is out of the picture for good, I'll tell her everything."

"Everything?" Mia challenges. "About GameStream too? About how you've technically been Eli's boss this whole time?"

I wince. That particular revelation is going to be the hardest to explain. "Yes, everything. No more secrets."

"Good," she says. "Because she deserves better than what she's had. Better than what either of you has given her so far."

The truth of that statement stings, but I can't argue with it. "I know," I say for the third time. "I'm going to make it right."

After we hang up, I pull up the hospital's security cameras on my laptop. It takes a few minutes to bypass their firewall, but soon I have a grasp of Lila's exact location. Room 312, East Wing. A police officer is stationed outside her door, a standard procedure in domestic violence cases.

Through the window, I can see her lying in bed, her phone clutched in her hand as she stares at the ceiling.

Is she thinking about my message? About Eli? About what happens next?

I close the laptop, suddenly uncomfortable with my own surveillance. She deserves privacy now more than ever. The time for watching from the shadows is over. When we meet again, it will be face to face, man to woman, with nothing hidden between us.

I walk to the kitchen and pour myself a glass of butterscotch bourbon, but don't drink it. Instead, I stare at the amber liquid, thinking about choices and consequences.

Everything that's happened; from that first meeting at the bookstore to today's violence, has led us here. Now I have to trust that when Lila knows the whole truth, she'll understand why I did what I did. And maybe, if I'm incredibly lucky, she'll forgive me for the parts where I failed her.

I set the untouched bourbon aside and pick up my phone again. There's work to do. Eli needs to be put away for a very long time, and I have resources that can make that happen. Amanda Finley deserves justice, and Lila deserves freedom. I can help with both.

It's time to step out of the shadows and into the light. Whatever comes next, I'll face it head-on, without masks or hidden cameras. Just a man trying to make amends for his mistakes and prove he's worthy of a second chance.

For Lila, I'd do anything.

26
Lila

THE HOSPITAL ROOM CEILING has exactly forty-three tiles. I've counted them three times now, tracing the fluorescent lights that make everything too harsh, too real. My ribs scream with every breath, a constant reminder of how close I came to never breathing again. The hospital gown scratches against my skin, and I can feel the weight of bandages wrapped around my wrist. But it's the weight of my phone in my good hand that feels heaviest of all, the messages it contains, the decisions I need to make, the future waiting on the other side of these sterile walls.

I shift slightly, wincing as pain shoots through my side. The doctor said I have two broken ribs, a sprained wrist, and enough bruises to make me look like a walking watercolor painting. Plus a mild concussion that has my head throbbing in time with my heartbeat. All courtesy of my *loving* husband.

My eyes catch on a small black dome in the corner of the ceiling. A security camera. I stare at it for a long moment, wondering if he's watching. Not Eli... they wouldn't let him near computers in jail, but my other watcher. My stalker. My masked man.

'I'm sorry I couldn't protect you today. I should have been there sooner.'

His text still burns in my mind. Hours later, and I'm still not sure how I feel about it. Grateful? Angry? Confused? All of the above, plus a heavy dose of painkillers making everything fuzzy around the edges.

The camera's small red light blinks steadily, a mechanical heartbeat. Is he watching me now, seeing me broken and bandaged? Something in my chest aches at the thought, and it's not just my ribs. But then I remember his last message:

'Take all the time you need...I'll be here when you're ready.'

No, he wouldn't watch me like this. Whatever else he might be, he's decent enough to give me privacy when I'm at my most vulnerable.

The room feels emptier without Mia and Valerie. They stayed as long as they could, Mia holding my hand while the doctor explained my injuries, Valerie pacing by the window, fury radiating from her like heat. Mia left first, apologizing profusely about some family emergency. She wouldn't say what, just promised to be back first thing tomorrow. Valerie stayed longer, only leaving after I'd gotten that text and insisted I needed rest.

"I'll be back at eight," she said, gathering her purse. "With coffee and those croissants you like from the bakery by the print shop."

"You don't have to—"

"Shut up," she cut me off, but gently. "I'm bringing you croissants. Deal with it."

I smiled then, despite the pain it caused in my bruised cheek. Having friends who love me enough to bulldoze through my protests is a luxury I'd forgotten I deserved. I would do the same for them.

Now, alone with the steady beep of monitors and the distant sounds of the hospital at night, I can't stop my thoughts from circling back to him. To my stalker. My protector? The man who's been watching me for months, who touched me on those steps, who made me feel alive in that VIP room.

I should be horrified by him. That's what any normal person would feel. But nothing about my life has been normal for so long that the thought of him. Of his hands on me, his voice in my ear, brings a warmth that has nothing to do with my injuries.

'I've removed all of his spyware from your phone. He can't track you or read your messages anymore.'

I check my phone again, scrolling through the messaging app. It looks the same as always, but something feels different. Lighter, somehow. For years, I've typed every message with the awareness that Eli might read it. Now I could text anything to anyone, and he'd never know. The freedom is dizzying.

The TV remote sits on the bedside table, just within reach of my good hand. I grab it, needing a distraction from the throbbing pain that's starting to break through the medication. The TV mounted on the wall flickers to life, sound low enough not to disturb the quiet of the hospital night.

A game show where contestants scream over spinning wheels. Click. A cartoon with bright colors that hurt my eyes. Click. A cooking competition where someone's crying over a fallen soufflé. Click.

Nothing holds my interest. My mind keeps drifting back to the moment at the top of the stairs. Eli's face twisted with rage, his hands in my hair. The sickening feeling of falling, of impact after impact. The certainty, in those seconds, that I was going to die.

I turn off the TV, plunging the room back into semi-darkness, lit only by the machines monitoring my vitals and the soft glow from the hallway. In the sudden quiet, a question pounds in my head, louder than the pain: How the fuck did I let it get this far?

Ten years. Ten years of my life given to a man who could throw me down a flight of stairs and then try to rape while I'm that bloodied and bruised. A man who tracked my phone, read my messages, controlled my bank accounts. A man who made me believe I deserved nothing better.

I wasn't always this person. Before Eli, I had dreams, ambitions. I laughed easily. I made decisions without checking with anyone first. I wore clothes I liked instead of clothes he approved of. When did I disappear so completely into his shadow?

The signs were there from the beginning, I see that now. The way he'd check my phone when I was in the shower. The subtle comments about my friends, my clothes, my weight. The way he'd raise his voice during arguments, just enough to make me back down. Small things that grew so gradually I didn't notice I was being consumed until there was almost nothing left of me.

I think back to our early days, when he still wooed me with grand gestures and promises. He seemed so perfect. Successful, handsome, attentive. By the time I realized the attention was control, the handsome face hid an ugly soul, I was already trapped.

Or did I trap myself? Did I ignore the warning signs because I wanted so badly to believe someone could love me that much? Did I make excuses for his behavior because admitting the truth meant admitting I'd made a terrible mistake?

"How the hell could I have avoided this?" I whisper to the empty room, my voice sounding strange to my own ears.

The answers don't come. Maybe there aren't any, or maybe they're too simple to accept. Maybe I could have left the first time he screamed at me over a dinner I'd burned. Or the first time he "accidentally" broke something I loved. Or the first time he pushed me, not hard enough to hurt, just enough to show he could.

My sprained wrist throbs, the bandage too tight and too loose all at once. I adjust it with my good hand, wincing at the pain that shoots up my arm. At least the physical wounds will heal. The doctor said six to eight weeks for the ribs, less for the wrist and bruises. The other wounds... the ones you can't see on an X-ray. I'm not sure about those.

Tears burn behind my eyes, but I blink them back. I'm done crying over Eli Fischer. He's taken enough from me.

My phone screen lights up with a notification. It's not a text, just a reminder from my calendar app about a print job due next week. Something so normal, so mundane, it almost makes me laugh. The world keeps turning, even when yours stops.

I open the browser on my phone and type "Maryland divorce papers" into the search bar. The state website comes up first, and I click it, watching as the page loads. There they are, PDF forms with titles like "Complaint for Absolute Divorce" and "Financial Statement."

My thumb hovers over the download button. Once I start this, there's no going back. But then, there was no going back the moment Eli threw me down those stairs. Maybe there was no going back years ago, and I just couldn't see it.

I download the forms, a small act of defiance that feels monumental. Tomorrow, I'll ask Valerie to print them at the shop. She can mail them as soon as I'm discharged. I don't need a fancy lawyer, at least not yet. This is just the first step, filing the paperwork myself to make it official that our marriage is over.

My stomach churns at the thought of Eli's reaction when he's served with divorce papers. But then I remember the police officer stationed outside my hospital room door, the restraining order they helped me file this afternoon, the charges stacking up against Eli. Assault. Attempted sexual assault. False imprisonment. The detective mentioned they're looking into other potential charges as well, though he couldn't elaborate.

For once, Eli can't hurt me. He's in a cell, and I'm free. Broken and bruised, but free.

The pain medication in my IV is starting to work again, dulling the sharp edges of my injuries. My eyelids grow heavy, but I fight the drowsiness. I'm not ready to sleep, not ready to risk the nightmares I know are waiting.

Instead, I open my e-reader app, scrolling through my library for something to distract me. My finger pauses over a dark romance I'd been reading before... before every-thing. The irony isn't lost on me, escaping into fictional tales of obsession and dangerous men while living my own twisted version. But these stories always had one crucial difference: the men in them, no matter how dark, never truly hurt the women they loved.

I open a different book instead, a mystery I've been meaning to read for months. Something with no romance, no obsession, just a puzzle to solve. The words swim before my eyes as the medication pulls me deeper toward sleep.

As I drift off, my thoughts turn once more to my masked man. To the promise in his text:

'I'll show you who I am. No more masks, no more secrets.'

Part of me is afraid of that revelation, afraid that the reality won't match the fantasy I've built in my head. But another part, growing stronger by the minute, is ready to see him again, without the mask.

The phone slips from my fingers, landing softly on the blanket covering my legs. Tomorrow will bring Valerie with croissants, Mia with her fierce protectiveness, and the first steps toward my new life. For now, I let the medication pull me under into darkness.

My last conscious thought before sleep claims me is simple: I survived. And that's enough for today.

27

Lila

TRIGGER WARNING: NON CONSENT, RECORDING
WITHOUT CONSENT

I STAND IN THE kitchen, staring at the coffeepot as it finishes
its cycle. The house is the same as it will always be. Silent,
sterile, cold. My hands are steady as I pour Eli's coffee. Two
sugars, a splash of cream, just how he likes it. I wipe the rim of
the mug before picking it up, careful not to leave any spillage.

I carry the cup upstairs, every step rehearsed. Every footstep
echoes, even the soft ones. Eli's office door is closed. Always
closed. I hold the coffee in one hand and knock with the other.

No answer. I wait. I listen. Nothing.

I count to five, then turn the knob. The office is dark except
for the glow of Eli's computer monitors. There are several of
them, angled so he can see everything at once. The screensaver
is off. He's there, slouched in his chair, one ankle crossed over his
knee. He's wearing sweatpants and a t-shirt.

He doesn't turn when I step inside, but I know he knows
I'm there. The desk is dark wood, wiped clean. I see my own

reflection in the screen: red hair pulled back, pale face, eyes already wide.

He's watching something on one of the monitors. I see flashes of skin and movement, hear the faint, rhythmic moaning. He turns the volume up a notch, and the sound gets clearer. She's not moaning, she's crying.

"Set it down," he says, not looking at me.

I place the coffee on a coaster at the edge of his desk. I keep my eyes down, but I can't help seeing the screen. There's a woman on her knees, her mouth wide open, her face streaked with makeup and tears. Eli doesn't even bother to mute it. He just keeps watching.

I take a step back, toward the door. My breath is thin and tight in my chest.

"Stay," he says. His voice is flat, bored, but there's a sharp edge to it.

I stop, like I've hit an invisible wall.

He leans back in the chair and finally turns to face me. His eyes are glassy, cold, like the blue of winter sky. He looks me up and down, then back at the screen.

"You ever think about doing something like this?" he asks, nodding toward the monitor.

I shake my head before I can stop myself. "No."

He smiles, but it's not a smile. "Why not? You've got the mouth for it. Big lips, perfect for sucking cock. If you lost twenty pounds, you could probably make a living."

I flinch, but he keeps going.

"Maybe that's your true calling. God knows you're not cut out for anything else. When's the last time you made a dime on your own, Lila? Oh, that's right. Never."

The woman on the screen is still crying, but the man behind the camera just keeps pushing her head down and calling her names. Eli laughs under his breath, low and mean. *"You think she's faking? I bet she's faking. You can always tell."*

I wish I could be anywhere but here. I wish I could close my ears to the sounds, close my eyes to the sight of him, but I can't. I'm frozen, stuck in this spot like a bug on a pin.

He turns the chair, so he's facing me square. He picks up the coffee and takes a sip, never breaking eye contact.

"You're such a prude," he says. "Such a stick-in-your-ass, bitch. No wonder your adoptive parents disowned you."

My face burns. I want to leave. I want to run. But I just stand there, silent, hoping he'll let me go.

He sets down the mug and stands up. He's taller than me, so much bigger, but he moves slow, like a cat stalking something trapped. He closes the distance in two steps and stops with his chest inches from my face.

"Do you know how lucky you are?" he says, voice almost gentle. "Most women would kill to have a husband who lets her stay home. Most women would be grateful for what I give you. Instead, you mope around the house all day, reading your stupid books and pretending you're too good for me."

I shake my head. "What?"

"Don't what me," He grabs my chin, hard, his fingers digging into the soft flesh. "Don't pretend. I know you think you're better than me."

His eyes are too close. I can see the flecks of gray around the pupil, the way his brow furrows when he's angry. I can smell the coffee on his breath, sour and bitter.

"I'm sorry," I say. It's all I ever say.

He lets go of my face and laughs, then nods toward the screen. "You should watch. You might learn something."

I don't move.

He sighs, like I'm a disappointment. "Go ahead. Watch."

I take a half-step backward. Not wanting to see any more.

His hand comes up behind me and grabs the back of my neck, shoving me forward. Then he presses close enough that I can feel the heat of his body. He puts one hand on my shoulder, the other on the small of my back.

"You see how she takes it?" he says. "No gagging, no whining. Maybe you should try being more like her."

My hands start to shake. I grip the edge of the desk so I don't fall over.

He leans in, his lips brushing my ear. "I could have married anyone, you know. But I picked you. I thought you'd be grateful. Turns out you're just a fucking parasite."

I flinch again, but he laughs. "You like that word? Parasite. It fits you."

He presses his hips against me, and I can feel he's hard. I want to scream, but I know better. The last time I screamed, he locked me in the bathroom for two days. No food, only tap water, and the smell of bleach. My only company was his voice through the door, telling me over and over what a burden I was and how I should have just let him do what he wanted.

He slides his hand up under my shirt, fingers cold and rough. "You want to earn your keep for once?" He squeezes my breast so hard it hurts.

I shake my head, but he ignores it.

He pushes me forward, so my stomach hits the edge of the desk. The wood digs into my skin, hard enough to leave a mark. He keeps one hand on the back of my neck, pinning me down, while the other pulls at the waistband of my pants.

"Stop," I say. My voice is small, weak. "Please."

He laughs again. "You don't get to say no. You're my wife. You're mine."

He spits in his hand, rubs it on me. I know that's not going to be enough lubrication. I know this is going to hurt. Then rams himself inside me, tearing me open in one brutal thrust. The pain is blinding, white-hot, and I scream before I can stop myself.

He clamps a hand over my mouth, muffling the sound, and hisses, "No screaming. You want the viewers to hear what a whore you are?"

Viewers? Tears stream down my face. I can't breathe. I can't think. I just focus on the wood grain on the desk, the cold, the way my breath fogs and fades, fogs and fades.

"Look right there," he shakes my head toward a camera set up on a tripod on the other side of the room. Right across from the desk with a full view of my body.

Put on a good show.

He fucks me with short, vicious thrusts, each one punctuated by another insult.

"Fat bitch."

"Ungrateful cunt."

"Fucking parasite."

With every word, he slams into me harder. The edge of the desk cuts into my hip, the hardness of it biting through the thin cotton of my shirt. My skin will bruise, I know it, but I don't care. All I want is for it to be over.

I try to go somewhere else. I stare at the photo on the wall in front of me, the only personal thing in the office. It's from our honeymoon, before the money, before the house, before he started hating me. I'm smiling in the picture, standing in front of a courthouse in a white dress. Eli is next to me, his arm around my waist, chin resting on my shoulder.

In the photo, he looks happy. I look happy. I try to remember what that felt like, but the memory won't come.

He pulls out just long enough to spit on his hand again and smear it between my legs, then shoves back in, raw and burning. I bite my tongue to keep from screaming. The taste of blood is sharp, real, grounding.

My body goes limp now. I let him do what he wants. It's easier that way. If I resist, he'll just hurt me more.

He finishes fast, hips jerking against my ass, fingers digging so hard into my shoulders I know they'll leave bruises. He shudders, grunts, then pulls out and lets me collapse onto the floor. My legs shake so badly, I can barely stand. I don't move. I just stay there, staring at the photo.

He tucks himself back into his sweatpants, wiping his hands on my shirt before stepping away. He grabs the coffee, now cold, and takes another sip like nothing happened.

"You made a mess," he says, voice flat. "Clean it up before you go."

I don't answer. I just pull up my panties, wincing at the pain, and reach for my pants on the floor. I hold them up, assessing the damage and then use them to wipe the mess from his desk and the floor.

Eli sits back down at the computer and keeps watching the video. The woman on the screen is still crying, still on her knees. I wonder if she ever got to leave. How long did she go through this?

I walk out of the office, legs numb, head spinning. The hallway is empty, the house silent except for the sound of Eli's video changing to his voice calling me a whore. He recorded himself raping me and made it obvious that he plans to post it.

I make it to the bathroom before I puke. When I'm done, I rinse my mouth, wash my face, and stare at the girl in the mirror for a moment before I cover it with a towel. Her eyes were red, skin blotchy, lips swollen where his ring caught them. She looked weak. Pathetic.

I ball up my ruined pants and hide them at the bottom of the trash. I put on a fresh pair, smooth my hair, and try to erase the last half hour from my mind. Thanking whatever god out there that hasn't allowed Eli to find out about my IUD.

But I can still feel him inside me, the echo of his voice flowing down the hallway.

Fucking parasite.

I go back to the kitchen, start dinner, and pretend nothing happened.

28

Lila

TODAY I USE THE front door instead of coming through the back. Stepping into the familiar warmth of the print shop. Two months away and nothing's changed; same smell of paper and toner, same hum of appliances in the back room, same stack of orders waiting to be processed. But everything's different too. I'm different. The woman who walked out of Mia's house that day to pack her bags and leave her husband is gone. In her place stands someone new, someone still figuring out who the hell she is without Eli's shadow looming over her.

"You guys are early," Valerie calls from behind the counter, her smile wide and genuine. "Couldn't sleep?"

"No, Lila refused to let us leave late. You know how she is about being early," she laughs. But I can't disagree.

I shrug, wincing slightly at the lingering tenderness in my ribs. "Mia snores."

"I do not!" Mia walks in behind me, feigning offense. "I breathe with enthusiasm, that's all."

The laughter comes easily, surprising me. Two months ago, I wasn't sure I'd ever laugh again. The doctors had fixed my broken ribs and sprained wrist. Yet here I am, smiling in the morning light that streams through the shop windows, feeling something close to normal.

"I got coffees," Valerie says, pushing a fancy cup across the counter toward me. "Your usual—vanilla with an extra shot of espresso."

The warmth of the cup against my palm is comforting, familiar. I take a sip and close my eyes, letting the rich flavor wash over me. "God, I missed this."

"The coffee or work?" Mia asks, nudging my shoulder gently.

"Both," I admit. "But mostly the coffee."

They laugh again, and I feel a tightness in my chest that has nothing to do with my healing ribs. These women rammed a car through a gate to save me. They've housed me, fed me, held me through nightmares and panic attacks. They've never once made me feel like a burden, even when I know I've been one.

We fall into our morning routine as if I'd never left. Valerie sorts through the orders that came in overnight, separating them by priority. Mia checks the inventory, making notes of supplies we need to reorder. I settle at my desk, powering up my computer and reviewing the day's appointments.

"Mrs. Chen's coming at ten for her business cards," Valerie says, passing me a file. "And the Harper wedding invitations need to be finished by closing."

I nod, already pulling up the design templates. This is what I need. The comforting rhythm of work, of tasks with clear beginnings and ends. No complicated emotions, no masked men watching from the shadows. Just paper and ink and deadlines.

The morning passes in a blur of customers and orders. Mrs. Chen loves her new business cards, the delicate floral design perfectly matching her tea shop's aesthetic. The Harper invitations turn out beautifully, cream cardstock with gold foil lettering. I find myself getting lost in the work, hands steady as I adjust settings on the printer, mind focused on colors and margins instead of tomorrow's court date.

At lunch, we close the shop for an hour and retreat to the small break room in the back. Mia unpacks containers of homemade pasta salad, passing them around with plastic forks.

"So," she says, settling into the chair across from me, "how's it been, living with me for two months? Be honest."

I twirl pasta around my fork, considering. "Well, aside from the snoring."

"Enthusiastic breathing," she corrects.

"Right, that. It's been... good." The word feels inadequate. "Better than good. I don't know how to thank you."

Valerie reaches across the table, squeezing my hand. "You don't have to thank us. That's what friends do, and I know you'd do the same for either of us."

I absolutely would.

"Still," I say, blinking back the sudden moisture in my eyes. "Not everyone would make room in their life for a broken woman with a psycho husband and almost no money."

"First of all," Mia says firmly, "you're not broken. Bent maybe, a little cracked around the edges, but not broken."

"And second," Valerie adds, "your psycho husband is in jail, where he belongs. And after tomorrow, he won't even be your husband anymore. You can partner with the business. He can't control your money after that."

Tomorrow. The word sends a shiver down my spine, equal parts fear and anticipation. "Do you really think the judge will grant it? Just like that?"

"With the charges against Eli? Absolutely," Valerie says, her tone leaving no room for doubt. "Plus, you're not asking for anything. No alimony, no property other than your books. Just a clean break."

"Your books," Mia reminds me. "Don't forget about those."

My books. My sanctuary in that house of horrors. I've missed them more than I've let myself admit. "I just want to get my books and never set foot in that house again."

We finish lunch talking about easier things. A difficult customer Valerie dealt with last week, Mia's newest Netflix obsession, plans for redecorating the guest room I've been staying in to make it more "me." They're doing what they've done every day since I left the hospital. Treating me normally while giving me space to heal.

As we clean up and prepare to reopen the shop, my thoughts drift to him. My stalker. My masked man. True to his word, he's given me the time I asked for. No texts, no calls, no shadowy figures watching from afar. I've caught myself reaching for my phone a dozen times, fingers hovering over his number before pulling back. Part of me has wanted to reach out, to hear his voice, to feel that strange connection that sparked between us. But I've stopped myself each time. I made a promise. To him and to myself, that I'd wait until the divorce was final.

After tomorrow, it will be.

The afternoon passes quickly, filled with the satisfying rhythm of completed orders and happy customers. By closing time, my back aches from standing at the printer, but it's a good ache, honest and earned. As I help Valerie count the register and Mia locks the front door, a sense of peace settles over me.

"You good for tomorrow?" Valerie asks, eyeing me carefully as she tucks the day's earnings into the safe. "9 AM at the courthouse. I'll pick you both up at eight."

After the incident, Valerie's insurance covered a new car for her. Which I'm grateful for. After that fiasco, she deserves it.

I nod, pushing down the flutter of nerves in my stomach. "I'm ready. I just want it to be over."

"It will be," Mia says, slinging an arm around my shoulders. "And then we're going out for a proper celebration. No more looking back, only forward."

As we walk to Mia's car, I glance up at the sky. The sun is setting, painting everything in shades of gold and pink. Tomorrow, I'll be Lila Fischer for the last time. After that, I'll be Lila... someone else. Someone new. Someone free.

The thought carries me home, through dinner and a shower, all the way to the guest bed that's become mine these past two months. I lie awake long after Mia's gone to sleep, staring at my phone in the darkness, thinking about the text I'll send tomorrow. Thinking about finally seeing his face again.

The courthouse looms in front of us, all cold stone and imposing columns. My stomach twists itself into knots as Valerie finds a parking spot, and I have to wipe my sweaty palms on my skirt. I've worn the only professional outfit I own, a navy pencil skirt and matching blazer. It hangs a little loose now; I've lost weight since everything happened. Mia reaches over from the backseat and squeezes my shoulder.

"You got this," she says, her voice steady and sure. "We're right here with you."

I nod, not trusting my voice. The three of us climb out of the car and make our way up the stone steps. My legs feel like they're made of jelly, and I'm grateful for Valerie's arm linked through mine, keeping me upright. Security is a blur of metal detectors and badge-flashing officers, and then we're inside, following signs to Family Court.

The hallway outside Courtroom C is crowded with people, other couples ending their marriages, lawyers in expensive suits, court personnel hurrying from one room to another. We find three empty seats on a wooden bench, hard and uncomfortable as church pews. Fitting, I suppose, for the dismantling of a sacrament.

"You okay?" Valerie asks, eyeing me with concern. "You're shaking."

I am. My hands tremble no matter how tightly I clasp them in my lap. "What if the judge says no?" I whisper, giving voice to the fear that's been growing since we got in the car. "What if I have to stay married to him?"

"Not gonna happen," Mia says firmly. "Not with what he did to you. The restraining order, the charges—there's no way a judge will force you to stay in that marriage."

"But what if—"

"No what-ifs," Valerie cuts me off gently. "One step at a time, remember? That's how we've gotten through everything else."

She's right. One step at a time is how I survived those first days in the hospital, how I made it through giving my statement to the police, how I've navigated each day since. I take a deep breath, trying to steady my racing heart.

"Fischer case?" A court officer calls from the doorway, scanning the crowded hallway.

"That's us," I say, rising on shaky legs. Valerie and Mia flank me as we follow the officer into the courtroom.

The room is smaller than I expected, with worn carpeting and fluorescent lighting that makes everyone look sickly. The judge, an older woman with silver hair pulled back in a severe bun, glances up from her papers as we approach the front.

"Mrs. Fischer," she says, her voice neither warm nor cold. "I understand you're seeking an absolute divorce from Eli Fischer, currently awaiting trial on multiple charges including assault and attempted sexual assault."

"Yes, Your Honor," I reply, my voice barely above a whisper.

"Speak up, please," she instructs, not unkindly.

I clear my throat. "Yes, Your Honor."

She shuffles through some papers. "And you're not seeking any financial settlement or division of property?"

"No, ma'am," I say, standing straighter now. "I don't want anything from him. Not the house, not the car, not his money. Nothing." I pause, then add, "Except my books from my library in the house. Those are mine. They've always been mine."

Something in the judge's expression softens slightly. "I see. And Mr. Fischer is not contesting the divorce?"

"No, Your Honor. He's been served the papers in jail, and his lawyer indicated he won't contest it."

Of course he won't. Eli's fighting much bigger battles now. The assault charges, the attempted rape charges, and whatever else the police are investigating. A divorce is the least of his worries.

The judge makes a note, then looks up at me again. "Mrs. Fischer, I've reviewed the circumstances of your case, including the police reports and hospital records." Her gaze drops to my wrist, where the bandage has been removed but a faint discoloration still lingers. "Based on the evidence of extreme cruelty and the ongoing criminal case against your husband, I'm granting your petition for absolute divorce, effective immediately."

The relief hits me so hard I actually sway on my feet. Valerie's hand steadies me as the judge continues.

"You'll be notified if Mr. Fischer is moved to a different facility or if he's released on bond, though given the severity of the charges, that seems unlikely. You're free to collect your personal belongings from the marital home at any time, though I'd recommend having a police escort if you're concerned about your safety."

"Thank you, Your Honor," I manage, blinking back tears.

"And Mrs. Fischer," she adds, "or I should say, Ms. Angelo now?"

I nod, the sound of my maiden name strange but welcome.

"I wish you all the best." She bangs her gavel once, gently. "Case closed."

Just like that, it's over. Ten years of marriage dissolved in less than fifteen minutes. I turn to Mia and Valerie, both of them beaming at me, and the tears I've been holding back finally spill over.

"Come on," Mia says, pulling me into a quick hug. "Let's get out of here."

We push through the heavy courtroom doors and back into the hallway, which seems brighter somehow, less oppressive. I feel lighter with each step, as if I've set down a weight I've been carrying so long I forgot it was there.

Outside, the sun is shining; the air crisp winter air hits differently now. I stop at the top of the courthouse steps, breathing deeply, filling my lungs with free air.

"How does it feel?" Valerie asks, watching me with a smile.

"Weird," I admit. "Good-weird, but still weird. I keep waiting for it to hit me that I'm really divorced."

"Maybe you need a divorce party," Mia suggests as we head back to the car. "We could invite the whole print shop crew, get a cake shaped like Eli's head and stab it repeatedly."

That startles a laugh out of me. "That's dark, even for you."

"Just an idea," she says, grinning. "Consider it on the table."

Back at Mia's house, they hover for a bit, making sure I'm okay before leaving me alone with my thoughts. Valerie heads back to open the print shop for the afternoon, while Mia retreats to her home office to catch up on paperwork, but not before making me promise to tell her if I need anything.

I curl up on the couch, still in my court clothes, staring at my phone. It's time. No more waiting, no more excuses. I'm free now, legally and completely free. My finger hovers over his contact for a long moment before I finally type:

> **Me:** It's done. The divorce is final. I'm ready to see you now, if you still want to meet.

His response comes almost immediately, as if he's been waiting by his phone:

> **Unknown Number:** Name the place and time.

My heart beats faster as I type:

> **Me:** The bookstore. Tonight at 7?

Another quick response:

> **Unknown Number:** I'll be there. No masks this time. Just me.

I set the phone down, my hand trembling slightly. After all this time, I'm finally going to see his face again. But as I stare out the window at Mia's backyard, where the few trees outside are now bare, I realize something strange: I already know who he is.

Little clues have been adding up. Things Mia has said, the way she sometimes looks at her phone with an expression I can't quite read, the "family emergency" that pulled her away from the hospital the night Eli attacked me. And sometimes, when he texted me, I can almost hear the voice from the bookstore, from my back steps, from the club, and at Akira Sushi.

Tonight, I'll know for sure.

29

Anthony

M Y PHONE BUZZES AGAINST my palm, and my heart nearly stops when I see her name. Lila. After two months of silence, of giving her the space she asked for, she's finally reaching out. I read her message three times, making sure I'm not imagining things:

> **Lila:** It's done. The divorce is final. I'm ready to see you now, if you still want to meet.

My fingers tremble as I type back, trying to sound calmer than I feel, like I haven't been checking my phone every five minutes for weeks hoping to hear from her.

> **Me:** I've been waiting to hear from you. Name the place and time.

Simple. Direct. Not revealing how my stomach is doing somersaults or how my pulse is racing like I've just run a marathon.

Her response comes almost immediately:

Lila: The bookstore. Tonight at 7?

The bookstore. Where this all began. Where I first saw her, first spoke to her. It feels right, bringing this full circle. I glance at my watch, 4:30. Two and a half hours to prepare for the moment I've been both dreading and longing for.

Me: I'll be there. No masks this time. Just me.

I set the phone down on my kitchen counter and let out a long, shaky breath. This is it. No more hiding, no more secrets. After tonight, Lila will know for sure who I am. Not just the masked man who's been watching her, but Anthony Russo, GameStream owner, Mia's brother, and the man who's fallen hopelessly in love with her.

What the fuck do I wear to reveal myself to the woman I've been essentially stalking? As much as I hate using that word. The thought is so absurd I actually laugh out loud; the sound echoing in my empty townhouse. I head to my closet, pushing aside the dark clothing I wore for my nighttime watches. Tonight, I need to look like myself.

I settle on dark jeans and a charcoal gray button-down, simple but nice. A heavy jacket and my helmet. Not trying too hard, but not casual either. I want her to see me as I am, the real Anthony, not the mysterious figure who followed her or the businessman who runs GameStream.

In the shower, I let hot water pound against my shoulders, trying to wash away the anxiety building in my chest. What if she actually hasn't figured out who I am, and she's angry when she sees me? What if she's disappointed? What if she's expecting something better than me?

No. I can't go down that road. Whatever happens tonight, at least it will be honest. At least we'll finally face each other without masks or secrets between us.

I dress carefully, taking more time than usual. Check my reflection in the mirror, I look nervous, which feels appropriate. I run a hand through my still-damp hair, wondering if I should have gotten it cut. Too late now. Besides, this is who I am.

The mask sits on my dresser, those green X's staring up at me. I should leave it here. Show up as myself, no props, no dramatic reveal. But something tells me to bring it. One last time, to close this chapter properly. I slip it into my jacket pocket, the familiar weight oddly comforting.

Before I leave, I need to do one more thing. I grab my phone and pull up Mia's contact.

> **Me:** Going to meet Lila at the bookstore at 7. She's ready to see me. Tonight she finds out her stalker is her best friend's brother.

I hit send before I can overthink it. Mia and I have had several conversations about this moment, about when and how I would reveal myself to Lila. She's been surprisingly supportive, given how furious she was when she first discovered my identity at the club. I think she understands now that my feelings for Lila are real, not some twisted game.

My phone buzzes with Mia's response.

> **Mia:** About time. Don't fuck up... again. She deserves the truth.

I smile at her directness. Mia never sugarcoats anything, which is one of the things I love about her. And she's right. Lila deserves the complete truth, every uncomfortable, messy detail of it.

> **Me:** I know. I'll tell her everything. Wish me luck.

> **Mia:** You don't need luck. You need honesty. But good luck anyway. Call me after.

I tuck my phone into my pocket and grab my motorcycle keys. The ride to the bookstore will give me time to collect my thoughts, to prepare what I'll say when I'm finally face to face with her, no masks between us.

The winter air hits me like a slap when I step outside, cool and crisp with the promise of spring not far behind. I zip my jacket against the chill and swing my leg over my bike, the familiar leather seat steadying me. The engine roars to life, and I pull away from the curb, heading toward The Dark Chapters Bookstore.

Traffic is light, and I find myself taking the long way, extending the ride to give myself more time to think. What will I say to her? "Sorry I stalked you, but I love you" doesn't exactly roll off the tongue. Yet that's essentially the truth of it. I've watched her, followed her, invaded her privacy. All while telling myself it was to protect her. And somewhere along the way, protection became devotion, obsession became love.

Will she see it that way? Or will she see a man who couldn't respect her boundaries, who appointed himself her protector without her consent? I wouldn't blame her if she walked away tonight and never looked back. But God, I hope she doesn't.

I pull into the bookstore parking lot at 6:45, cutting the engine and sitting for a moment on my bike. My heart hammers against my ribs so hard it almost hurts. I scan the lot for her car but don't see it. Maybe she's not here yet. Was she dropped off? Maybe she changed her mind.

I get off the bike and pull the mask from my pocket, turning it over in my hands. One last time. I slip it over my face, feeling the familiar press of it against my skin. It feels different now, like a costume I've outgrown.

The door sensor plays a short jingle as I push it open, the smell of books and coffee washing over me. The bookstore is quiet tonight, just a few customers browsing the shelves. I scan the space, looking for her red hair, those distinctive blonde streaks.

She's not at the front. Not by the registers. Not in the main aisle. I move deeper into the store, past self-help and history, toward the back corner where I know the romance section is. That's where I found her that first day, browsing dark romances with their dramatic covers and tangled lovers.

And there she is.

She stands with her back to me, one hand tracing the spines of books on a shelf at eye level. Her hair is pulled back in a loose ponytail, those blonde streaks catching the light. She's wearing a simple black dress that hugs her curves and a heavy black sweater, making my mouth go dry. Even after everything,the club, the hospital, the divorce and everything in between. The sight of her still hits me like a physical force.

I approach quietly, not wanting to startle her. When I'm just a few feet away, she turns, as if sensing my presence.

Her eyes find mine through the mask, and the corner of her mouth lifts in a small, knowing smile.

"I thought you said no masks," she says, her voice softer than I remember.

"I thought it would be fitting," I reply, taking another step closer. "To end this the way it began."

She nods, understanding in her eyes. "Then let me see you. The real you."

I stand perfectly still as she closes the distance between us. Her hands rise slowly, hesitating just before they touch the mask. I can smell her perfume. Something light and floral, honeysuckle and jasmine. It makes me think of spring, of new beginnings.

"May I?" she asks, her fingers hovering at the edges of my mask.

"Please," I whisper, the word catching in my throat.

Her fingers are warm against my skin as she carefully lifts the mask away. I keep my eyes on hers, watching for her reaction, for any sign of disappointment or anger. Instead, I see recognition, then confirmation, then something softer I don't dare name.

"Anthony," she says, and hearing my name on her lips for the first time nearly undoes me. "I knew it was you." The mask dangles from her fingers now, forgotten between us.

"How?" I ask, genuinely curious. "What gave me away?" Hinting a smile.

She smiles, and it transforms her face, making her look younger, freer. "I started to put it together after... after that night on the steps. When you waved to me at the restaurant. And Mia has photos of you in her house. The way she reacted when she saw you at the club, the 'family emergency' that pulled her away from the hospital. Those things started to fit. But, I think you wanted to be found out."

"Are you angry?" I need to know. Need to hear it from her.

She considers this, her head tilting slightly. "I was. For a while. But then I remembered how you protected me, how you called the police when Eli—" She stops, takes a breath. "I think I understand why you did it your way, even if it wasn't... conventional."

"You did refuse to talk to me," I say with a small laugh.

"Most people haven't lived my life," she counters, and there's a strength in her voice that wasn't there before. "They haven't been through what I've been through."

I want to touch her. To take her hand, brush her cheek, anything... but I hold back, not sure if we're there yet. "I'm in love with you," I say instead, the words tumbling out before I can consider them. "I knew I loved you that day you threatened me with the knife. It doesn't make what I did right, but I need you to know that it's not just about obsession, lust, or control."

Her eyes widen slightly, and for a terrible moment, I think I've said too much, too soon. But then she smiles again, that beautiful, transformative smile. "I know," she says simply. "I think I've known for a while. You kept your word when I said I needed space."

"And Mia?" I ask, remembering the other piece of this complicated puzzle. "Are you angry with her for keeping my secret?"

Lila shakes her head. "No. She was caught in the middle, trying to protect both of us. I understand why she didn't tell me."

Relief washes over me, so powerful it makes me dizzy. I reach out, finally allowing myself to touch her, just the lightest brush of my fingers against hers. "What happens now?"

"Now," she says, taking my hand properly, her fingers intertwining with mine, "we start over. No masks, no secrets. Just Anthony and Lila."

The feeling of her hand in mine is better than anything I could have imagined. Warm and real and present. "I'd like that," I say, giving her hand a gentle squeeze. "Maybe we could start with dinner? Akira Sushi is just down the street. We can walk."

"I'd like that too," she says, and there's a lightness to her voice I've never heard before. "But first, I want to ask you something."

"Anything," I promise, meaning it completely.

"All those books you left me. Did you choose them on purpose?"

I nod, surprised she's bringing this up now. "Yes. I wanted to... I don't know, plant seeds, I guess. See what things you might be okay with. It was my way of getting to know you. And I wanted you to see that you deserved better than Eli, that you had the strength to leave."

She considers this, then says, "Thank you. For seeing that strength in me before I could see it in myself."

Something shifts between us in that moment, some final piece falling into place. She tugs gently on my hand. "Come on. I'm starving, and you owe me at least one proper date after all the drama."

We walk toward the front of the store, still hand in hand. I glance down at the mask she's still holding. "What do you want to do with that?"

She looks at it for a moment, then tucks it into her purse. "Keep it as a reminder, I think. Of where we started. Maybe you can wear it again, but just for fun."

Outside, the evening air has grown colder, but I barely notice. We walk the short distance to Akira Sushi, making small talk about the chill in the air and whether or not we think it will snow soon. Normal conversation, the kind people have when they're getting to know each other the normal way. It feels strange and wonderful all at once.

As we wait for the hostess to seat us, Lila turns to me, her expression suddenly serious. "I want you to know something. I'm not... fixed. What happened with Eli, it left scars. Not just the physical ones. I'm still working through a lot of things."

"I know," I say, matching her seriousness. "And I'm not asking you to be fixed. I'm just asking for a chance to know you, the real you. The rest we'll figure out together, at whatever pace you need."

Her smile returns, smaller but no less genuine. "I'd like that," she says, echoing my words from earlier. "One day at a time."

"One day at a time," I agree, and as the hostess leads us to a table by the window, I feel a sense of rightness, of coming home. No more masks, no more shadows.

30

Lila

T HE RESTAURANT IS WARMER than I expected, or maybe it's just my nerves heating me from the inside out. Anthony sits across from me, no mask between us now, just his actual face, handsome and open, watching me with those intense eyes that seem to see straight through me. I fidget with my chopsticks, unsure what to do with my hands when they're not hidden under a table or wrapped around a coffee mug. This is strange. Being on an actual date with the man who's been watching me for months, who's seen me at my most vulnerable, who knows more about me than anyone. Except maybe Mia and Valerie. And yet, it also feels like the most natural thing in the world.

"I recommend the dragon roll," Anthony says, breaking the silence that's settled between us. "And the spicy tuna. Both are excellent here."

I nod, grateful for the mundane topic. "I trust your judgment."

When the server comes and Anthony orders for both of us, the rolls he mentioned plus miso soup, edamame, and sake that arrives warm in small ceramic cups. I take a sip, letting the alcohol burn down my throat, steadying my nerves.

"So," I say, setting down my cup, "is this weird for you too? Sitting across from me instead of... watching from a distance?"

His laugh is rich and genuine, crinkling the corners of his eyes. "Definitely weird. But the good kind of weird."

"The best kind," I agree, feeling some of the tension dissolve between us.

The server returns with our edamame, and we fall into the rhythm of pulling the beans from their pods, a simple activity that gives our hands something to do while we navigate this new territory.

"I should probably tell you something," Anthony says after a moment, his expression turning slightly strained. "About Eli."

My stomach tightens. "What about him?"

"Well, he streamed with GameStream... I own that company. I actually came home to do an internal investigation and his named popped up. I thought you should know that before we continue."

"All right, is there anything else?" I ask, unsure whether I want to know or not.

"Not much that I know of right now. I can tell you that Eli may be linked to a missing person's case."

I sit quietly for a moment, letting that information sink in. All the times he'd left, was he hurting other women and not just cheating?

Anthony cuts through my thoughts, changing the subject. Sensing that I'm starting to spiral. I can't handle any more information about Eli right now. I just got free from him.

"And Mia," he says

"What about her?"

"She threatened to tell you everything if I didn't do it myself." He pops an edamame into his mouth, chewing slowly. "After that night at the club, when she recognized me, she gave me an ultimatum. Said if I didn't come clean by the end of the month, she'd tell you herself."

I laugh, picturing Mia's fierce expression as she laid down the law to her brother. "That sounds like her."

"She was right, of course," he continues, leaning forward slightly. "You deserved to know the truth. But then... everything happened with Eli, and it didn't seem like the right time to dump more complications on you."

The mention of Eli's name again sends a chill through me, despite the restaurant's warmth. I take another sip of sake, letting its burn chase away the cold memories.

"Is that why you stayed away?" I ask. "These past two months?"

Anthony's eyes soften. "I wanted to give you space. I knew being with Mia and Valerie would help you heal better than anything I could offer at the time. And I didn't want you to feel pressured or confused about... whatever this is between us."

The consideration in his words touches me. After years with Eli, who only ever thought about his own needs and desires, Anthony's thoughtfulness is like water in a desert.

"I appreciate that," I say quietly. "The space helped. But I also missed... something. Someone. I just didn't let myself acknowledge who."

Our miso soup arrives, steaming in small black bowls. I wrap my hands around mine, soaking in the warmth.

The server brings our sushi, colorful rolls arranged artfully on black platters. We eat in comfortable silence for a few minutes, the delicate flavors of fresh fish and rice filling my mouth. Anthony wasn't wrong about the dragon roll. It's delicious.

As I watch him across the table, chopsticks moving with grace between plate and mouth, something shifts inside me. The attraction I've felt since that first meeting at the bookstore hasn't faded with time or distance. If anything, it's grown stronger, deepened into something more substantial. This isn't just physical desire or the rebellious thrill of doing something Eli would hate. It's not a rebound or a desperate grab for affection after years of emotional starvation.

It's real. Real enough to survive two months of silence. Real enough to make my skin flush hot when Anthony's gaze meets mine.

"What are you thinking?" he asks, catching me staring.

The truth tumbles out before I can stop it. "That I want you. That these two months haven't changed that."

His chopsticks pause halfway to his mouth. "I thought you wanted to take things slow."

"I did. I do." I search for the right words. "But I also spent ten years of my life not doing what I wanted. Not being who I wanted to be. I'm done with that."

Anthony sets down his chopsticks, his eyes never leaving mine. "What are you saying, Lila?"

The sound of my name on his lips still sends a thrill through me. "I'm saying that I know what I want. And slow doesn't have to mean... glacial."

A smile spreads across his face, lighting up his features. "Noted."

We finish our sushi, talking about easier things, like what books we've read. A few days after he'd left those books for me, he went back and bought them for himself and read them at the same time as me. All so we could talk about them when this day came. We talked movies, and TV shows we binged. I was not a fan of the character replacement for one of my favorite shows and even though he had never seen it; he agreed with me.

The conversation, though not at all sexual, has me clenching my thighs. His laugh, his happiness. The way he makes me feel like he really does enjoy spending time with me.

"Next time," he says, handing his credit card to the server without looking at the total. "You can get the next one."

Next time. The casual certainty of it warms me more than the sake did.

Outside, the January air hits me, cold and bracing after the restaurant's warmth. I pull my sweater tighter around me, wishing I'd thought to bring something heavier.

"I just realized I need a ride back to Mia's," I say, my breath forming white clouds in the air. "She dropped me off, and I haven't bought a new car yet."

After the divorce, I didn't want anything to remind me of Eli at all. It was legally in his name anyway, and I wanted as clean a break as possible. Mia and Valerie have been driving me around, but I know I need to get my own transportation soon.

"I'd be happy to take you," Anthony says, gesturing toward the parking lot. "But all I have is the bike. Are you okay with that? It's pretty cold tonight."

I glance toward the sleek black motorcycle parked at the edge of the lot. I've never ridden one before, but the thought of pressing myself against Anthony's back, feeling his body heat through our clothes, is too tempting to resist.

"I'm okay with it if you are," I say, trying to sound casual.

He studies me for a moment. "You sure? January isn't exactly ideal for your first motorcycle ride."

"I'm sure." I take a step toward the bike, then add, "Unless you're trying to get out of giving me a ride?"

Anthony laughs, the sound warming the space between us. "Definitely not. Come on, then. Let's get you geared up."

At the motorcycle, he grabs his helmet off the seat. "This should fit well enough," he says, placing it over my head. "And here, take my jacket, too. You'll freeze in just that sweater. We'll have to get you your own set as soon as possible."

Before I can protest, he's shrugging out of his leather riding jacket. Underneath, he's wearing only a grey button-up shirt that clings to his chest and arms, highlighting the defined muscles I'd glimpsed that night in the VIP room. My mouth goes dry at the sight.

"Won't you be cold?" I ask, even as he gently pulls the sleeves on each of my arms.

He shakes his head. "I'm used to it. And it's not that far."

The jacket is still warm from his body as I slip it on. It's too big, of course, the sleeves hanging past my fingertips, but it's heavenly warm and smells like him, that clean linen, woodsy scent I remember from the club.

"It looks good on you," he says, something in his voice making me look up. His eyes have darkened, and I suddenly remember how he looked at me on those back steps, how he knelt before me in that VIP room.

I swallow hard. "Thanks."

He helps me with the helmet, his fingers brushing against my neck as he fastens the strap. Then he swings his leg over the bike with practiced ease and looks back at me.

"Hop on and hold tight," he instructs. "Lean with me when I lean, but otherwise just relax and let me do the work."

I climb on behind him, settling myself on the small passenger seat. There's nowhere to put my hands except around his waist, so I slide my arms around him, feeling the solid warmth of his body through his shirt. The contact sends electricity shooting through me, awakening parts of myself that have been dormant.

Anthony starts the engine, the motorcycle rumbling to life beneath us. The vibration travels up through my body, an unexpected sensation that makes me tighten my grip on him. I hear him inhale sharply and realize my hands are pressed against his abs, feeling the muscles tense under my touch.

"Ready?" he calls over his shoulder.

I nod, forgetting he can't see me, then remember to shout, "Ready!"

We pull out of the parking lot and onto the main road, the cold air rushing past us. Despite the jacket and helmet, my legs are freezing where they're exposed to the wind. I press closer to Anthony, seeking his warmth.

As we ride, something shifts inside me. Maybe it's the vibration of the engine, or the feel of Anthony's body against mine, or just the freedom of speeding through the night with nothing between me and the world except this man and this machine. Whatever it is, it makes me bold in a way I haven't been in years.

I slide my hands lower, feeling Anthony's body tense as my fingers trace the waistband of his jeans. We're at a stoplight, the red glow painting everything crimson. I lean forward, my chest pressed against his back, and try to make sure he can hear me when I say, "Take me to your place instead."

He turns his head slightly, trying to see my face through his helmet visor. "You sure?"

In answer, I slide my hand between his legs, feeling the hardness already growing there. I palm him through his jeans, a rush of power surging through me as he groans, the sound barely audible over the engine.

"I'm sure," I say, giving him a gentle squeeze. "Very sure."

The light turns green, and Anthony accelerates perhaps a bit faster than necessary, the sudden burst of speed making me cling tighter to him. I keep my hand where it is, massaging him through the denim, feeling him grow harder under my touch.

We turn off the main road onto a street that leads toward the bay. The homes here are larger, with well-maintained lawns and expensive cars parked under their stilts.

After a few minutes, Anthony slows and turns into a driveway leading to a modern townhouse with large windows facing the water.

He cuts the engine, and the sudden silence is almost jarring. Neither of us moves for a moment, my hand still resting between his legs, his body still radiating heat into mine.

"This is me," he says finally, his voice rougher than before.

I reluctantly withdraw my hand so we can dismount. As I pull off the helmet, I realize I recognize this neighborhood. "Wait, this is only a few houses from Mia's place."

Anthony nods, taking the helmet from me. "Yeah, we're practically neighbors. I bought this so I could live closer to my sister."

The thought makes me laugh. "So all those times you were watching me, you were just... crossing over the bridge from the bay to oceanside?"

"Yeah," he admits, looking slightly embarrassed. "It's only about a fifteen-minute ride."

I shake my head, still smiling. "Unbelievable."

I look up at him, at this man who's been a shadow and a mystery for so long, now solid and real before me. His eyes are dark with desire, his breath quickens. I reach up and touch his face, tracing the spot where the mask used to sit.

He leans down, hesitating just before our lips meet, waiting for permission. I close the distance, pressing my mouth to his. The kiss is gentle at first, almost tentative, but quickly grows deeper, hungrier. His hands tighten on my hips, pulling me closer until I'm pressed against him from chest to thigh, feeling the hardness I'd been teasing on the ride here.

When we finally break apart, we're both breathing hard, our exhales mingling in the cold night air.

"We should go inside," Anthony says, his voice rough with want. "Before we give the neighbors a show."

I nod, suddenly eager to see his home, to be alone with him properly for the first time. "Lead the way."

He takes my hand, intertwining his fingers with mine, and leads me toward the front door. As we climb the steps to his door, I feel a flutter of nerves mixed with anticipation. This is it, the beginning of something new, something chosen freely and without fear.

And I can't fucking wait.

31

Anthony

I UNLOCK THE DOOR and guide Lila inside, my hand still intertwined with hers. The click of the door shutting behind us feels monumental. The sound of a threshold being crossed, not just physical but something deeper. My townhouse is dark except for the faint blue glow of the bay waters visible through the wall of windows overlooking a spacious balcony, casting everything in soft shadows. Neither of us reaches for a light switch. In this half-dark, with her hand warm in mine and her breath coming quick and shallow, I don't need to see clearly. I just need to feel.

"Your place is beautiful," she whispers, eyes taking in the open layout of the main floor, the moonlight dancing on the water outside.

"Not as beautiful as you," I say, and it sounds cliché, but fuck, I mean it. Standing here in my entryway, still wearing my too-big leather jacket, her red hair loose around her shoulders, she's the most beautiful thing I've ever seen.

She turns to me, a small smile playing at her lips. "Smooth."

"Not trying to be." I step closer, drawn to her like gravity. "I call it like I see it."

Her eyes hold mine, searching for something. Whatever she's looking for, she must find it, because she reaches up and hooks her arms around my neck, pulling me down to her level.

"Take me upstairs," she whispers against my lips. "I want to see your bedroom."

My heart hammers against my ribs as I lead her toward the stairs. Each step we climb feels heavy with anticipation. I've imagined this moment. Bringing her here, to my space, my bed, more times than I can count. But the reality of her hand in mine, her feet on my stairs, outshines every fantasy.

My bedroom takes up most of the top floor, with floor-to-ceiling windows facing the bay just like downstairs and a large ensuite bathroom. The king-sized bed sits centered on one wall. Simple dark sheets made this morning without knowing they'd see her tonight. The moon is bright enough that we still don't need lights, just silver-blue glow washing over everything.

Lila moves to the window, looking out at the water. "The view is incredible."

I come up behind her, sliding my arms around her waist. "I know," I murmur, but I'm not looking at the bay. I'm looking at her reflection in the glass, the way the moonlight catches in her hair, illuminates the curve of her cheek.

She turns in my arms, her back to the window now, face tilted up to mine. There's vulnerability in her eyes, but no fear. Just trust and want and something deeper I don't dare name yet.

"I've been thinking about this since that night at the club," she says, her voice barely above a whisper. "About your hands on me. Your mouth."

The memory of that night, her soft gasps, the taste of her lips. The way she came apart under my tongue sends heat rushing through me. "I haven't thought about anything else."

She rises on her toes and kisses me, soft at first, then deeper as her hands find my hair, tugging me closer. I moan against her mouth, hands sliding down to cup her ass, lifting her slightly. She's so fucking perfect in my arms, like she was made to be there.

I walk her backward toward the bed, never breaking the kiss. When her legs hit the mattress, I ease her down, following her body with mine, careful not to crush her with my weight. The feel of her beneath me, soft curves pressed against me. It's intoxicating.

"Too many clothes," she murmurs against my mouth, tugging at my shirt.

I sit back on my heels, straddling her thighs, and slowly unbutton my shirt. Her eyes follow my fingers, hungry and appreciative. When I shrug it off, her hands immediately go to my chest, tracing the muscles there, fingertips ghosting over my skin.

She sits up enough for me to pull her dress over her head, revealing a simple black bra underneath. My breath catches at the sight of her. The full curves of her breasts rising above black lace, the soft swell of her stomach, the way her skin glows in the moonlight.

"You're so fucking beautiful," I breathe, unable to keep the reverence from my voice.

A shadow crosses her face. "Eli always said I was too fat."

Anger flares hot in my chest at the mention of his name, at the knowledge that he made her feel anything less than perfect. "Eli was a blind, stupid asshole," I say firmly, placing my hands on her waist. "Every inch of you is exactly how it should be."

I lean down and kiss her collarbone, the soft skin above her breasts, the valley between them. Her breath hitches as I reach behind her to unhook her bra, sliding it down her arms and tossing it aside. Her breasts fall free, full and perfect, nipples hardening in the cool air of the room.

"God, look at you," I murmur, cupping one breast in my palm, brushing my thumb over the nipple. She arches into my touch, a soft moan escaping her lips.

I lower my head and take the hardened peak into my mouth, sucking gently, then more firmly as her hands find my hair again, holding me against her. The sounds she makes, little gasps and whimpers, drive me wild. I switch to her other breast, giving it the same attention while my hand continues to massage the first.

Her hips are moving restlessly beneath me, seeking friction. I slide one hand down her stomach to the waistband of her panties. She lifts her hips to help me remove them, leaving her in nothing.

I sit back again, drinking in the sight of her naked on my bed. "I've dreamed about this," I admit, running my hands up her thighs. "About having you here."

The sight of her completely naked makes my cock throb painfully against the confines of my jeans.

I slide down the bed, positioning myself between her legs, pushing her thighs gently apart and lifting her legs over my shoulders. She's already wet, glistening in the moonlight. I blow softly against her core, watching her shiver at the sensation.

"Please," she whispers, hips rising slightly.

"Please what?" I ask, needing to hear her say it. "Tell me what you want, baby."

"Your mouth. I need your mouth on me. Don't make me wait."

I lower my head and lick a slow, deliberate stripe from her entrance to her clit. She gasps, body tensing at the contact. I do it again, slower this time, savoring the taste of her on my tongue. She's sweet and perfectly Lila, and I could happily drown in her.

I focus on her clit, circling it with my tongue, then sucking gently. Her thighs tremble on either side of my head, her breathing coming in short, sharp gasps. I slide one finger inside her, then another, curling them forward to hit that spot that makes her cry out.

"Anthony," she moans, the sound of my name on her lips sending a surge of pride through me.

I work her with my fingers and mouth, finding a rhythm that has her writhing beneath me. Her hands fist in the sheets, then in my hair, pulling almost painfully.

I love it.

I want her to lose control, to take what she needs from me.

I can feel her getting close. Her inner walls tightening around my fingers, her clit swelling under the pressure. I suck it into my mouth and gently bite down, flicking it with my tongue.

"Oh God," her body arching off the bed as she comes, a cry tearing from her throat. I don't let up, working her through the orgasm, only easing off when her spasms subside.

I kiss my way back up her body, her inner thigh, her hipbone, her stomach, between her breasts, her neck, until I reach her mouth. She kisses me hungrily, tasting herself on my tongue, her hands already working at my belt.

"I want you inside me," she says against my lips. "Now."

I stand to shed my jeans and boxers, my cock springing free, hard and aching. Her eyes widen slightly at the sight, a small smile curving her lips.

"I knew you were big, but I didn't see everything at the club, with your pants still on," she says, reaching for me as I crawl back onto the bed.

I position myself between her thighs, the head of my cock brushing against her entrance. "You sure you're ready for this?"

Her answer is to wrap her legs around my waist, pulling me toward her. "Fuck me, Anthony. And *don't* be gentle."

Her words send a surge of heat through me. I push into her slowly at first, giving her time to adjust to my size. She's tight and hot and wet around me, and it takes everything I have not to lose control immediately.

Once I'm fully seated inside her, I pause, forehead pressed against hers, both of us breathing hard. "You feel so fucking good," I murmur.

She urges, digging her heels into my lower back. "Hard."

I pull back and thrust into her, harder than before. She gasps, nails digging into my shoulders.

I find a rhythm, each thrust driving deep inside her. Her breasts bounce with the force of my movements, the most beautiful sight I've ever seen. I can't take my eyes off them, off her face twisted in pleasure.

"Harder."

I push in deeper, pounding into her with enough force to make the headboard bang against the wall. "Like this?" I growl.

"Mmm," she hums.

Her hand comes up to guide mine to her throat. I hesitate for a split second, but the look in her eyes is clear—she wants this. I wrap my fingers around her neck and squeeze.

The effect is immediate. Her eyes roll back, her inner walls clenching around me. "That's it," I say, watching her face. "That's my good fucking girl."

She moans at the praise, her body responding beautifully. I maintain the pressure on her throat, still thrusting into her, watching as her cheeks flush and her eyes glaze with pleasure.

"You take my cock so well," I tell her, leaning down to kiss her parted lips. "Such a good girl for me."

I release her throat, watching as she gulps in air, her eyes focusing on mine again. Without breaking my rhythm, I lower my head to her breast, taking a nipple between my teeth, biting just hard enough to make her gasp. I suck the tender flesh, marking her, claiming her in a way Eli never could.

"Mine," I growl against her skin, leaving another mark on the swell of her other breast. "All mine."

She hums in agreement, the sound rough and raspy.

I pull out suddenly, ignoring her whimper of protest. "Turn over," I command, my voice rough with need. "Hands and knees."

She complies eagerly, positioning herself before me, ass raised invitingly. I run my hands over the smooth curves, squeezing gently. "Look at you," I murmur. "So perfect."

I line myself up and push back into her, the new angle allowing me to go even deeper. She cries out, pushing back against me, taking me fully.

"That's it," I say, setting a brutal pace, my hands gripping her hips hard enough to leave marks. "Take all of me."

My hand comes down on her ass with a sharp crack, the sound echoing in the room. She moans, pushing back harder.

I spank her again, watching the pale skin turn pink under my hand. "You like that, don't you? Like it when I mark you?"

"Yes," she gasps.

I continue fucking her hard, one hand slapping her beautiful ass, the other reaching around to find her clit. She's soaking wet, so sensitive that she immediately reacts to my touch.

Her moans are getting higher in pitch as she approaches another orgasm.

"Lila, come on my cock," I growl in her ear. "That's my good fucking girl."

Her body tenses, then shudders violently as she comes. Her inner walls clamping down on my dick like a vice. The sensation pushes me over the edge, and I follow her into oblivion, a guttural moan tearing from my throat as I empty myself inside her.

For a moment, we stay frozen like that, both panting, bodies still connected. Then, I carefully pull out and collapse beside her, drawing her into my arms. She nestles against my chest, her body warm and soft against mine.

We lie there in comfortable silence for a few moments, our breathing gradually slowing. I disentangle myself from her.

"I'll be right back," I promise, pressing a kiss to her lips before heading to the bathroom.

I return with a warm washcloth and gently clean between her legs, taking care not to be too rough with her oversensitive skin. She watches me with heavy-lidded eyes, a small smile playing at her lips.

"What?" I ask, catching her expression.

"Nothing," she says. "Just... I didn't expect this after what we just did."

I toss the washcloth into the hamper and climb back into bed, pulling her close again.

"I didn't scare you, did I?" she asks.

Confused, I pull her against me and hold her. "What do you mean, scare me?"

"I like rough sex. I enjoy choking, spanking, and even some bondage. I enjoy being submissive with someone I trust. We didn't talk first, so I had no way of telling you that."

"I was afraid I'd trigger you. I have no idea what trauma you went through before I started watching you. But this is nice to know, because I enjoy being dominant." I reply.

"I've never been with anyone I trusted enough for this type of sex." She trails off for a moment, thinking about how to word the next part of what she's saying. I wish I could read her mind. "I never trusted Eli not to hurt me.

He always did. Every time, he'd hurt me and he wouldn't stop."

This knowledge sends a rush of anger through my blood. There is a time and place to let out this feeling and it is not here and now, with Lila. I force it down, for now. Maybe I'll pay him a little visit in jail.

We lay together in silence for so long that I thought she had fallen asleep, but she shifts next to me like she's about to leave.

I pull the covers over us, tucking her in more securely next to me. "Stay the night?" I ask, trying to keep the hope out of my voice.

In answer, she snuggles closer, throwing her leg over mine, head nestled in the crook of my neck. "Wild horses couldn't drag me away."

I listen as her breathing deepens and slows, feel the moment she drifts into sleep. I stay awake a little longer, savoring the weight of her against me, the scent of her hair, the warmth of her skin. After months of watching from a distance, of wanting but not having, the reality of her in my arms, in my bed, feels like a miracle.

She's mine now, I've got her. Not the masked man or the stalker, but the real me. And somehow, impossibly, she wants me anyway.

I send a quick text to Mia so she doesn't worry about Lila. She answers with a wink face emoji that makes me chuckle. The movement making Lila shift against me.

It doesn't take long before I'm drifting off to sleep with her.

32
Lila

I WAKE UP TO the sunlight in my eyes and Anthony's arm heavy around my waist, pulling me in like I'm something precious. For a second, I don't know where I am, and I panic. Expecting the chill of my library, or the scratch of hospital sheets, or Eli's voice hissing in my ear. But then the smell of clean cotton and his skin hits me, and everything from last night floods back, electric and real.

I turn my head, and he's already awake, watching me with a ridiculous intensity. A way no one has ever looked at me before. He smiles, the kind that's all teeth and wickedness, and leans in to kiss my shoulder.

"Morning, gorgeous," he says, voice gravel from sleep.

"Morning," I answer, and for once, the word feels right. I stretch, every muscle humming with the ache of what we did last night. The sheets are twisted between my legs.

He traces a line from my collarbone to my chest, then lower, his hand big and heavy and possessive. "You have any idea how fucking beautiful you are first thing in the morning?" he says, voice low. "You should see yourself. All soft and sleepy. I want to keep you like this."

My face flushes, but I can't stop grinning like a moron. "You're such a liar," I mumble, but I don't mean it.

He kisses my jaw, then my throat, then bites my earlobe just hard enough to make me gasp. "I wouldn't lie about that, Lila." His hand slides down over my stomach, then up under the edge of the blanket. "You want a shower?"

"Yes," I say, and I do, but I don't want to leave this bed. "But you're coming with me. You're the reason I need one."

He laughs and throws off the covers, rolling out of bed naked, not even pretending to be shy. He stretches, arms over his head, and I stare at his back. Broad, scarred, and cut like something out of a movie. He catches me looking, turns, and grins. "Like what you see?"

"Not bad," I say, and make a show of rolling my eyes, even though I want to devour him.

He crosses the room and scoops me up bridal-style, like I weigh nothing. "Anthony!" I yelp, half-laughing, "Put me down, you psycho."

"Not a chance," he says, carrying me into the bathroom.

His shower is stupidly huge, with a bench built in. A glass wall on one side and tile on the other. Everything fogs up the second he turns on the water. He sets me down on my feet inside, then steps in after me, reaching up to adjust the rain shower head so it pounds down over both of us.

The first hit of hot water is almost too much after the cold air, but then it's perfect, washing away sweat and sleep and everything else.

Anthony leans into the spray, water streaming down his face and chest, and sighs like he's in heaven. I just watch him, memorizing every detail. The curve of his shoulders, the way the water beads on his eyelashes, the light scar running from his right pec down to his ribs. He's the kind of beautiful that makes you want to do something stupid. Like fall in love.

He notices me staring and comes over, trapping me against the warm tile. "What are you thinking about?" he asks, forehead pressed to mine.

I slide my hands up his chest, feeling his heartbeat under my palm. "That I could get used to this," I admit.

"Yeah?" He kisses my temple. "Me too."

We stand there for a minute, just letting the water run over us. Then he turns me around so my back's to him and starts soaping my shoulders, slow and careful. His hands are rough, but gentle, kneading out every knot of tension I have left. He works down my spine, then around to my stomach, not hurrying, just exploring.

He slides his arms around my waist and pulls me against him, his cock hardening between us. He bends down and kisses my neck, biting just enough to leave a mark. I shiver, pressing back into him.

"You know what I used to think about, when all I could do was watch you?" he says, voice low in my ear.

I shake my head, not trusting myself to speak.

He runs his hand up to my throat, holding it just tight enough to make my breath catch. "I used to jerk off thinking about you on your knees," he whispers. "Right here in my shower. Mouth open, taking me all the way down, gagging on it. I had to stop myself from coming over to your house and making it real."

The words hit me like a punch. I'm so wet already, I don't know how I can possibly want him more, but I do.

He lets go of my neck and turns me around to face him. "You don't have to," he says, thumb brushing my cheek. "I don't expect anything from you. Ever. But fuck, I want it."

I drop to my knees on the tile, the steam swirling around us. His cock is right in front of my face, thick and leaking and perfect. I wrap my hand around the base and stroke him once, twice, watching his eyes go half-lidded.

I look up at him. "Tell me what you want," I say, voice steady even though my heart's racing.

He threads his fingers through my hair, not pushing, just holding. "Open up, baby. Show me how pretty you look with my cock in your mouth."

I do. I run my tongue over the head, then take him in as far as I can. He groans, low and guttural, and tightens his grip on my hair.

"Fuck, Lila," he says, voice rough. "You're fucking perfect."

I hollow my cheeks, loving the way his whole body tenses. I use my hand for what I can't fit in my mouth, twisting and stroking in time with my lips. He looks down at me, eyes wild, and I feel powerful for the first time in forever.

"God, you're gonna make me come," he says, and I don't stop. "Uuhh-yes" he breathes out. Then sucks air in through his teeth. "That's it. Good girl," he says, breathing out again.

I love it, I want to make him lose control. He groans my name, and comes hard, hot on my tongue. I swallow every pulse of it, looking up at him while I do it.

He stares at me like he's never seen anything so beautiful. "You're fucking unreal," he says, helping me up. "Come here."

He pulls me into his arms and kisses me hard, like he can't stand to be apart for even a second.

Then he sits down on the bench and drags me onto his lap, facing away from him. His cock is still slightly hard, pressed between us. He leans back, hand on my hip, and nuzzles his face into my neck, biting down on the soft flesh.

He slides two fingers between my legs and starts circling my clit, slow and deliberate. I gasp, hips rocking forward, but he holds me in place, not letting me move.

"You like that?" he asks, voice dark.

"Yes," I say, barely able to breathe.

He adds a third finger, pressing inside, and I moan, clenching around him.

He wraps his other hand around my throat, squeezing just enough to make the room spin. "You're gonna come for me," he says. "Right here. Right now. Show me how good you can be."

I see stars, my whole body shaking. He loosens his grip on my throat, and the pulsing in my body draws out longer than I thought possible. Fingers working me until I can't take any more.

When I finally stop trembling, he pulls me close and kisses the top of my head. "Good girl," he says. and I can feel my face flush.

He has to help me stay upright as we rinse off together, soaping each other's hair and skin. He takes his time, fingers gentle as he works the conditioner through my tangled mess of red and blonde. When we're finally clean, he wraps me in a huge towel and carries me back to the bedroom.

We towel off and get dressed in a lazy, half-hearted way. He puts on pajama pants and nothing else. I steal a faded t-shirt from his closet and pull it on over my bare skin.

He leads me downstairs to the kitchen, where he starts to make scrambled eggs and coffee like it's the most normal thing in the world to have me here. The house is silent except for the sizzle of eggs hitting the pan and the gurgle of the coffee maker.

I sit at the island and watch him move around, feeling like I'm in someone else's life. A better one.

He brings me a plate piled high with eggs and toast, then sits across from me, his feet brushing mine under the table. He's so casual about it, like we've been doing this for years.

I dig into the food, starving. The coffee is strong and perfect, exactly how I like it. I take a long drink, then sigh.

"You know what's wild?" I say, looking up at him.

"What?"

"I don't remember the last time I took a hot shower and didn't run out of water halfway through. Or had breakfast made for me. Or woke up next to someone who actually wanted me there."

He gives me this look, soft, but a little sad. "Get used to it," he says. "Because I plan on keeping you around."

I laugh. "You're such a sap."

He grins. "Only for you."

We eat in silence for a short while, just enjoying the food and the sunshine coming in through the windows.

After breakfast, I pull out my phone and call Mia. She answers on the second ring.

"Hey, my beautiful bitch," she says. "You alive?"

"Barely," I say, smiling. "Can you pick me up for work?"

She snorts. "You're not coming in today, are you?"

"I need to. I'm saving for a car remember?"

Anthony gives me a look over the rim of his coffee mug. "I can give you a ride," he says.

I shake my head. "No way. It's like twenty degrees out, and I'm not ruining my hair with your helmet."

He smirks. "You just want to ride in Mia's car so she can talk shit about me."

"Obviously," I say. The banter is so easy to get used to now that I'm not walking on eggshells. I can be myself.

Mia laughs on the other end. "I'll be there in twenty. You want coffee?"

"I'm good," I say, glancing at the mug in my hand. "Just bring yourself. And maybe some leave-in conditioner."

She hangs up, and I set my phone down, feeling strangely... content. Happy, even.

Anthony comes around the counter and pulls me into his arms, holding me tight. "You sure you don't want to stay here today?"

"I'll see you tonight," I promise, kissing his chest.

He kisses the top of my head, then whispers, "I'm proud of you, you know."

"For what?"

"For being brave," he says. "For surviving. For letting yourself be happy."

I close my eyes, holding onto that feeling. The truth is, I'm not brave. I'm still terrified, still waiting for the other shoe to drop. But right now, with his arms around me and the taste of coffee on my tongue, I almost believe him.

Maybe, for once, I really do deserve this.

33
Anthony

THE WEATHER APP SAID today would break seventy for the first time all year. I get up before the sun, fill a cooler with way too much food, grab some blankets and cushions, then drive to the trailhead. The whole way there I'm buzzing. Not the caffeine kind. The kind that only kicks in when I know I'm about to do something that'll make her smile.

I park at the end of the lot where no one ever bothers with this trail, it's a bit too long and sandy for most people. The sand's still cold under my boots. The first time I ever saw was after Mia told me she had been here, so I came to check it out and it's been one of my favorite places to sit and read ever since. Then, I thought: Lila would love this place. Even then, before I'd ever touched her, I thought like that.

The wind's up, but it's not miserable. I drag everything to the gazebo, set up the blankets on the side that gets the sun, wedge the cushions so she can lounge without getting sand in her hair. The cooler's mostly charcuterie and little finger sandwiches I made at 5 a.m., plus two thermoses. One coffee, one the kind of hot chocolate she likes, which tastes like pure sugar to me but she's obsessed with it. I set out strawberries too, because I saw her pick them off the cheese platters at a few gatherings.

I finish and make my way back to the parking lot as her car pulls into the lot. Mia's car, actually. She's been borrowing it ever since she divorced Eli. I watch her step out, sunglasses already on even though it's early, hair up in a loose knot, a hoodie zipped all the way to her chin. She spots me, waves, then starts up the path, sneakers already sinking in the soft sand.

I meet her halfway. "Hey, gorgeous."

She takes off the sunglasses and gives me this look, a full-body scan up and down, like she's making sure it's really me. "You look like a handsome lumberjack," she says, but she grins as she says it.

"Better than looking like, I don't know, a masked stalker" I laugh and wink at her, her grin widens. "How's the drive?"

"Long. I hate driving in sand; it's like walking on the moon."

I laugh and take her hand, leading her down the trail. "You ever been to the moon?"

"I don't need to, I have you for that. You find the weirdest places."

"Yeah, but this one's special," I say, and I mean it. "Wait until you see the view."

She looks at me over her sunglasses. "You sound like a realtor. Next you'll tell me the HOA fees are low."

"Only fee is you have to eat everything I packed," I say, and she laughs, really laughs. It's the best sound I've ever heard. I'd kill to make her do it more.

She slows down and tugs on my hand. "Can we take a break? My calves are dying."

I let go and wait while she sits down on a chunk of driftwood. She pulls the hoodie sleeves down over her hands and just sits there for a minute, staring at the ocean.

"You want a piggyback?" I offer.

She snorts. "You want to carry my fat ass through a mile of loose sand?"

"First of all, don't call my girl that. Secondly Fuck yeah. You think I can't?"

She gives me this sly look, and for a second I know exactly what she's thinking: she wants me to prove it. So I do. I squat down, let her climb on, and stand up with her arms locked around my neck.

She squeals, but not loud enough for anyone to hear, because there's no one out here this early. "I was kidding! Jesus, Anthony, you're gonna throw your back out."

"Please. You weigh less than a rescue dummy," I say, and she smacks me on the chest. "Hold tight."

I walk the rest of the way to the gazebo, her clinging to me and giggling in my ear. The last stretch is the hardest, but I'm not letting her down until I reach the blanket. When I finally do, I kneel and let her slide off onto the cushions. She's breathless and a little pink in the face.

"God, you're a showoff," she says, but there's pride in her voice.

I sit next to her, open the cooler, and hand her the thermos. "Try it."

She takes a sip, eyes going wide. "You made it with oat milk. You remembered."

"I always remember."

She sips again, then looks out at the ocean. "It's beautiful," she says, and this time she means it. "You can't see any houses or people. Just water and sky."

"That's why I like it."

She tucks her legs up under her, careful to keep her shoes off the blanket. "Did you ever come out here when you were, you know, watching me?"

"Yeah," I say, no point lying. "A few times. When things got rough."

She turns to look at me, chin on her knees. "How the fuck did you even move through this sand without getting totally exhausted and without me hearing you?"

I grin. "I'm *very* athletic and very sneaky."

She rolls her eyes. "No, really. You're huge and you walk like a cat. It's unnatural."

"It wasn't easy. But it was worth it."

She stares at me for a second, then shakes her head. "You're insane."

I reach into the cooler and hand her one of the sandwiches. "Eat. You'll feel better"

She takes a bite, chews thoughtfully. "Did you make this?"

"Yeah."

"It's really good. Like, suspiciously good."

"I used to cook for my team," I say. "They'd kill each other if I didn't keep them fed."

She snickers. "Were you the mom of the group?"

"I guess you can say that. I was the boss. The boss always feeds the crew."

She holds up a strawberry. "And these? Is this some kind of metaphor?"

"Nope. You just always eat them first."

She pops it in her mouth, chews, then licks her fingers. "You're a weirdo, but I like it."

We eat for a while, not talking much. The wind picks up a little, but the sun is strong enough to keep us warm. She leans back on the cushions and closes her eyes, face tipped up to the sky.

I watch her for a long time, just breathing her in. The way she relaxes when she's with me, the way her lips part a little when she's thinking, the way she fidgets with the edge of the blanket when she's not sure what to say.

After a while, she cracks one eye open. "What are you staring at?"

"You."

She smiles. "You're sappy as hell, you know that?"

I shrug. "Only for you."

She sits up and pours herself more hot chocolate. "So. Tell me about your rescue missions. You never talk about that stuff."

I hesitate. I don't like talking about work, especially not the black ops shit. But she asked, and I'd rather she hear it from me than anyone else.

"It's mostly retrievals," I say, keeping it simple. "People get lost, or taken, or sometimes they just run from their consequences. We go in, get them out, bring them home. Sometimes it's kids, sometimes it's adults, sometimes it's..." I stop, not sure how much to say.

She waits, patient.

"Sometimes it's ugly," I finish. "But it's better than leaving them there."

"Did you ever get hurt?"

I laugh. "All the fucking time."

She eyes my chest, where the scar runs from my pec down to my ribs. "Is that one from a rescue?"

I nod. "Yeah. Guy didn't want to come back. He had a knife, and I let him get close. Stupid move, but it worked."

She traces the scar with her finger through my shirt, soft and slow. "I like it. Makes you look dangerous."

I raise an eyebrow. "You like dangerous?"

She grins. "Only when it's you."

I lean in, kiss her hard. She tastes like strawberries and chocolate and a little bit like sunshine. She kisses back, hungry and rough, biting my lip just enough to hurt.

I pull her into my lap, wrap my arms around her, and squeeze until she squeaks. "Can I tell you a secret?" I say, mouth against her ear.

She shivers. "Always."

"I used to come out here and jerk off thinking about you. On this exact fucking beach."

She laughs, loud and sharp. "You're disgusting. Where didn't you jerk off to me?"

"Yeah, I am," I agree. "But you love it."

She kisses me again, and this time it's slow, drawn out. Her hand slides under my shirt, fingers cold on my skin. I let her explore, let her take what she wants.

After a while, I pull back, eyes dark. "I want to fuck you," I say, voice low.

"Here?"

I nod. "I want to remember this day forever."

She doesn't argue. I lay her down on the blanket, kneel between her legs, and strip off her hoodie and shirt in one move. She shivers in the breeze, nipples already hard. I kiss

ANTHONY   291

down her neck, over her collarbones, down to her chest.
She arches up, hands in my hair, pulling me closer.

I make quick work of her jeans, dragging them down
her legs. She kicks them off, shoes and all, and laughs as
they land somewhere in the sand.

"You're going to lose those," I say, but she doesn't
care.

She tugs at my shirt, and I pull it off, tossing it behind
me. She stares at my chest, runs her hands over my abs,
then lower. She wants me bad, and I want her worse.

I slide her panties down, slow, watching the way her
thighs tremble. She's already wet, dripping for me. I lick
a stripe up her inner thigh, then blow cold air on her clit.
She jerks, grabbing my head.

"Don't tease," she says, voice rough.

"You love when I tease."

She moans, legs spreading wider. "I love when you
fuck me."

I lick her beautiful pussy and suck and flick her clit
until she comes apart. But I'm not done.

I flip her onto her stomach and pull her ass up, just
like she likes. I line up and push in, slow, letting her feel
every inch. She gasps, face buried in the blanket, hands
fisted in the fabric.

I pound into her, hard enough to shake the whole
fucking gazebo. She tries to muffle her screams, but I
know she wants to let them out.

I lean over her, hand on the back of her neck. "You're
so fucking good for me," I whisper.

She pushes back, meeting every thrust.

I give her what she wants. I fuck her so hard the blanket
slides on the wood. She's loud, but I cover her mouth with

my hand so no one can hear her. Her eyes go wild, and I know she loves it.

"Take it," I say, voice low in her ear. "Take all of me, baby."

She comes so hard her whole body shakes. I keep going, chasing my own release. When I come, I grab her hip, digging in hard enough to leave marks. She moans into my hand, then goes limp, spent.

I pull out slowly, then lay down next to her, both of us breathing hard. She rolls onto her back, face flushed and eyes glassy.

"I hope no one else is out here," she says, voice barely there.

I grin, brush the hair off her face. "You're fucking perfect."

She laughs, soft this time. "You're gonna kill me one of these days."

I pull her close, wrap her up in my arms, and stare out at the ocean. "Not today."

She's here, and that's all I ever wanted.

34
Lila

THE SALESMAN'S VOICE FADES into the background as I run my fingers along the smooth hood of the Subaru. Chameleon blue to purple, depending on how the light hits it. My car. Mine. Not Eli's, not a rental, not borrowed from Mia or Valerie, mine. Five months of saving every penny from my paychecks at the print shop has led to this moment. My heart beats a little faster as I picture myself behind the wheel, windows down, answering to no one.

"Ms. Angelo? Did you hear what I said about the all-wheel drive system?" The salesman, Brad, according to his name tag. Steps closer, clipboard in hand.

"Sorry," I say, offering a smile that feels only slightly forced. "I was just admiring the color."

"It's one of the rarest finishes. Changes like a mood ring, doesn't it?" He taps the hood. "Want to take her for a spin?"

I nod, suddenly unable to speak past the lump in my throat. This is happening. I'm buying a car. Such a normal thing for most people, but for me, it's monumental. Another step away from the woman who needed Eli's permission for everything.

Brad hands me the keys, and I close my fist around them, feeling the metal bite into my palm. Five months since the divorce was finalized. Five months of rebuilding my life piece by piece. Five months of Anthony.

Anthony. Even now, his name sends a flutter through my chest. After our first night together in January, I'd thought things would move quickly, that giddy rush of new love sweeping us along. But he surprised me, agreeing that we take things slow. "You've been through hell," he said, holding me close in the gray morning light. "I don't want to be just a reaction to that. I want to be a choice you make every day."

So I stayed at Mia's. We arranged to be roommates. I decorated my room with a new bedspread and curtains in shades of green that remind me of forests. Anthony and I have dinner together most nights, sometimes at his place, sometimes out. We go to movies and bookstores and dancing at the same club where we'd met in the VIP room. But most nights, I go back to Mia's. Enjoying getting to know myself again.

It's not that I don't want to be with him all the time. God, I do, and the sex is incredible. Tender when I need it, rough whenever I want it, always exactly what I ask for and never too far. But there's something healing in having my own space, in knowing I can walk away if I need to. Anthony understands that better than I do sometimes.

"Should I start explaining the features, or do you want to just get a feel for it?" Brad asks, pulling me back to the present.

"Let's drive," I say, more confident than I feel.

The interior of the Subaru smells like new car. That mixture of leather and plastic that somehow signals "beginning." I adjust the seat closer to the pedals than Brad had it and take a deep breath. My hands find the wheel, and I'm struck by how right it feels.

"Take a left out of the lot," Brad instructs, buckling his seatbelt. "We'll do a loop around town, hit some open road if you'd like."

I nod, starting the engine. It purrs to life, smoother than the SUV I used before. That car was always his, even though only I drove it. He made sure I knew it, too. I had the plain car and he had the BMW.

This Subaru wagon is nothing like that SUV. It's practical but stylish, with enough room for me to start getting all my books when I finally go back to the house to get them. Anthony offered to help me with that weeks ago, but I wasn't ready. The thought of stepping back into that house, even with Eli locked away awaiting trial, made my skin crawl. But now, with my car, my freedom. It feels possible.

I navigate through the dealership lot and onto the main road, feeling the car respond to my touch. It's responsive but stable, grounded. The exact opposite of how I felt for most of my marriage.

"Handles nice, right?" Brad says from the passenger seat. "This model's really popular with people who want something reliable but still fun to drive."

Fun. When was the last time I did something just for fun, just because I wanted to? Before Eli, probably. But

these last months with Anthony have been reintroduc-
ing me to the concept. Like when he took me for a picnic
on a private ocean-side trail a couple of weeks ago. I
complained most of the hike down, but then he carried
me the rest of the way. I wondered how he did it so easily
all those nights he was hiding in the dunes. The view
was amazing and the picnic he'd packed; he had made
all the food himself. So it was worth it.

I make a right turn, following Brad's directions, and
catch sight of Anthony's motorcycle in my rearview mirror. He promised he'd meet me here, said he wouldn't
miss this for the world. I'd told him I could handle it
alone, that I didn't need him to hold my hand through
buying a car. He'd just smiled and said, "I know you can
handle it. I just want to see your face when you drive it
off the lot."

Now he's pulling into the dealership parking lot,
right on time. Something warm unfurls in my chest at
the sight of him. Five months, and I still get butterflies.

"Mind if we head back?" I ask Brad. "I think I've seen
enough to know this is the one." Never mentioning that
I had seen this car online and had already come to this
decision.

His face lights up at the prospect of a sale. "Absolutely. If you're ready to talk numbers, we can get the
paperwork started."

I drive back to the dealership, parking in the spot
marked "Customer Test Drive." Anthony is waiting by
his bike, helmet tucked under his arm, hair slightly
mussed. He's wearing dark jeans and a thin leather riding jacket, looking like every bad decision I should have
made in my twenties instead of getting married.

"Hey," he says as I climb out of the car. "How's she drive?"

"Perfect," I answer, unable to keep the smile off my face. "It feels right."

"You look happy."

"I am." And I realize with a start that it's true. Not just in this moment, but in general. Somewhere along the way, happiness has become my default state again, not something I have to chase or pretend at.

Inside the dealership, the paperwork goes quickly. I've saved more than enough to buy the car outright. No loan, no monthly payments tying me to debt. Just mine, free and clear. When Brad hands me the final form to sign, I hesitate for just a second.

"Second thoughts?" Anthony asks quietly from the chair beside me.

I shake my head. "No. Just... taking it in. This is big."

"It is," he agrees. "But you've got this."

I sign my name, Lila Angelo, not Fischer, never Fischer again, and it feels like signing a declaration of independence.

An hour later, I'm driving my new Subaru out of the lot, Anthony following behind on his motorcycle. The sun hits the hood, and the paint shifts from blue to purple like it's alive. I roll down the window, letting the spring air rush in, filling my lungs with the scent of possibility.

For the first time in a long, long time, the road ahead feels like an adventure rather than an escape route. And that, more than anything, tells me I'm finally heading in the right direction.

The printer hums steadily as I adjust the settings for Mrs. Chen's latest batch of business cards. The familiar sounds of the print shop wrap around me like a blanket. Paper cutter slicing through stacks with a satisfying chunk, Valerie's fingers tapping at the register keys, Mia's voice greeting customers with practiced warmth. This place saved me long before I knew I needed saving. Before Anthony, before the masked man, before I found the courage to leave Eli. It was here, among the paper and ink and steady rhythm of ordinary days, that I first remembered who I was.

"Earth to Lila," Valerie says, snapping her fingers near my face. "You've been staring at that same print job for five minutes."

I blink, pulling myself back to the present. "Sorry. Just thinking."

"About your stalker boyfriend bringing you flowers again?" There's a teasing edge to Valerie's voice, but I catch the undercurrent of something else. Five months, and she still hasn't fully made peace with how Anthony and I started.

"He's not my stalker," I correct automatically. "He's my... Anthony."

Valerie raises an eyebrow. "Your Anthony who watched you through windows? Who left books on your nightstand while you slept? Who tracked your phone until, oh wait, your abusive husband was already doing that?"

"Val," Mia warns from across the shop, where she's arranging a display of greeting cards. "We've been through this. If I thought Tony could have hurt Lila, I would have told you."

"I know, I know." Valerie holds up her hands in surrender. "And I'm happy for you, Lila, really. It's just weird that the creepy masked guy turned out to be my best friend's slash business partner's brother, and she knew for weeks and didn't say anything."

There it is, the real issue. Not Anthony's behavior, but Mia's secrecy. When the truth came out about Anthony being my masked man. Valerie wasn't just shocked, she was hurt that Mia had kept it from her. Their friendship has recovered, but sometimes the wound still shows.

"She was protecting him," I say, not for the first time. "And me, in her own way."

"I know." Valerie sighs. "And look at you now, all loved up and driving a fancy new car. I guess it worked out. Now you can be part owner if you want to buy in. You'd be making enough for your own place."

I smile, choosing to focus on her acceptance rather than the lingering doubts. "I'll think about it," I say, smiling at Valerie. "Speaking of the car, want to take a ride during lunch? It's got this amazing sound system."

"Hell yes," she agrees, instantly brightening. "Can we blast Slipknot with the windows down like we're teenagers again?"

"Is there any other way to drive a new car?"

We fall back into our comfortable rhythm, Valerie helping a customer choose the right paperweight for their resume, me finally finishing Mrs. Chen's business cards, Mia calling suppliers about a late delivery. The morning passes in a pleasant blur of routine tasks and friendly banter.

Just before lunch, the bell above the door jingles. I look up from the binding machine to see Anthony walking in, a bouquet of bright yellow wildflowers in hand. He's wearing a dark blue button-down that brings out his eyes, sleeves rolled up to expose his forearms. Five months together, and the sight of him still makes my heart skip.

"Ladies," he greets, handing a single flower to both Mia and Valerie before his gaze finds mine. His smile deepens, reaching his eyes in that way that makes me feel like I'm the only person in the room.

"Delivery for Ms. Angelo," he says, crossing to my workstation and presenting the flower and a bag of my favorite chewy candy with a slight bow.

"What's the occasion?" I ask, taking the bouquet. The wildflowers are vibrant and cheerful, their bright faces turned up like they're seeking light.

"Do I need an occasion to bring flowers to the most beautiful woman in the world?" He leans in, pressing a quick kiss to my cheek.

Valerie makes a gagging noise from behind the counter. "God, you two are nauseating."

"You love it," Mia calls to her, coming around to give her brother a hug.

"I do." Valerie concedes.

I catch Anthony's eye over the flowers, sharing a private smile. This easy banter, the way he fits into my world. It still feels miraculous sometimes. After years of Eli isolating me from everyone, having someone who genuinely likes my dearest friends and wants to be part of my life is both foreign and wonderful.

"Still on for after work?" Anthony asks me, his voice dropping slightly. "I can meet you at the house, or we can go together from here."

The house. My stomach tightens at the thought. I haven't been back since that day Eli threw me down the stairs. The day I escaped through the library window. The police had gathered evidence for weeks afterward, and then the lawyers had to sort out the property issues. Even though it's legally mine now as part of the divorce settlement, I've been avoiding it because I never wanted any of it. But my books are still there, in the library that was my only sanctuary in that house of horrors.

"Together," I say firmly. "I don't think I can go there alone."

He nods, understanding in his eyes. "I'll be here at five then."

"Lila," Mia says, her expression serious. "You don't have to do this today. The house isn't going anywhere."

"Neither are my books," I reply. "But it's time. I'm ready."

Anthony's hand finds mine, fingers intertwining. "I'll be right beside you. And we'll only stay as long as you want."

"I know." I squeeze his hand, drawing strength from his steady presence. "It's just books. In and out."

But it's not just books. It's facing the scene of my near-death, the place where Eli tried to destroy me. It's reclaiming the only part of that house that ever truly belonged to me.

"I'll bring boxes," Valerie offers suddenly. "For the books. And I can come too, if you want backup."

The offer touches me deeply. Despite her reservations about Anthony, Valerie has never wavered in her support of me.

"Thanks, but I think this is something Anthony and I need to do together." I glance at him for confirmation, and he nods slightly. "But the boxes would be great."

"Consider it done." She disappears into the back room, presumably to find suitable boxes for a library's worth of books.

Mia looks between Anthony and me, concern evident in her eyes. "Just... be careful, okay? That place holds a lot of bad memories. You have PTSD, you may have flashbacks."

"I do have some good memories there of my favorite books. But, maybe I can make some good ones on the way out," I remind her, thinking of my library, of the books that kept me sane through years of Eli's control. Too bad the new memories can't be of me burning it to the ground. "The books helped me survive. They gave me somewhere else to go when I couldn't physically leave."

Anthony's thumb traces circles on the back of my hand. "And now they're coming home with you. Where they belong."

We take the car for a spin and grab a pick up sushi order from Akira sushi. The rest of the day passes in a fog of anticipation and dread. I go through the motions—printing, binding, helping customers, but my mind keeps drifting to the house. Will it look the same? Will I see blood on the stairs, still? Will I feel Eli's presence lingering in the rooms like a ghost?

By closing time, my nerves are wound so tight I jump when Mia touches my shoulder.

"Hey," she says gently. "Anthony's waiting outside."

I look up from the order I've been fumbling with for the past half hour. "Already?"

"Time flies when you're having an anxiety attack," she jokes, but her eyes are soft with concern. "You really don't have to do this today."

"I do, though." I stand, gathering my purse and jacket. "If I don't do it now, I'll just keep finding reasons to put it off."

Valerie appears with a stack of flattened boxes under her arm. "These should hold a decent number of books. Need help assembling them?"

"We've got it," I assure her, taking the boxes. "Thanks, Val. For everything."

She pulls me into a tight hug. "You call me if you need anything, okay? I don't care what time it is."

"I will," I promise, throat suddenly tight with emotion.

Outside, Anthony waits beside my new Subaru, keys in hand. "Figured you might want me to drive," he says, holding them out.

I shake my head, taking a deep breath. "No. I need to drive myself there. Take control of how this goes."

He nods, understanding without needing explanation. "I'll follow on the bike, then."

As I slide into the driver's seat, placing the folded boxes on the passenger side, I catch a glimpse of myself in the rearview mirror. My eyes are steady, my jaw set with determination. This isn't the same woman who fled through a window five months ago. That woman was broken, terrified.

This woman is driving herself back to face her demons, with the man she loves following behind. Not to rescue her, but to stand beside her while she rescues herself.

I start the engine, watching as Anthony mounts his motorcycle. The Subaru shifts colors in the late afternoon sun, blue to purple, and back again. Like me, changed by circumstance, but still fundamentally myself underneath.

It's time to go get my books.

35

Anthony

I FOLLOW LILA'S SUBARU as it shifts from blue to purple in the late afternoon sun, keeping my bike close behind her. Every few seconds, I check to make sure she's okay through the rear window, watching for any sign that this trip to her old house is too much for her. The road winds along the bay, familiar territory from all those nights I spent watching her, but everything is different now. No more masks, no more secrets between us. Just Lila driving toward her past, and me following, ready to help her face whatever ghosts still linger in that house.

When we reach the long private drive leading to her old home, she slows almost to a stop. For a moment, I think she might turn around. Her brake lights glow red in the fading daylight, and I can see her silhouette as she sits there, hands gripping the wheel. Then, with what looks like a deep breath, she continues forward, the electronic gate grinding loudly against the pavement as it opens. I follow her through, the space between tall dune grass opening up to reveal the house where she nearly died.

It looks different in daylight. Less ominous, more ordinary. Just a modern two-story with large windows and a deck that leads down to a patio on stilts. Hard to believe this was the setting for so much pain. But houses don't cause suffering, people do. And Eli is locked away, awaiting trial for what he did to Lila and potentially others. The evidence against him keeps mounting, especially after they linked him to Amanda Finley's disappearance. Dillian thinks it's just a matter of time before they find her body.

Lila parks in the circular driveway, and I pull up beside her, cutting the engine on my bike. Through her window, I can see her white-knuckled grip on the steering wheel, her eyes fixed on the front door. I give her a moment, not rushing her. This has to happen at her pace.

When she finally opens her door and steps out, her face is set in determination, though I catch the slight tremble in her hands as she smooths down her skirt.

"You okay?" I ask, dismounting from my bike.

She nods, not quite meeting my eyes. "Let's just get this over with."

I grab the stack of flattened boxes from her passenger seat, tucking them under my arm. "Lead the way."

Her key slides into the lock with a soft click. The sound seems to echo in the stillness around us, like the house itself is holding its breath. When the door swings open, Lila hesitates at the threshold, and I wonder what she's seeing. The foyer where she once lived, or the battlefield where she fought for her freedom?

"I'm right here," I tell her, not touching her, just reminding her of my presence.

She steps inside, and I follow, closing the door behind us. The house is unnaturally quiet, that particular silence of a place long unoccupied. Dust covers the surfaces, and the air smells stale, like memories left too long unexamined. Lila stands in the entryway, her gaze fixed on the staircase leading to the second floor. The staircase where Eli tried to kill her.

"I don't have to go up there," she says, her voice small.

"You don't have to go anywhere you don't want to," I agree, setting the boxes down on a side table. "We're here for your books, nothing else."

She takes a deep breath, her eyes still on the stairs. "I remember every second of it, you know. The fall. How each step felt hitting my body on the way down. The look on his face when he stood over me."

I stand beside her, close enough that she can feel my presence but not crowding her. "He can't hurt you anymore, Lila."

"I know." She turns to me finally, a small, sad smile playing at her lips. "It's not him I'm afraid of. It's... this." She gestures around us. "This house. These memories. I was so small here, Anthony. So scared all the time."

The urge to pull her into my arms is nearly overwhelming, but I hold back. This moment isn't about me comforting her; it's about her confronting her past on her own terms.

"You're not small anymore," I remind her. "And you're not scared. You drove yourself here to take back what's yours. That's fucking brave."

Her smile grows a little stronger, a little more genuine. "I guess it is, isn't it?"

"Damn right it is."

She squares her shoulders, seemingly coming to a decision. "Okay. Let's get this done."

I follow her down a hallway lined with generic artwork that screams "Eli's taste" all stark lines and cold colors. When she stops at the closed door connected to the livingroom, her hand hovers over the knob for a moment before she pushes it. The door nearly falls off the hinges as it swings open.

The library is nothing like the rest of the house. Where the other rooms we passed were sterile and impersonal, this space feels lived in, loved. Floor-to-ceiling bookshelves line the walls, filled with volumes of every size and color. A large window looks out over the bay, the water glimmering in the distance beyond the dune grass. And in the center of the room sits a massive lavender chair, the size of a twin bed, draped with throw blankets.

"This was where I slept," Lila says, her voice stronger now. "After things got really bad. I'd barricade the door with that chair and sleep in it, surrounded by my books."

I stay in the doorway, giving her space to reacquaint herself with this sanctuary and go through her memories one at a time. She moves through the room, trailing her fingers along book spines, adjusting a lamp, picking a blanket up from the floor. Reclaiming her territory.

"I never lived here," she says suddenly, turning to face me. "Not really. I existed here. I survived here. But I didn't start living until I left."

"And now you never have to come back," I tell her, bringing in the flattened boxes. "Once we get your books, you can close this chapter for good."

She nods, helping me unfold and assemble the first of the boxes. As we work side by side, I notice the tension gradually leaving her shoulders, her movements becoming more fluid, less guarded. This room, at least, doesn't hold the same terrors as the rest of the house.

When the boxes are ready, she stands in the center of the room, hands on her hips, surveying her collection. "I don't even know where to start."

"Anywhere you want," I say. "We've got all evening."

Her eyes drift to the lavender chair, and something shifts in her expression. "This chair," she says, her voice taking on a quality I haven't heard before, "was the only place in this house where I felt safe."

I watch as she runs her hand along the plush fabric, her touch almost reverent. "It held me when no one else did."

"It kept you safe," I say, understanding the significance of this piece of furniture in a way I hadn't before. It wasn't just a chair, but was her refuge. Her protector when I couldn't be.

She turns to me, her eyes darker now, intent. "I want to make a new memory here. Before we take the books and leave this place behind for good."

My pulse quickens at her tone. "What kind of memory?"

She sits on the edge of the chair, spreading her legs slightly, her skirt riding up her thighs. "I want you to fuck me here. Hard and rough. Make me forget every bad thing that ever happened in this house."

Jesus Christ. My cock stiffens immediately at her words, at the sight of her on that chair, looking at me with hunger in her eyes. "Are you sure? Here?"

"I've never been more sure of anything." She leans back, her hands gripping the arms of the chair. "I want you to take me right here, where I used to hide from him. I want to replace those memories with you. With us."

I cross to her in three strides, my hands framing her face as I kiss her hard, swallowing her gasp of surprise. Her lips part for me instantly, her tongue sliding against mine as her hands fist in my shirt, pulling me closer.

"Tell me what you want," I growl against her mouth. "Exactly what you want."

"I want you to be rough," she whispers, her breath hot against my lips. "Choke me. Bite me. Spank me. Make me yours, Anthony. Erase him completely."

Something primal roars to life inside me at her words. I've always been careful with Lila, mindful of her past, but she's asking for something different now. She's asking me to help her reclaim not just her books, but her sexuality, her power.

"Stand up," I order, my voice rough with desire.

She complies instantly, her eyes wide and dark as she looks up at me. I spin her around, pressing her back against my torso, one arm wrapped around her waist while my other hand finds her throat. Pulling her close, I apply just enough pressure to make her breath catch, my lips at her ear.

"I'm going to fuck you so hard you'll forget your own name," I promise, feeling her shiver against me. "But you'll remember mine, because I'm going to make you scream it."

"Yes," she gasps, arching into me. "Mmm," she hums.

I release her throat to spin her around again, my hands finding the hem of her skirt and yanking it up around her waist. Her panties are simple black cotton, practical for a workday, but the sight of them still makes my mouth water.

I hook my fingers in the waistband and drag them down her legs, dropping to my knees to help her step out of them.

While I'm down there, I can't resist pressing a kiss to her inner thigh, feeling the muscle jump under my lips. She's already wet. I can see her arousal, and it drives me fucking crazy knowing how much she wants this, wants me.

"Anthony," she moans, her fingers threading through my hair. "Don't tease me. Not today."

I stand, unbuckling my belt with quick, efficient movements. "On the chair. Face down, ass up."

Her eyes widen at the command, but she moves quickly, positioning herself on the lavender chair exactly as I instructed. The sight of her like that. Bent over, skirt bunched around her waist, perfect ass exposed. It nearly makes me lose my mind.

I free my cock from my jeans, already hard as steel and leaking at the tip. In two steps I'm behind her, one hand gripping her hip while the other slides between her legs, finding her soaked and ready.

"Fuck, Lila," I groan, sliding two fingers into her pussy. "You're dripping for me."

She pushes back against my hand, desperate for more. "Anthony. I need you inside me."

I withdraw my fingers, replacing them with the head of my cock, teasing her entrance. "Look at you, begging for my cock on the same chair where you used to hide from him. You're not hiding anymore, are you?"

"No," she gasps as I push just the tip inside her.

"Good girl," I praise, then thrust into her hard, burying myself to the hilt in one powerful stroke.

She cries out, her body clenching around me, adjusting to the sudden fullness. I give her only a moment before I start moving, setting a punishing pace that has the chair shifting beneath us. My fingers dig into her hips hard enough to leave marks, claiming her in the most primitive way.

"Is this what you wanted?" I ask, punctuating each word with a thrust. "To be fucked hard in your safe space?"

"Yes," she moans, pushing back to meet each thrust.

I reach forward, gathering her hair in my fist and pulling just hard enough to arch her back. My other hand slides around to her throat. I squeeze hard enough that I can feel her pulse beneath my fingers.

"You're mine now," I tell her, my voice rough with exertion and emotion. "Say it."

"I'm yours," she gasps, the words slightly choked by my hand on her throat. "Anthony."

I release her hair to reach beneath her, finding her clit with practiced ease. She jerks at the contact, a high, keening sound escaping her lips. I circle the sensitive bud with my fingers, matching the rhythm of my thrusts, feeling her body tighten around me.

"That's it," I encourage, releasing her throat to lean down and bite the junction of her neck and shoulder, hard enough to leave a mark but not break skin. "Come for me, Lila. Let me feel that beautiful pussy strangle my cock."

The bite does it. She comes with a scream, her body clamping down on my cock like a vise, pulsing around me in waves that nearly trigger my own release. But I'm not done with her yet.

I slow my thrusts, giving her a moment to come down from her peak, then withdraw completely. She whimpers at the loss, looking back at me over her shoulder, her face flushed and eyes glazed with pleasure.

"Turn over," I command, already helping her shift onto her back. "I want to see your face when you come again."

She complies, spreading her legs for me as I position myself between them. This time when I enter her, it's slower, more deliberate, watching her face as I fill her inch by inch. Her mouth falls open in a silent moan, her eyes locked on mine, and the connection between us in that moment is so intense it nearly breaks me.

"You're so beautiful," I tell her, bracing my weight on my forearms, caging her beneath me. "So fucking perfect."

I start moving again, finding a rhythm that's less frantic but no less intense. My mouth finds hers in a deep, passionate kiss that swallows her moans. When we break for air, I trail my lips down her neck, stopping to suck a mark just below her ear.

"Anthony," she breathes, her nails digging into my back through my shirt.

I slip a hand between us, finding her clit, still swollen and sensitive from her first orgasm. "Come on, baby," I urge, circling the bundle of nerves with my thumb. "Be a good girl and come on my cock."

Her body responds instantly to my words, her back arching off the chair as another orgasm rips through her. This time, I let myself follow her over the edge, my hips jerking erratically as I spill inside her, filling her with pulse after pulse of my release.

"Fuck, Lila," I groan, collapsing on top of her, careful to keep most of my weight on my arms.

We lie there for a moment, our breathing gradually slowing, bodies still connected. I press soft kisses to her

face, her neck, anywhere I can reach. A gentler counter-
point to the roughness of our lovemaking.

When I finally pull out, I watch my come start to
leak from her, a primal part of me deeply satisfied by the
sight. She's marked inside and out as mine now.

"Stay here," I tell her, pressing one more kiss to her
lips. "I'll get something to clean you up."

She nods, looking too blissed out to move anyway. I
tuck myself back into my jeans and head to the bathroom
attached to the library, wetting a washcloth with warm
water and grabbing a dry towel. When I return, she's in
the same position, a contented smile playing at her lips.

"Feel better?" I ask, gently cleaning between her
legs.

"Much." She sighs as I tend to her, the intimacy of
this moment just as powerful as the sex we just had. "I
think I've successfully made a new memory here."

I laugh, helping her sit up and straighten her clothes.
"Happy to be of service."

Once she's put back together, we turn our attention to
the books. She moves around the room with new energy, pulling volumes from the shelves and placing them
carefully in the boxes. I follow her lead, helping where
I can, struck by how much more at ease she seems now,
how the tension that gripped her when we first arrived
has melted away.

"This one was my favorite," she says, handing me a worn paperback with a dark cover. "I read it the night you first watched me through the window. I could feel you out there, you know."

"I hoped you couldn't," I admit, taking the book from her. "I thought I was being stealthy."

She laughs, the sound echoing in the room. "Not even close. But I wasn't scared, strangely enough. It felt... different from when Eli watched me. Less threatening, somehow."

We work in comfortable silence for a while, filling box after box with her collection. Romance novels, thrillers, classics, poetry, her taste is eclectic and fascinating. Another glimpse into the complex woman I've fallen in love with.

By the time we've worked our way through half of one wall, the boxes are full, stacked by the door ready to be loaded into her car.

"We're going to need more boxes," I observe, looking at the still-packed shelves.

Lila nods, surveying what's left. "I didn't realize I had quite so many."

"Want me to run back to the print shop and grab more boxes? You can stay here and sort through what you want to take next. You don't have to stay here alone if you don't want to."

She considers this for a moment, then nods. "That would be great. The keys are in my purse on the chair. Could you drop these books at Mia's while you're out so we have room in the car?"

I kiss her quickly, grabbing her keys. "Yup, I'll be back in twenty minutes. Keep sorting and think about what new memories you want to make when I get back."

"I like the sound of that," she says.

I fill the back of her car with the boxes of books we'd packed and head for the door one last time before heading out. My heart is so full of pride for her. This is a huge step in her healing and I'm so glad I could be a part of it.

36

Lila

I RUN MY FINGERS along the spines of my books, feeling the familiar textures under my fingertips. Some are worn smooth from countless readings, others still crisp and new. Each one holds a piece of me, a memory, an escape route from the hell my life had become. The house is quiet around me, just the soft sound of my breathing and the occasional creak of the old shelves as I remove another volume. Every few minutes, my eyes drift to the lavender chair, and heat rises to my cheeks as I remember Anthony's body against mine, the way he made me feel safe even in this place that had been a prison for so long.

My body still tingles from his touch, that delicious soreness between my thighs a reminder of what we shared here. I pull down another book, a worn paperback with a cracked spine and smile at the memory of reading it during one of Eli's business trips, curled up in this very chair while rain lashed against the windows. That night had been mine alone, a rare moment of peace during years of walking on eggshells.

Now every night can be mine. With Anthony or without him, my time belongs to me again.

I place the book carefully in a half-filled box, marveling at how many I've collected over the years. Romances with their passionate embraces on the covers. Thrillers that kept me up all night. Poetry that gave words to feelings I couldn't express. They've been my friends, my counselors, my escape hatches from reality. And now they're coming with me to my new life.

"Where am I going to put all of you?" I murmur to the remaining shelves, still heavy with books. My room doesn't have space for this many volumes. I've been saving for my own place, but I'm still months away from a down payment.

Maybe Anthony would let me store some at his place. The thought brings another flush to my cheeks. We haven't talked about moving in together, five months is too soon. Especially after what I've been through, but I'm at his townhouse more nights than not lately. My toothbrush has a permanent spot in his bathroom. My favorite tea sits in his kitchen cabinet. Plus, the things he's bought for me to make me comfortable at his house. Little pieces of me migrating into his space. Just as he's carved out space in my heart.

I pull down another book, this one a battered copy of Jane Eyre. The irony isn't lost on me, a woman escaping one controlling man only to fall for another mysterious figure. Except Anthony never locked me away, never lied about who he was at his core. His methods were unorthodox, sure, but his heart was true.

The sound of my own laughter startles me. When did I become such a romantic? Probably around the time I let my stalker fuck me on this chair and loved every second of it.

I glance out the window, half-expecting to see Anthony in my Subaru pulling back into the driveway, but the space remains empty. The sun is lower now, casting long shadows across the dunes beyond the house. We should wrap this up before dark; I don't want to be here any longer than necessary.

Setting Jane Eyre in the box, I move to another shelf, this one holding the fantasy novels that were my most frequent escape. Dragons and magic and worlds where good triumphs over evil. If only real life worked that way. But then again, I did escape my monster. Eli is locked away, and I'm free. Maybe happy endings aren't just for books after all.

The house creaks around me, settling as the temperature drops with the setting sun. It's an old sound, familiar but no longer comforting. This place doesn't feel like mine anymore, if it ever truly did. It's just a shell now, holding the last pieces of my old life until I can carry them away.

A soft thud from the foyer breaks the silence.

"Anthony?" I call, setting down the book in my hands. "That was fast."

No answer comes. Maybe he's struggling with the boxes. I set the book I'm holding into the nearest box and head for the door, eager to help him.

"I've got at least another wall to organize," I say as I step into the hallway. "We're definitely going to need—"

I freeze mid-sentence, my blood turning to ice in my veins. It's not Anthony standing in the foyer.

It's Eli.

"You didn't think you were getting away that easy, did you?" His voice is the same. That cold, controlled tone that always preceded the worst violence. But he looks different. Harder, his usually immaculate appearance now ragged around the edges. Prison hasn't been kind to him.

My mind can't process what I'm seeing. Eli is supposed to be in jail awaiting trial. Eli is supposed to be gone from my life. Eli cannot possibly be standing here, looking at me with those ice-blue eyes that have haunted my nightmares.

"How..." The word comes out as a whisper, my throat suddenly desert-dry with fear.

"You know what they say," he replies, taking a step toward me. "Money talks. And I've always had friends in the right places."

Run. The command flashes through my brain like a neon sign. I spin on my heel, bolting back toward the library. If I can get inside, barricade the door like I used to.

His footsteps pound behind me, gaining quickly. I'm halfway to the library when his hand catches in my hair, yanking me backward with enough force to make me cry out. Pain lances through my scalp as he drags me against him, his other arm snaking around my waist.

"I don't think so," he hisses in my ear, his breath hot against my skin. "You've caused me enough trouble."

I struggle against his hold, kicking backward, trying to connect with his shins, his knees, anything. "Let me go! Anthony will be back any minute—"

"Your stalker boyfriend?" Eli laughs, the sound sharp and humorless. "I'm counting on it. But we'll be long gone by then."

Fear floods my system, turning my muscles to water. Long gone? Where is he planning to take me? I try to twist in his grip, to face him, maybe reason with him.

Something hard connects with the side of my head. Stars explode across my vision, the pain immediate and blinding. My knees buckle, but Eli's arm around my waist keeps me upright.

"I told you what would happen if you ever tried to leave me," he says, his voice sounding far away now as darkness edges into my vision. "You're mine, Lila. You'll always be mine."

The last thing I see before the darkness claims me is the hallway tilting sideways, my body suddenly weightless as Eli lifts me into his arms.

Then nothing.

Pain. That's the first sensation that filters through. A throbbing ache at the side of my head that pulses in time with my heartbeat. I try to reach for it, to touch the source of the pain, but my hands won't move. They're stuck behind my back, something biting into my wrists when I try to separate them.

Zip ties. The realization seeps through the fog in my brain. My hands are bound with zip ties.

I try to call out, to ask what's happening, but my voice catches on something in my mouth. Fabric, wadded tight against my tongue, secured with what feels like tape across my lips. A gag.

My eyes snap open, panic surging through me, but there's nothing to see. Just darkness, complete and disorienting. I'm lying on my side on a hard surface that vibrates beneath me. The air is stale, hot, and there's barely enough room to move. Every few seconds, the whole space jolts, my body bouncing painfully against the unforgiving surface.

A trunk. I'm in a car trunk.

The realization hits me like another blow to the head. Eli has me. He's taken me from the house. We're driving somewhere.

I try to control my breathing, to fight down the panic threatening to choke me around the gag. Think, Lila. Think. My feet are bound too; I can feel the same plastic cutting into my ankles when I try to move them. The space is too small to maneuver, barely big enough for me to lie curled on my side.

How long have I been out? Minutes? Hours? The side of my head throbs, and I can feel something sticky in my hair. Blood, probably. The car hits a bump, and I'm thrown against the side of the trunk, a muffled cry escaping around the gag as pain lances through my already injured head.

Anthony. The thought of him returning to the house, finding the boxes but not me, sends a fresh wave of panic through me. Will he know what happened? Will he realize Eli has taken me? Or will he think I've changed my mind, run away, abandoned him?

The car slows, the change in momentum sliding me forward slightly. Are we stopping? Where has he taken me? Fear claws at my throat as possibilities flash through my mind, each worse than the last. Is he going to kill me? Hurt me? Take me somewhere no one will ever find me?

We make a turn, the force of it pressing me against the side of the trunk. Then another. The road beneath us changes, I can feel it in the vibrations, smoother now, like we've moved from a highway to a smaller road.

I strain my ears, trying to hear anything beyond the rumble of the engine and the rush of blood in my head. Music filters through faintly, something classical, piano notes rising and falling. Eli's music. He always played it when he was angry but trying to control himself. The sound of it now makes my stomach clench with remembered fear.

The car slows again, then stops completely. The engine cuts off, and silence falls. I hold my breath, straining to hear what comes next. A car door opens and closes. Footsteps on gravel, coming around to the back of the car.

A key in the lock. Metal against metal. And then....

Light floods the trunk as the lid opens, blinding me after the complete darkness. I squint against it, my eyes watering, trying to make out Eli's silhouette against the dimming sky behind him. He must have been driving through the night.

"Home sweet home," he says, reaching down to grab my bound ankles. "For now. Tomorrow you'll find out just how tainted my love is."

He drags me toward him, my body scraping painfully along the rough carpet of the trunk. When I'm halfway out, he hoists me up, throwing me over his shoulder like I weigh nothing. The blood rushes to my already aching head, and for a moment, I think I might pass out again.

As he carries me, I catch glimpses of our surroundings. A gravel driveway, trees thick around us, no other houses in sight. A cabin, rustic and isolated, looms ahead of us. We're in the middle of nowhere.

No one knows where I am. Not Anthony, not Mia, not Valerie. No one will find me here.

As Eli kicks open the cabin door and carries me inside. Harshly dropping me on the livingroom floor, one thought crystalizes through the fear and pain:

I might not survive this time.

37

Anthony

I PUSH THE FRONT door open with my foot, arms loaded with empty boxes. "Lila? I think I got more than enough boxes this time," I call out, stepping into the foyer. The house is quiet. Too quiet. Something feels off right away, like the air itself has changed since I left. "Lila?" I call again, setting the boxes down by the door. No answer comes back, just the hollow echo of my voice bouncing off the walls.

A chill runs down my spine as I take another step into the house. My eyes scan the entryway, looking for any sign of her. That's when I see it, a dark smear on the hardwood floor. Small, but unmistakable. Blood.

"Lila!" I shout, my voice cracking with sudden panic. I run toward the library, feet pounding against the floor, heart hammering in my chest. "LILA!"

The library door stands open, just as I left it. Inside, the boxes she'd started packing while I was gone only have a few books inside. Some books are scattered on the floor near one of the shelves, as if dropped in a hurry. The lavender chair where I'd made love to her just an hour ago sits empty, the throw blanket half on the floor.

I spin around, rushing back into the hallway. "Lila, where are you?" My voice echoes through the empty house, mocking me with its empty return. I check every room on the first floor. Kitchen, dining room, living room. Nothing. No sign of her.

Taking the stairs two at a time, I race to the second floor, throwing open doors, calling her name with increasing desperation. The master bedroom is empty, bed still made. Eli's old office sits untouched, dust covering the surfaces. Bathroom empty.

Back downstairs, I stand in the foyer, trying to make sense of what I'm seeing. The blood on the floor. The empty house. Lila, gone.

"Fuck," I whisper, my mind racing through possibilities. Did she leave on her own? No. Not without telling me. Not with her books still here. Not with blood on the floor.

My stomach drops as the most obvious answer hits me. Eli. But he's in jail. He can't have taken her. Unless...

My hands shake as I pull out my phone, scrolling to Dillian's number. He picks up on the second ring.

"Anthony? What's up, man?"

"Lila's gone," I say, my voice tight with fear. "I left her at the house for twenty minutes to get more boxes, and when I came back, there's blood on the floor and she's nowhere to be found."

"Shit." Dillian's voice changes instantly, all casual friendliness gone. "I'm on my way. Where are you?"

"Her old house. The one she shared with Eli." I pace the foyer, eyes locked on that small bloodstain. "I think he took her, Dillian. I know he's supposed to be in jail, but I can't think of who else would—"

"Stay put," Dillian cuts me off. "I'm bringing backup. I'll call it in officially, get local PD there too. Don't touch anything. Could be a crime scene."

"Hurry," is all I can say before hanging up.

My next call is to Jonathan. Unlike Dillian, he's not a cop, but he's the most level-headed person I know, and right now, I need that. He answers immediately.

"What's wrong?" he asks, no greeting, no preamble.

"Lila's been taken," I tell him, the words burning my throat. "I think Eli has her. I need your help."

"Where are you?" His voice is calm, focused.

"Her old house. Dillian's on his way with police." I run a hand through my hair, my whole body vibrating with adrenaline and fear. "Jonathan, there's blood."

"I'm on my way," he says. "Twenty minutes. Don't do anything stupid before I get there."

"I won't," I promise, though every fiber of my being wants to tear out of this house and hunt Eli down myself. "Just hurry."

After hanging up, I stand in the foyer, staring at that small smear of blood. Her blood. The thought of Eli putting his hands on her again makes something dark and violent rise inside me. I squeeze my eyes shut, trying to calm the rage threatening to consume me. I need to think clearly. I need to be smart about this.

I dial Cainen's number next. If anyone can find electronic breadcrumbs, it's him.

"I'm in the middle of something," he answers, voice clipped.

"Drop it," I command. "Lila's been taken. I need you to get into the police database, the court system, anywhere you can. Find out if Eli Fischer has been released from jail."

I would normally have Dillian do this to avoid Cainen's exposure, but Dillian is on his way to me right now. Cainen knows I wouldn't ask him to do this unless it was necessary.

There's a brief pause, then the sound of typing. "Give me two minutes."

While I wait, I walk carefully around the foyer, looking for any other clues. The front door wasn't broken. She must have opened it, thinking it was me. Or someone had a key. The blood is a small amount, not enough to suggest a fatal injury. Maybe she fought back. The thought gives me a flicker of hope. My Lila is a fighter.

"Anthony." Cainen's voice pulls me back to the phone. "Eli Fischer posted bond six weeks ago."

The words hit me like a physical blow. "What? That's impossible. Lila would have been notified. She's the victim, she would have been told he was out."

"Checking notification system now," Cainen says, more typing sounds in the background. "There's a flag on his file. All notifications regarding his case were turned off or routed. Lila's phone and email were removed from the notifications list."

"Routed where?" I demand.

"Working on it." More typing. "It's a dummy account. Someone with access to the system redirected her notifications and removed her information."

Cold dread washes over me. "He's had six weeks to plan this. To watch her. To wait for the perfect moment."

"I'm digging deeper," Cainen says. "Looking for any properties in his name, any transactions, anything that might tell us where he'd take her."

The sound of sirens in the distance interrupts my spiraling thoughts. "Police are almost here. Keep digging. Call me as soon as you find anything."

"Wait," Cainen says sharply. "There's something else. I'm looking at Lila's divorce file. Her maiden name is Angelo, right?"

"Yeah," I confirm, confused by the change in topic. "Lilian Mae Angelo. Why?"

"And she's from Florida originally? Adopted around age five?"

My brow furrows. "Yes. How is this relevant right now?"

Cainen's breathing changes, becoming faster. "Holy shit. I think—I think she might be my sister."

"What?" The word comes out like a punch. "What are you talking about?"

"My father had another child not long after me," Cainen explains, speaking faster now. "A daughter. My half-sister. Her mother took her and disappeared when she was little. My father's been looking for her for years. The timeline matches. The location matches. And Angelo is mine and my dad's last name."

The sirens are getting louder, police cars pulling up outside. "Are you sure?"

"No," Cainen admits. "But it fits. I've been looking for my sister for years too, and now—fuck, if it's her, and that bastard has her—"

"Focus," I snap, though my mind is reeling from this revelation. "We need to find her first. Confirm the family connection later."

"I'm on my way," Cainen says. "I'll be in Maryland in three days. Keep me updated. I'm sending everything I find to your phone and Dillian's."

I hang up as the first police officers enter the house, Dillian right behind them. He spots me and crosses the foyer, eyes immediately going to the blood on the floor.

"Tell me everything," he demands, waving over a crime scene technician.

I explain what happened, how I left to get more boxes, how I returned to find Lila gone and blood on the floor. I tell him about Cainen's discovery that Eli has been out on bail for six weeks, how the notification system was compromised.

"We should have been more careful," I say, self-loathing burning in my gut. "I should have checked myself to make sure he was still in jail."

"This isn't on you," Dillian says firmly. "Eli is a resourceful son of a bitch with money and connections. We'll find him, and we'll find Lila."

The police work efficiently around us, photographing the scene, collecting samples of the blood, dusting for prints. I stand in the middle of it all, feeling helpless and terrified. Jonathan arrives as they're finishing up, his solid presence a small comfort in the chaos.

"We've put out an APB on Eli Fischer and his vehicle," Dillian informs us after conferring with the lead detective. "All available units are on alert. We're checking traffic cameras, toll booths, everything."

"It's not enough," I say, pacing now. "He's had this planned for weeks. He wouldn't use his own car. He wouldn't take her somewhere obvious."

"We'll find her," Jonathan says, his calm voice cutting through my panic. "We've tracked down people with a lot less to go on."

My phone buzzes with a text from Cainen.

> **Cainen:** Sending you coordinates for three properties that might be connected to Eli. Off the books, paid for through shell companies. I'm on my way.

I show the text to Dillian and Jonathan. "We need to check these places. Now."

Dillian nods, already moving toward the door. "I'll co-ordinate with local PD, get teams to each location."

"I'm coming with you," I insist, following him.

"No," Dillian turns to face me. "You're too emotionally involved. Let us handle this."

"Fuck that," I growl. "She's out there, scared, hurt, with that monster. I'm not sitting this out."

Jonathan steps between us. "He's coming," he tells Dillian. "But he'll stay in the car unless we give the all-clear. Right, Anthony?"

I nod, willing to agree to anything that gets us moving faster. "Right. Just please, let's go. Now."

As we head for the door, I take one last look at the library doorway, where just hours ago Lila and I were happy, planning our future. The rage and fear inside me turn into something harder, more focused. I will find her. I will bring her home. And if Eli has hurt her, I will make him wish he'd never been born.

"Hang on, Lila," I whisper as we step out into the gathering darkness. "I'm coming for you."

Acknowledgements

Thank you to those who supported me. A couple of friends and a mentor whose class on publishing really pushed me forward. Trying to do this alone was the hardest thing I've ever done, and it took me over three years to write and finish this book. Thankfully, book two is already partially drafted!

To the readers who liked this book, thank you so much.

Where to Follow Me

If you liked my book, please spread the word and leave me a review. You can also show your support by following my socials.

For up-to-date information on my socials, visit: https://mythicbad.com/unadove

You can also join the Discord server through my website.

www.ingramcontent.com/pod-product-compliance
Lightning Source LLC
Chambersburg PA
CBHW021241190726
48289CB00005B/1435